TH
GALLOWS

By the same author

Nonfiction

Scandal of the West

With F. E. Boswell

Nonfiction

Hanging the Sheriff: A Biography of Henry Plummer
John David Borthwick: Artist of the Gold Rush
Gold Camp Desperadoes
Vigilante Victims: Montana's 1864 Hanging Spree

THE BANNACK GALLOWS

A NOVEL

BY

R. E. MATHER

Historical Note
By F. E. Boswell

History West Publishing Company
Oklahoma City, Oklahoma
1998

In-house editing by Louis Schmittroth

Cover design by Margaret Anderson

Cover photograph by F. E. Boswell

Copyright 1998 History West Publishing Company
Oklahoma City, Oklahoma, USA
All rights reserved

LIBRARY OF CONGRESS CATALOGING-IN-PUBLICATION DATA

Mather, R. E. (Ruth E.), 1934-
   The Bannack gallows / R.E. Mather ; historical note by F.E. Boswell.
      p. cm.
   ISBN 0-9625069-3-1 (pbk. : alk. paper)
   1. Gold mines and mining–Montana–Bannack–Fiction.
2. Vigilantes–Montana–Bannack–Fiction. I. Title.
PS3563.A83542B3   1998
  813'.54–dc21   98-24666
                                                            CIP

Printed in Canada

DEDICATION

This book is dedicated to editor Louis Schmittroth and artist Margaret Anderson, for their devotion to truth and beauty, which according to Keats are one and the same thing.

CONTENTS

Author's Note / *1*

The Bannack Gallows / *3*

Historical Note / *205*

AUTHOR'S NOTE

In a remote little ghost town in Montana, events stranger than fiction once took place. I have often walked Bannack's abandoned lanes, soaking up a brooding past that hovers over the narrow valley and, like white alkali dust, saturates every gangly sagebrush and weathered log cabin lining main street. I have stood under a harsh sun and shaded my eyes to gaze up the barren gulch, transfixed by the sight of a delicate pine gallows outlined against the drab hills beyond.

In some school textbook you may have read about the gripping events that occurred at the Bannack gallows more than a century ago. But I doubt the account you read was correct. For years I have lived with the burden of knowing the truth. And the truth is that a haunting crime was committed at Bannack and then painstakingly covered up for decades.

The story told in the following pages lays bare a troubling secret. And if the story seems excessively violent, it is because it took place during violent times.

R. E. Mather

CHAPTER ONE

A gust of wind swept up the trampled lane and peppered the frail gallows with a cloud of gritty dust. The large crowd of gold miners and main-street merchants tensely waiting to see the hanging ducked their heads and turned away from the grainy assault.

Above the gray hills that confined the valley, an autumn sun was just beginning to sprout a few feeble rays. Against the coming light, the gallows crossbar and the slight figure of the young convict posed on a makeshift platform stood out like a black silhouette.

This was Deputy Buck Stinson's first execution and he was nervous as a cat. In fact he wasn't sure he could make it through the hanging. He'd always been prideful about his reputation as one of the most fearless men at the gold mines, but now all of that was shot to the smithereens. It had to be obvious to everybody watching that he was more jittery than the stiff figure waiting on the high dry-goods box with his thin legs bound together and his hands tied behind his back.

For the tenth time Stinson twisted around to look at the trail winding down cemetery hill but there was still no sign of Sheriff Plummer. He should have been back hours ago. What made it so worrisome was a rumor Stinson had heard about the Stranglers, how they were laying plans to get rid of the miners' Sheriff.

And there were other things bothering Stinson too. For starters, he was only a few years older than the teenager he was supposed to hang. Even more embarrassing, he was several inches shorter. And he wasn't half so good looking as the boy convict. Stinson was fully aware that his stubby frame was too stocky, and even as a boy he'd been self-conscious about his bad forehead. It was too high and it bulged out a little. He'd always felt uncomfortable when he was on display before an audience but now it was close to being more than he could stand because he couldn't keep his hands from shaking.

Stinson glanced up at his prisoner standing on the high box. The boy reminded him of a startled jackrabbit that had frozen in its tracks because it was terrified out of its wits. What was gnawing at Stinson most of all was the doubt he had about that skinny boy standing up there ... because there was really no guarantee he was actually guilty. To Stinson's way of thinking the jury members had made up their minds long before the trial started, probably the same day the boy was captured and brought into town perched atop his scrawny mule. When the trial testimony was over the eight jury men were in such a hurry to announce their guilty verdict they didn't even take time to discuss the facts of the eerie case.

As if all those things weren't enough to set any raw deputy on edge, Sheriff Plummer wasn't here, and they needed him to run things and tell everybody just what to do. And without Sheriff there to put the fear of God into the lynch crowd, there was a real danger the Stranglers would make a stab at yanking the execution right out of Stinson's hands.

From the minute Plummer had ridden out to find the priest, the Stranglers commenced bragging all over town about how they intended to carve the boy up. They said while his eye sockets and the stub of his tongue were still dripping blood, they'd noose him and gradually hoist him off the ground. They claimed that one quick snap of the neck was far too easy for his punishment. Besides, choking a criminal to death very slowly and observing him while he twisted and danced at the end of the rope for a long spell made a lot more lasting impression on other roughs who were watching.

Some of the most enthusiastic Stranglers had even boasted they might go one step further. They might leave the two deputies dangling on the crossbar alongside the boy, just as a sign to the gold miners that their lawmen were past history now and a new tougher bunch was in control of law and order here at the mines.

The crowd was getting restless because Stinson was so slow and some of them began to shout jeers at him. He knew he had to get on with it whether he liked it or not. In these parts it didn't take much for a group of men as big as this to work themselves into such a lather that before they knew it they'd turned into a howling mob.

Stinson didn't like turning his back on such an uncertain audience but he had to so he could climb up on the box and noose the boy. First he made one final survey of the men flooding the lane that led off of main street and up to the gallows. Then he fixed his eyes on the front semicircle, where two known Stranglers were shuffling around in the ankle-deep dust. Hank Crawford, the town butcher, didn't appear to be armed. And his sidekick, a short spindly mule-packer named Xavier Beidler, didn't have his tall shotgun propped up beside him like he usually did. Apparently he'd left it back at the saloon. Of course Beidler might have another gun tucked away somewhere in his clothes because his dingy-black overcoat was several sizes too big for him. It hung almost to the ground and was so long in the sleeves that only his fingertips stuck out of the frayed cuffs.

Beidler noticed that Stinson was observing him. He gave an impish grin and then eased one small hand inside the bulky overcoat and began groping around for something. Stinson tensed and immediately the four lawmen posted behind the gallows swung their double-barreled shotguns on Beidler. But he only pulled a small metal flask out of his pocket. Then he grinned again and tipped his head back and gulped down a long swig.

"Hey, don't git s' damn jumpy!" he called out to Stinson, "jist needed me a li'l smile out o' th' bottle."

The butcher, a lank wiry frontiersman, let out a guffaw at how his little sidekick had fooled Stinson and then reached one big-knuckled hand out for Beidler to share the flask. The little carpenter with the black beard and spectacles was squeezed in next to the butcher, but of course nobody offered him a drink. He was too queer. Besides, he'd been the first suspect and some people still thought he was the real murderer instead of the boy on the box. Deputy Stinson was surprised the little carpenter had the nerve to come to the hanging.

A few feet beyond them, Stinson spotted a battered Henry rifle that was wavering back and forth but appeared to have him as the target. It belonged to old Justice Edgerton, who fancied he was helping keep order. The tall stoop-shouldered Justice had a tight grip on the rifle but his gaunt hands were trembling worse than Stinson's. The old man didn't have the foggiest notion how to handle a weapon and there was a real danger he was so fidgety he might accidentally fire the gun and injure some innocent bystander, either that or else set off a stampede. Or it wouldn't be beyond him to take it into his white old head to purposely fire a shot in Stinson's direction as a warning to quit stalling.

Stinson blamed Abraham Lincoln for the miners being stuck with the old Justice and the whole pack of grief he'd brought to Bannack with him. The President had sent Edgerton to the Territory to set up a permanent justice system but other than criticizing the miners' lawmen, the crotchety old lawyer hadn't made any progress. That was because on his very first day in Bannack he caught a bad case of gold fever and ever since then he'd been busy trying to get rich. Early every morning he sent his greenhorn nephew, a gawky young lawyer named Wilbur, off chasing after mining claims for the two of them. While Wilbur was out dangling his gangly legs on each side of a hired jackass and trying his darnedest to follow gold stampedes, but instead getting himself lost in the wilderness, Edgerton would leave his wife and children at the cabin and amble onto main street wearing his rumpled black suit and his limp white shirt. He said he felt obligated to dress like a gentleman so he could separate himself from the ignorant miners with their muddy trousers and red flannel shirts and black slouch hats.

The Justice was a teetotaler so he didn't want to lounge around the saloons like the other loafers in Bannack. Instead he spent most of his time at Chrisman's general store. Stinson hated how you couldn't go into Chrisman's to buy something without seeing old Edgerton sitting by the fire with his feet propped up. And while you were picking out what you wanted and paying for it you had to listen to the Justice crow to his nephew about his glory days in Congress back in the city of Washington, D.C. The old man was always complaining he didn't much care for this barbaric wilderness, including the way Sheriff Plummer and his bumbling deputies handled law and order. He said they were too slow. He was always rambling on and on about politics and the war back in the States too. After he wore those topics out he'd go back to spouting off about his belief in speedy executions. And when any crisis erupted in town he'd run home and drag out the battered Henry rifle he'd bought secondhand as soon as he arrived at the mines. Then he and Wilbur would stalk the streets and claim the two of them were keeping order. Stinson knew all they were really doing was causing more worry for the miners' lawmen.

But since the Chief Justice was sent by President Lincoln himself, there wasn't much anybody could do to protect the citizens from Edgerton's wavery old gun. Deputy Stinson took his eyes off the Henry rifle long enough to shoot another glance over his shoulder at the cemetery hill trail. There was still no sign of Sheriff Plummer and the priest.

Through clenched teeth Stinson let out a long whistling sigh. It was so shrill it echoed on his own ear drums. He was shivering from the chilly breeze but he had to pull out the black bandana he'd brought for the execution and use it to wipe sweat from his bad forehead. He could tell by the catcalls coming from the crowd that it was dangerous for him to keep on stalling. Their carping about how he should get on with the hanging turned louder inside his own head and made him want to cover his ears. He turned back toward the wooden dry-goods box and cleared his throat several times.

The wind moaned and the moan stayed in his ears and got louder. Then another strong gust of wind clouded the gallows in dust and he couldn't see a thing. Stinson was wishing he'd never let the gold miners talk him into being a deputy. He wasn't cut out for it. He just didn't have it in him to choke the life out of another human being, especially one who didn't look more than sixteen. And when something like this got Stinson on edge, strange things happened to him. His ears magnified every single sound and then the noise rolled around and around inside his head till it almost drove him crazy.

With the back of one knotted fist he rubbed grains of sand from his eyes and did his best to put on an air of casualness. Then he determinedly scrambled up beside the condemned murderer.

"Y'all gotta be a man now," he warned the boy. He knew the warning applied just as much to himself but he hoped the boy didn't realize that.

The young convict didn't so much as move a muscle of his body, except for shifting his eyes toward the cemetery hill trail. The trail was still empty. The boy set his frail jaw and nodded his head at Stinson, but tears were already beginning to form in his eyes.

"Y'all fixin' t' die game now aintcha?" Stinson went on. "Gotta be a man, now."

The crowd had stopped their restless motions and dropped their yammer for him to get on with the hanging. They stood in complete silence. Stinson turned away from them but he could feel their eyes boring into his back. The wind that had been blowing all morning suddenly stopped and it was so quiet in the gulch he could hear himself breathing. The boy beside him was rigid as a corpse and Stinson drew himself back so their bodies didn't touch. Then he lifted one arm toward the noose dangling over their heads. It was just out of his reach and he had to stand up on his tiptoes and then stretch some more to get hold of it. The instant his fingertips brushed the coarse fibers, he watched his own hand jump back like a rattlesnake had bit it. He could see there was no way he could force himself to slip that rough old noose around the boy's skinny little neck so he leaped back down to the ground.

As he lit, he wheeled around so he could keep an eye on the spectators. He saw they were still safely frozen in position so he began edging his way toward First Deputy Ray, the rangy long-haired New Yorker who was holding a shotgun on the crowd. Not that having the Yankee there was any great comfort. Ray came West to be a civil engineer and he might know how to build a bridge all right but he didn't know the first thing about frontier law. It was only by chance he ended up as a lawman. He and the three jailers had their shotguns at the ready because Ray was just as worried as Stinson that the Stranglers would try to take over and gouge out the convicted boy's eyes and slice off his tongue before they strung him up.

Stinson kept his eyes pinned on the section of the front row where the butcher and the little mule-packer were huddled together and slowly sidled his way over to the deputy who outranked him.

"Reckon we mustn't wait on Sheriff?" he murmured to Ray.

The crowd began shifting in their places again and started up more grumbling about the delay. They knew the condemned boy wasn't going anywhere with his legs hobbled so they weren't looking at him anymore. They were watching to see what the two deputies were up to.

Ray seemed to be pondering Stinson's words, then he tensed and took a firmer grip on his shotgun. He stood there with a thoughtful look on his face and at the same time kept on surveying the anxious bunch facing them. For what seemed like a very long time to Stinson, Ray considered the suggestion.

Finally he said, "No ... go ahead. Get it over with."

The order left Stinson a bundle of raw nerves. He glanced down at his own shotgun, which he'd left resting near Ray's feet. Then he flashed another glance up cemetery hill and another one back down to the two Stranglers and then skipped his eyes across to the Henry rifle in Edgerton's shaky old hands.

"Somethin's cockeyed here," Stinson muttered to Ray. "Sheriff oughta be back. Y'all don't reckon them string-em-up yahoos went'n ... went'n ..." He heard his own voice trail off.

"Go on, Reb," Ray insisted, "get it over with."

But Stinson noticed there wasn't much conviction in the senior deputy's voice. Ray sucked in a deep breath and turned to Stinson for the first time and looked him in the eye. Then he waited, like he was giving Stinson a chance to speak his piece. It was a rare occasion when Ray thought his under-deputy had anything to say that was worth listening to. Everybody knew the two men were bitter enemies and didn't work together or even speak to each other unless they absolutely had to. It wasn't anything personal, just that back in the States their brothers and cousins and uncles were out on the battlefields trying to kill each other.

The crowd wasn't frozen any more but now Stinson felt like he was. He couldn't open his mouth.

"Well spit it out, Reb," Deputy Ray said, "or else hop back up on the box and get it over with."

Stinson couldn't speak or budge either. Big drops of sweat were rolling down the curve of his forehead. He tried to lick grains of sand off his front teeth but his tongue was too dry. Then suddenly the words came spilling out on their own.

"I ain't goin' t' noose 'im," he said. "If th' boy's innocent an' we kill 'im, well ... well then somethin' ba-a-ad's fixin' t' happen. I just kno-o-ow so."

At first Ray looked startled but he got hold of himself. "Superstitious," he said. His voice was as dry and indifferent as usual. "Superstitious, that's what the hell's wrong with you, Reb."

Stinson was too absorbed in his worries to argue the point. On their own say-so, his short arms clasped his thickset body to try to keep it from shivering and his torso began rocking slightly back and forth while the words kept gushing out of his mouth. "Felt it from th' git-go ... soon as they foun' that nekkid body."

Stinson couldn't loose his grip on himself and he couldn't keep his torso from rocking and he couldn't stop the words that were pushing their way out of his dry mouth. "An' then y'all an' Sheriff rode in with th' boy."

Stinson was speaking in a low voice but to his own ears it sounded too loud. The wind started up again and blew dust in his face and moaned and wailed around the gallows posts. For just a second Stinson blocked out the uneasy crowd and gazed off into the empty gray space above their heads. Suddenly it was all too clear to him why there was so much noise in his ears. It was because he was afraid he himself deserved the shameful noose more than the boy did.

He was thinking how when he first came West he'd shucked off all the sweet things his Mama had always taught him and hitched up with some ugly old roughs who did their share of gambling and drinking and shooting up the gold camps. Now because of Sadie's jabs and pushes he'd finally gotten around to straightening himself up. But it was too late. Those rough old days were already recorded in the Book of Life and that left him without any right to hang a quiet timid boy who acted like he wouldn't so much as hurt a mosquito. Stinson could see it very plain now, that's what his ears were trying to tell him when they raised every noise up till it blared and echoed inside his head. It was his ears way of saying, "Oughta be y'all up there on th' drygoods box!"

He knew that somehow he had to convince Ray to call a halt to the hanging.

"Y'all go ahead on with this an' there ain't no turnin' back," he said to Ray. "It'll en' up takin' us down ... even y'all. I feel it in m' bones."

Stinson glanced over and noticed his own attack of nerves was taking its toll on the First Deputy. Ray was shifting his shoulders and moving his head in quick jerks. And at their stations the three jailers were listening to what he'd been saying too and they were also beginning to fidget.

Ray's eyes darted nervously over each of the jailers and on to the mass of milling people. Then he swung his head back toward the trail on cemetery hill. It was still empty.

"Guess maybe we'll wait on Sheriff Plummer," Ray said. "Grab up your shotgun there, Reb, and I'll announce it ... say it wouldn't be legal without the Sheriff here to give the order to hang the convict."

"Y'all do that, Yank," Stinson said.

Stinson's eyes had turned glassy on him but he managed to pick up his shotgun and level it in Beidler's general direction. Out of the corner of his eye was the blur of Ray giving instructions to the jailers. Ray wasn't talking loud but Stinson's ears were still boosting up every sound around him. The First Deputy's orders and the objections the jailers were firing back and his own fast breathing were all rattling around inside his skull. He wanted to clap his hands over his ears to keep out the din. But he couldn't.

He had to keep his shotgun pointed at Beidler.

And if Beidler reached inside the long black coat and went for a weapon this time instead of the whiskey, Stinson knew he'd have to blast him. He'd have to kill a man. There was no way out for any of them. They were all caught up in this spooky business and there was no safe way out.

Ray was showing the gumption to call a halt to the hanging but Stinson knew it was only temporary ... only a slight delay in the doom that was waiting for them. They were all trapped, just like the time he got hooked in the thorn patch when he was a little boy. Stinson switched his eyes over to Edgerton's rifle and then jerked them back to Beidler and Crawford. He wished his mind hadn't gone and fetched up the old thorn patch again because it had always been one of his worst memories. Sometimes he still had nightmares about it.

But this whole creepy business that started off when they found the naked corpse was just being hooked in another thorn patch, at least to his way of thinking, just another ugly old thorn patch. It was way back when he was only four years old and he'd been running along a path and he tripped and fell face down in some brambles. The thorns were almost an inch long and they pierced his forehead and his cheeks and went right through his clothes and stung into his arms and legs and belly and pinned him right there where he was. First he began to blubber and then he screamed at the top of his lungs and his Mama came running. He could hear her moaning up there above him and then he felt her hands clutching at his armpits. As she jerked him up, he heard the thorns ripping through his flesh and then she laid him on the ground and he could see blood oozing out of the gashes on the palms of his hands.

To this very day he still had the thorn scars on his face and body. Only this time it wasn't just him. The whole bunch of them were hooked in a thorn patch together ... the boy and the Stranglers and the deputies and Sheriff and the gold miners, and even old Edgerton and his gawky greenhorn nephew.

He could hear the jailers still trying to persuade Ray he'd be crazy to try to postpone the execution. They were saying it might start a riot and lots of people would end up getting killed. One jailer spit out that he didn't have to follow Ray's orders anyway because "he wasn't no Sheriff." Ray came back that all three of them damned well better follow his orders whether he was Sheriff or not or they'd damned well end up getting killed right here and now ... by him. The arguing was harsh in Stinson's ears and then he heard his own voice drowning the other voices out. His worries wouldn't put up with being cramped inside his mind any longer. They were bound they'd come out and he didn't bother to try and hold them back.

"More'n likely Sheriff's a corpse by now," he said.

He purposely said it loud enough for the jailers to hear and then went on. "Oughta warned Sheriff. Oughta warned 'im."

Ray and the jailers were quiet now, like they were listening to him, so Stinson kept on talking in the same raised voice. "We hang a innocent boy an' somethin' ba-a-ad's fixin' t' come down on us. Felt it from th' git-go ... soon as I laid eyes on that nekkid body."

CHAPTER TWO

It had all started only four days ago. And from the very first day, the queer little man who had just moved into the back of the carpenter shop was tangled up in the case. That was because he tried to build a coffin and get the corpse under the ground before the law officers could see it. Right after the doctor examined the nude corpse and found two hidden wounds on it, the dark-complected little carpenter became the chief suspect in the brutal murder. In fact some of the Stranglers still had suspicions he was guilty.

The past Sunday morning a train of Salt Lake freighters had been headed for Bannack with a long line of wagons filled with food and liquor and other essentials. First the freighters noticed scavenger birds circling in the sky up ahead of them. And a short time later the lead bullwhacker spotted a corpse lying beside the trail.

A heavyset old man with matted white hair and a grizzled beard was stretched out flat on his back on the ground. His legs were slightly spread and his upturned palms were extended out on each side of him like he was nailed to a cross. There were no eyeballs left in his eye sockets. And his parched lips were parted so the bullwhacker could see that part of his tongue was missing too. But the most eerie thing of all, the dead man was completely nude.

When the rest of the freighting party caught up, they all looked at the corpse and agreed the old man hadn't been dead very long. Then they examined him from head to toe but didn't see any gun wound or stab marks. The idea of the old fellow suffering some strange death in the very part of the wilderness they were traveling through unsettled them and since one member of the party was a Mormon elder, the others asked him to say a prayer for the dead man and for them too.

Later, the Mormon elder explained to the little man at the carpenter shop how he had pulled off his hat and knelt down beside the eyeless corpse. "Dear Heavenly Father," he said, "please bless the soul that has departed to the spirit world and please comfort some grieving family who is wondering where their missing relative is. We ask Thee now to protect us from such horrible savagery on the rest of the trail. Please deliver us safe to the mammon-loving town of Bannack. Amen."

The Mormon took two raggedy old blankets and tore them into long strips and wound them round and round the naked man like he was a mummy. Then the lead bullwhacker helped him lift the bound corpse inside the first wagon. One by one the bullwhackers cracked their long whips and spat out the usual vile curses at the oxen teams, and the caravan of tandem wagons gradually jerked forward and plodded on.

About a quarter of a mile down the trail, the lead bullwhacker stumbled across a badger hole with some cloth sticking out of it. When he knelt down and began pulling it out, he found the dead man's trousers and shirt and stockings and shoes. He didn't want to take time to dress the corpse so he just unwound a few of the blanket strips and stuffed the tattered clothes and shoes inside the mummy case with their owner and then wound the strips back up again and tucked in the loose ends.

It was early afternoon when the caravan rolled into Bannack. Since the freighters didn't know the miners had elected themselves a sheriff, they decided to deliver their pitiful bundle directly to the carpenter shop to have a coffin made.

A tidy little man with bushy black hair and eyebrows and a neatly trimmed black mustache and beard came bustling out the front doors to meet them. He welcomed them warmly, like he was anxious for some business. That made the freighters a little suspicious because the old carpenter was always so busy that when they needed some quick repair work, he wouldn't even give them the time of day. Besides, the new carpenter didn't have the look of a builder about him. He was frail and wore spectacles and was dressed in a neat suit and vest. And his hands looked soft and delicate.

When the freighters questioned him, he got nervous and began talking very fast and finally admitted he wasn't really a carpenter. He said he was a college professor. He'd come West to prospect for gold but the work was too demanding for him. Now he was trying to earn enough money to get back East to his wife and his parents.

To convince the skeptical freighters, he reached in his vest pocket and pulled out an ornately engraved gold watch attached to a chain. While he dangled it in front of their eyes, he told them he was so desperate to get home he'd even considered selling the beautiful watch to raise funds. It was a gift from Angeline, his little Creole wife. She gave it to him just before he left home and told him to keep it close to his heart so they'd always be together. So he couldn't bring himself to raise money by selling her gift.

Then he went on to tell how he'd heard there was a carpenter shop for lease in Bannack. Since his father was a carpenter, he figured he knew enough about the trade to get by. The only problem was that people in Bannack seemed to avoid him and his shop and that was why he was eager for business. He wanted to earn some money and start for home.

That explanation satisfied the freighters and they went back to the wagon to collect their bundle.

The professor stayed inside the shop and watched them through the front windows. During his months at the mines he'd been a loner and he'd gotten in the habit of talking to himself. Sometimes he forgot and talked to himself out loud even when other people were in earshot. He hadn't confessed his fault to the freighters, but he knew his bad habit of talking to himself was what made the people at Bannack shy away from him. They thought he was queer in the head. Just yesterday he'd overheard an illiterate mule-packer named Xavier Beidler insulting him in public. And to make it even more humiliating, everybody in hearing distance had burst out laughing.

As the professor watched the sober-faced freighters carry the wrapped body from the wagon and gently place it on his workbench, he said, "One died on the trail ... they're grieving for him."

He knew it wouldn't be proper to question grieving men about the death of their comrade so he didn't say a word, not even to himself. Then he noticed some strange lumps under one side of the shroud. It wouldn't be proper to comment about that either so he just took their fifty dollars in real currency and didn't ask any questions. But after they left, he was measuring the lumpy bundle to calculate dimensions for the coffin and he got to talking to himself about how the freighters had arrived on the Salt Lake trail.

"Probably Mormons," he said. That thought made him very uneasy.

He'd been in the West less than a year but that was more than enough time to hear rumors about the Mormons, how they were liars who claimed they'd found a golden book some angel without any wings had buried in a hill. He didn't have any grounds for disputing that claim but it was fairly obvious the Mormons were a bunch of murderous jackals who couldn't be trusted under any circumstances. As everybody knew, one naive wagon train had made the fatal mistake of trusting them. It was a terrible story because the entire party of immigrants, even the women and children, ended up massacred in a meadow up in the mountains. The Mormons tried to deny it and blame it on the Indians, but nobody believed them.

The professor needed the fifty dollars from the coffin in the worst way, but he kept picturing the bodies of women and little children, bloody with hatchet wounds and scattered over a green mountain meadow. Finally his conscience got the best of him.

"Better step next door and get Doctor Glick," he said, "ask him to take a peek inside the shroud."

Glick was upset at being disturbed in the middle of a card game. He didn't hesitate to let everybody in the Elkhorn Saloon know about it. But after he finished the long tirade about how the inconsiderate people in this town wouldn't let him enjoy a moment's rest, he threw down his cards. He left his half-finished drink waiting on the table and followed the professor next-door to the shop.

"Probably brought me for nothing," he grumbled as he bent over the bound body lying on the workbench.

As Glick spoke, the professor noticed a strong scent of alcohol and when the doctor began unwinding the blanket strips from the corpse, his slender fingers seemed clumsy.

"You could have done this yourself." Glick said, "and not troubled me."

There was so much contempt in the doctor's voice that the professor felt ashamed. He was beginning to understand why the doctor was about as unpopular in Bannack as he was himself.

While Glick was fiddling around with the cloth that had been wound over the big lumps, some dirty patched trousers, then a threadbare shirt, and finally a pair of nearly soleless shoes stuffed with muddy woolen stockings spilled onto the floor. Glick picked up the items and examined them one by one. He said he didn't see anything suspicious about the clothes ... no holes that might have been made by a gun or a Bowie knife or an arrow.

He went back to unwinding. "I told you so," he said, "you brought me over here for nothing."

As the doctor peeled off a strip of blanket that was tied around what appeared to be the corpse's head, the professor caught a glimpse of an eyeless face. He sucked in his breath so hard he nearly choked on his tongue.

"Believe I'll step outside for some fresh air," he said quietly to himself.

Because of the doctor's impaired condition the professor figured it would probably take quite some time to determine the cause of death, so he left the front doors open and began ambling back and forth on the uneven boardwalk in front of the shop while he tried to keep his mind on something besides the empty eye sockets. His favorite topic of course was going home.

"Just a few weeks," he said, "maybe even sooner." He patted the gold watch so it pressed up against his heart and kept on walking. "Please, Lord, see this prodigal son home safely. That isn't asking too much is it?"

Just then Glick called out the front door that he'd discovered a wound where a revolver ball had entered. It was at the back of the victim's mouth. That frightened the professor because it meant foul play and now he was involved. He had no desire to go back in the shop and look at the wound inside the mouth.

"I'll take his word for it," he said. He kept on pacing the boardwalk and trying to calm himself by talking about home. "I need to leave before cold weather sets in," he said. "Please, Lord, don't let the heavy snows set in too early."

He went on pacing the boardwalk and patting the gold watch Angeline had given him and thinking about home instead of the gun wound.

A few minutes later Glick stepped to the door. The professor noticed the doctor was so unsteady he had to lean against the door frame. "The ball entered the victim's mouth and passed out the back of his head," he said. His tongue seemed to be thick and he had to swallow a few times before he could go on. "I parted his hair at the back of the scalp and uncovered an exit hole."

Glick was in a surly mood and didn't bother to ask politely. Instead he demanded the professor come inside immediately and get him some writing paper and a pen.

After he had paper and pen in hand, he pulled a stool up to the workbench and sat down and began writing. "A Report on the Deceased," he said as he wrote.

The professor stood beside him and watched him scribbling out the lines in jerky motions. He concentrated on Doctor Glick because he didn't care to think about a wound made in a mouth by a revolver ball. It reminded him too much of mutilated women and children sprawled across a mountain meadow.

Glick stopped writing and put his left hand over his mouth and belched loudly. "Pardon," he said and then went on writing. The professor turned his face away so he didn't have to smell the alcohol released by the belch. He considered the doctor an interesting specimen of the radical change that human nature can undergo on the frontier. He'd heard that back in the States, Glick was a sophisticated and highly respected surgeon. And he still acted snobbish. But here it was early afternoon, and the snobbish surgeon was already so far under the influence he had trouble speaking and standing up.

Glick signed his report with a flourish and then dropped the paper on top of the corpse. Without bothering to say good-bye he headed out the front door and turned in the direction of the Elkhorn. He didn't even show the good manners to close the doors after him.

With the doctor gone, the professor had to face up to his dilemma alone. He gazed at the paper lying on the chest of the nude corpse and shivered. "Some dirty business here," he whispered, "another Mormon massacre and I'm caught up in it."

He couldn't stand to look at the body so he laid the clothes on top of it and began the rewrapping. Before he could finish, the freighters walked through the open front doors. They said they were in a hurry to get back on the trail and wanted him to take care of the burial too. That pretty well confirmed the professor's suspicions. He was thinking about darting past them and running out the door to find Sheriff Plummer, but one hefty freighter quickly blocked the doorway. Evidently he'd noticed the binding had been taken off the dead man, so he began relating the whole story. When he got to the part about the prayer, he even started reciting the lines he'd said over the body.

As he spoke the words "horrible savagery," that quite naturally brought Indians to the professor's mind. Then after the freighter had finished repeating the prayer that he'd said on the trail, he went on to mention how a few miles beyond where they found the victim, they spotted a party of armed warriors off in the distance. The freighter said he calculated that explained both the murder and the mutilation ... Indians ... savages.

The professor didn't want to be taken in by a lying and murdering jackal. But he'd always been an avid student of human nature and the hefty clean-cut Mormon standing in front of him and looking him directly in the eye appeared to be a decent man who was telling the truth. He thought the matter over for a while and then said yes, he'd take care of the burial too. He needed the money so he could get home.

After the freighters paid him another twenty dollars in real currency and left, he finished rewinding the blanket strips and brought the wheelbarrow and rolled the corpse onto it. Then he started carting the poor Indian-victim across to the other side of the creek. That was where Caroline Hall's establishment was located.

"Miss Hall's the logical person to take care of the laying out," he said as the wheelbarrow bumped across the dust-chinked ruts gouged into main street. "She's neat and clean herself."

At the creek he located the rocky section where he'd seen the Salt Lake stage cross and began pushing the wheelbarrow through the water. He didn't like getting his feet wet, and his load was so heavy he could barely shove it up the other bank. The effort made him out of breath and he had trouble speaking. "Miss Hall's the logical one," he panted. "She's a clean woman.... Besides, she won't be shocked to see a strange man with his clothes off."

When he got to the Bluebird, he could hear the fiddler sawing out a lively tune inside the log cabin. He rested the wheelbarrow down on its props and knocked on the back door. He had to pound for several minutes before anybody heard him over the music. Finally Caroline herself cracked the door and peered out.

"Front door's wide open," she said crossly.

The cool welcome made the professor nervous. He adjusted his spectacles and massaged his short black beard. "You see, Miss Hall," he said, "I'm in need of an angel of mercy."

"Then what'd you come here for?" she asked. She pushed the door open a little wider and stared down at the lumpy bundle balanced across the wheelbarrow.

The professor had never been this close to Miss Hall before and he couldn't help taking the opportunity to examine her closely. She was a tall well-shaped woman and her face would have been pretty if it didn't have such a harsh look to it. Her hair was her best feature, about the color of dark honey, and he noticed how her pale blue dress exactly matched the color of her eyes. It was impossible to guess her age because her face makeup was applied very skillfully, like she'd had lots of practice.

"A lady's touch, please, Miss Hall," the professor pleaded. "This dead man's a victim of the Indians. He'll have to go to the grave in a very pitiful condition unless you ..."

"We're awful busy," Caroline interrupted. But she continued gazing down at his bundle. "Say th' Indians killed somebody?"

"Yes, a poor old man ... stripped off his clothing ... mutilated the body."

"Well," she sighed, "hang on while I clear out a table." Then she slammed the door in his face.

When she came back, she stooped and slipped her bare white arms under the top half of the rigid bundle and he took the legs. She made carrying the heavy man look so easy it was obvious to the professor she was much stronger than he was.

Together they lifted the victim onto the green-felt surface of a table near the back door, with her carrying most of the weight. She'd set up two screens around the table so they had privacy. While he undid the blanket strips and placed the pile of clothing on the floor, she solemnly lit two candles and set them at the head and foot of the table.

"My Mama always lit candles when she was layin' out," she said, "out o' respect for th' dead."

Next she brought a wicker basket filled with small utensils and then two towels and a blue-flowered porcelain basin filled with sweet-scented water. By the candlelight she began carefully washing the remains. As the professor stood contemplating the rhythmic motions of her strong white hands and smelling the sweet water and running his eyes over the graceful blue flowers on the porcelain basin, images of sacred rituals flooded his mind. To his ears, the fiddler's raucous tune rang like majestic organ music.

Then the fiddle stopped and from the rooms behind them there was only the drone of unintelligible conversations. "Requiem for the dead," he said quietly.

Caroline seemed to understand he wasn't talking to her. She ignored him and began scrubbing one of the old man's gnarled hands with a soaked towel. A grave look came on her face. "Puts me in mind some o' my Papa," she said. She patted the hand with the dry towel. As she moved around the table to scrub the other hand, her motion caused the candles to flicker, and shadows of moving light played over the dead man's maimed features.

Before she began washing his face, she tried to close his mouth but his jaws were locked open. She couldn't get his eyelids to come down either so she just washed him the way he was. When she began swiping the wet towel down the chest and on toward the more private parts, the professor wanted to show he had respect for the dead too so he turned his head away.

After she'd finished the sponge bath, Caroline sloshed the dirty water in the basin out the open back door. The professor stood stroking his own beard and watching while she selected a comb from the basket and smoothed the matted white hair back off the old man's face. Then she took a pair of shears to the grizzled beard and evened it up, and last of all she pared the jagged fingernails with a penknife and scraped the rings of black dirt out from under them.

As she stepped back to judge her handiwork, the fiddler commenced "La Paloma." He wasn't sawing this time. He was gently coaxing the notes out of his instrument. And when the notion took him he'd chime in with a few words in a high rather nasal twang:

"... day that I left my home for the rolling sea, I said, 'Mother dear, oh pray to thy God for me.'"

As the professor knew all too well, homesickness on the frontier was more common than mountain fever and dysentery and cholera combined, and the moving song brought all conversations in the Bluebird to a halt. The rapt attention seemed to inspire the fiddler even more and he made his instrument throb with melancholy.

"... if I should die and o'er ocean foam ..." he sang. Then he followed up with a cascade of soft sweet notes.

"Too sad," the professor murmured, "too sad to bear ... like there's no home or happiness left in the world."

Caroline was still examining the neatened corpse. "Eyes n' mouth look awful bad," she said. She fished in the pocket of her pale blue dress and pulled out a white handkerchief that was embroidered with blue forget-me-nots and spread it over his face. "There, that's better."

At the show of tenderness from such a hard woman, the professor could feel a tightening in his throat and his eyes went a little watery. He didn't dare to wipe them though because she'd notice and think he was unmanly.

Caroline bent over to the floor and began sorting through the heap of dirty ragged clothing the bullwhacker had retrieved from the badger hole. "Give me a hand here," she ordered.

The professor hurried to help her but even with both of them working at it, they weren't able to tug the patched trousers past the knees. And when they examined the shirt and shoes it was plain they were too small also.

Caroline seemed to be puzzling over this strange turn of events but she didn't say anything. She just brought a clean white sheet and covered the old man up to the chin so it looked like he was sleeping peacefully with a daintily embroidered shade over his eyes. All the while she was smoothing the sheet though, she kept giving the professor side glances.

He guessed she was thinking that nobody in town really knew much about him, only that in the evenings he went to the Elkhorn and perched in the high barber chair so he could be above the rest of the crowd. Then he sat and drank the locally brewed beer and observed true frontier society in action. After a few drinks he couldn't help reflecting out loud on human nature and history and literature and philosophy. He'd warned himself not to do it but he was always forgetting, and his bad habit didn't set well with the saloon crowd. He knew so because just yesterday he'd walked into the Elkhorn and overheard Beidler calling him the "ejycated li'l fool." That was the time when everybody in earshot laughed. The insult hurt so much he had wanted to turn around and go back to the shop, and he would have except he knew that would only give them another laugh on him.

The fiddler ended his song and the conversations behind them started again. The professor caught Caroline sneaking another look at him. That set off a nervous twitch in his left eye and right away she observed it and strode to the end of the table where he'd laid Doctor Glick's paper. She snatched it up and began reading it.

"Damn little weasel, you!" she hissed. "Gettin' me mixed up in a damn murder."

She squeezed the paper in her hand and hurried out the open back door. "You stay put!" she yelled back. "I'm goin' for my husband. You damn well better stay put!"

The professor had heard that when Caroline referred to her husband she meant Edward Ray, and he knew Ray was a deputy for the miners' association so he didn't try to leave. He just walked to the open doorway and stood there watching and waiting for her to come back. He'd never pretended to be a brave man and it didn't surprise him when he felt his legs begin to tremble underneath him. He had visions of Deputy Ray forcing him to walk barefoot on hot coals to prove his innocence. "Oh dear Lord," he said, "deliver me from the fiery furnace."

The tic in his left eye was coming oftener and sharper and he tried to divert his attention to something else. He knew it was crucial he didn't appear nervous when the two of them got back. He tried to think of a specimen of frontier humanity who was interesting enough to keep him occupied.

The obvious person to mull over in his mind was the woman who'd just stalked out the back door. She was definitely an interesting specimen. He had some doubts the frontier experience had changed her though. Probably she had always been tough as nails and headstrong as a mule. He didn't know much about her, only that she and Ray lived together in great luxury in a small cabin on the banks of Grasshopper Creek. Evidently she'd fallen head over heels in love with the handsome engineer from New York and he appeared to be taken with her too. In fact he was so jealous she'd had to start disappointing her regular clients at the Bluebird. Only last night the owner of the Elkhorn, Cyrus Skinner, was taking bets that Ray would marry Caroline within a week. His customers thought Cyrus was crazy and began pulling out their pokes of gold dust faster than he could record the bets.

The professor tried to concentrate on what a strange couple the two of them made, a civil engineer from a prominent Eastern family and an unrefined madam from God knows where ... and how they'd been thrown together on the frontier and seemed to care for each other and get along fairly well. But what was really on his mind was his own predicament. "Dear Lord," he said, "please let Deputy Ray believe me." He readjusted his spectacles and tugged at his beard. Then he pulled out his gold watch and checked the time and slipped it back in his vest pocket and patted it to his heart.

But his left eye kept on twitching. "I'm innocent of any crime," he said and patted the watch to his heart again. The problem was he didn't feel innocent. He felt guilty. He was guilty of trying to bury a man without notifying the Sheriff about the gun wounds. "It's just that law officers make me nervous, Lord," he said. "How can I be sure they're honest?"

And he was also guilty of abandoning his wife and parents for no other reason than to satisfy his own selfish wants. "I only left them temporarily, Lord," he said. "How can I understand ancient history if I ignore the history taking place around me? I had to witness this fantastic rush for gold with my own eyes."

His vision seemed clouded and he took off his spectacles and cleaned them with his handkerchief. "Nothing to worry about ... innocent of murder. Completely innocent." Then he pressed the watch to his chest and held it there. Hearing the reassuring words and feeling the gift from his little Creole wife touching his heart soothed him so much his legs stopped trembling and his left eye quit twitching too.

When Caroline finally came in sight across the creek, he was horrified to see that Deputy Ray and Deputy Stinson and Sheriff Will Plummer were all trailing behind her. He could see that Stinson was holding a piece of white paper in his hand, evidently Glick's report. They'd read it. They knew it was murder. And they suspected he was the murderer. "So it won't be Deputy Ray," he said. "It'll be the notorious Sheriff Plummer who'll toss me into the lion's den ... Oh dear Lord, please spare me, ... for Angeline's sake."

He observed the four of them as they took turns walking single file across the log spanning the Grasshopper. He knew Stinson from another camp. And he knew the First Deputy by sight. Two nights ago while he'd been sitting in the barber chair at the Elkhorn, Ray had broken the faro dealer's bank.

But the Bannack Sheriff ... he was an altogether different case. The professor had never had a chance to study the man up close. All the merchants knew Plummer made his rounds of town on foot about dawn, but at that hour the professor was still sleeping in the bunk at the back of the shop. And when the Sheriff passed down main street during daylight hours, he was usually on top his shiny long-legged bay horse and surrounded by other riders.

Caroline and the three law officers were now on this side of the creek and headed toward the cabin, with the Sheriff walking off to one side of Caroline. Plummer was slim and a little above average height. It was a fairly long hike across Yankee Flat and there was nothing the professor could do but stand and wait and watch his accusers approach. He tried to calm himself by saying out loud that a face-to-face meeting with the most famous lawman on the frontier was the chance of a lifetime. From the day the professor had stepped off the steamer at Fort Benton, he'd heard bits and snatches of the legend that had grown up around William Henry Plummer. And now the enigmatic man himself was coming closer ... step by step.

The professor's legs were trembling again and he knew he had to avoid thinking about his own plight so he focused on the Sheriff. Plummer was a more interesting specimen than either Doctor Glick or Caroline because there was a great mystery about him. The Plummer legend began with the rush to the California gold fields, how a teenage law student from Maine made a name as a peacemaker in the lawless mining camps. Apparently the young Easterner thought his aristocratic background obligated him to assume civic responsibility on the frontier.

When he was only twenty he was elected a city manager and town marshal for one of the largest towns in California. He made a flamboyant lawman and stories of him capturing dangerous desperadoes spread throughout the West. Years later he dispersed a rabid lynch mob in Lewiston, Idaho with nothing more than an eloquent speech. He was completely unarmed at the time.

Plummer took his eyes off the path and studied the suspect waiting in the open doorway. Then he looked down again. There was no doubt the man who created the legend was a prepossessing figure. But the professor comforted himself by thinking about the stories of Plummer helping the needy, how once he'd ridden for miles along a wilderness trail to find a buffalo robe that a destitute miner had lost. And another time he'd come close to being shot himself while he was protecting a housewife whose gambler husband beat her regularly and occasionally tried to choke her to death.

As Plummer walked, he continued glancing up at the man he was coming to question, and the professor couldn't keep his eyes off the mysterious lawman either. By the easy way Plummer moved he appeared to be very athletic. Supposedly he was the best at everything from dancing or riding a horse to giving advice on mining or personal problems. Here at Bannack the miners referred to him as "the law of the country." It was common knowledge he was the best shot at the mines and apparently he'd had to prove it from time to time. But now he didn't even appear to be armed. There was no sign of a gun belt and holsters under his suit coat.

He was within yards of the back door of the Bluebird and in just moments he'd be starting the interrogation. The professor felt a chill run down his spine. Along with all the stories of heroic feats, there were also rumors ... rumors about a dark secret in Plummer's California days. There was also an account from Idaho about a shootout at the Orofino Corral and how Plummer had to escape a lynch mob by crossing to this side of the mountains.

Nobody really knew which stories were true and which weren't but most people seemed to think Plummer was a frontier hero. Still, there were a few skeptics who claimed he was a dangerous desperado himself. The professor couldn't help worrying over how a desperado went about questioning a murder suspect. The ordeal in store for him might be even more barbaric than walking barefoot on hot coals or being mauled by a lion in its own den.

Now Caroline and the three men following her were only a few steps from the cabin door. The professor readjusted his spectacles and tried to convince himself he was very lucky. Everybody at the mines hoped for a chance to have a private chat with Plummer. It would make a good story to relate when they got home. But on the other hand, who would want to go home and tell his wife and parents that Sheriff Plummer had questioned him as a murderer.

Caroline swished into the room, hiking up her long blue skirt as she stepped over the sill. The two deputies held back to let their dignified superior enter ahead of them. As the professor took his first close look at the Sheriff, the left eye went back to its twitching and he had to step inside and grip the green-felt gaming table with both hands for support.

First Plummer glanced down at the covered corpse and then he approached the professor and casually fixed his eyes on him. He extended one hand and said without much warmth, "Will Plummer." Everything about the man gave off an aura of Eastern gentility. It seemed impossible he could be a desperado.

The professor took the extended hand and answered quickly, probably too quickly, "Richard Rawley here." His voice wasn't nearly as steady as it was when he talked to himself. He concentrated on trying to control the eye tic. But Plummer's eyes seemed to be piercing right through to his very soul, and without any warning all of Professor Rawley's efforts at control suddenly collapsed.

He began blurting out that he was innocent of any crime and had never seen the poor old man before the freighters carried him into the carpenter shop for a coffin and how the hefty clean-cut Mormon mentioned horrible savagery in the prayer and that convinced him the victim had been killed by Indians. And if they didn't believe him then they could go over to main street right now and ask the Mormons about it because they were still unloading their wagons and if the Mormons denied it, then they were lying, just like they lied when they said they'd found a gold book a wingless angel had buried in a hill and when they said they didn't commit the massacre in the meadow when everybody knew they did. While he frantically went on pleading his innocence, Plummer kept him pinned down with a stern gaze.

Finally Professor Rawley blinked his eyelids shut and rocked back on his heels and drew a deep breath and forced himself to stop babbling.

"Appreciate the information," Plummer said quietly. His voice was soft and rather low but even in those few words Rawley could detect the rhythm peculiar to an upper-class Down Easter.

Caroline pulled the blue-flowered handkerchief off the face of the corpse and Deputy Stinson gave a loud gasp and grabbed hold of the table edge himself. Then Caroline folded back the white sheet. Stinson's eyes went glassy and he stood staring at the undressed corpse like he was in a trance.

Deputy Ray appeared taken back too, but apparently he was trying to give the impression that seeing a nude mutilated corpse was something a frontier law officer had to do every day of the year. He casually bent down and examined the ball wound in the partly open mouth. Then he rolled the stiff body to one side so they could find the exit wound in the back of the head. Stinson let go of the table long enough to come over and look at it.

The two deputies began quietly offering theories about the mutilations. Rawley noticed the Northerner and Southerner disagreed with each other on almost every point. From time to time the two of them glanced over at him with suspicious eyes, like they thought he might try to make a break for it. For a moment he did consider it, but then he decided the desperado life was not for him.

"Not Indians," Ray said. "Definitely not Indians." The words sent another chill running down Rawley's spine.

For the first time, Stinson nodded in agreement with Ray. Plummer was keeping his thoughts to himself.

"Aloof," Rawley whispered to himself as he stood gripping the table. "The genteel Mr. Plummer is aloof." He stared hard at the Sheriff's face and tried to read what he saw there. "Maybe just reserved," he said. "Anyway, in some world of his own."

The Sheriff and deputies walked from one side of the table to the other, minutely examining the corpse in the flickering candlelight and all the while Rawley was trembling and holding on to the table and minutely examining the Sheriff, the man who was about to decide his fate.

Rawley noticed that both deputies seemed to be somewhat in awe of Plummer themselves. They were anxious to do the dirty work for him, like handling the corpse. And he stood back and took it like it was his due.

"Focus on this interesting specimen," Rawley whispered to himself. Obviously Plummer more than lived up to his reputation for being good looking. His facial features were well cut and the gray eyes showed intelligence. When he bent toward the candle glow, his light brown hair gave off golden glints and a full drooping mustache was just as glossy.

Part of the legend was that Plummer never wore miners' garb or buckskin, not even when he was on the trail. In fact the stiff-collared white shirt and the dark suit with a diamond stickpin in the lapel made him look like he'd just stepped out of a San Francisco tailor shop. And Rawley couldn't imagine how anybody was able to keep black boots so shiny in the dusty streets of Bannack.

While the law officers were hovering over the corpse, the fiddler commenced playing "Nelly Was a Lady." It was another favorite and the crowd behind them fell silent so they could listen. The Sheriff had stopped moving from one side of the table to the other now and stood looking pensively down at the dead man.

Rawley was surprised. "Gentleness," he whispered. "I see gentleness in Plummer's face."

One of Caroline's girls peeked around the edge of a screen but when the officers noticed her, she bobbed her head back.

"Pretty sure this man's Old Turk Keeler," Ray said. "He and his partner work a fairly worthless claim out west of the Salt Lake trail."

"Hard t' tell who it is without no clothes on," Stinson said.

The fiddler played another cascade of notes and then sang "Last night she died" in a mournful tone. Rawley felt the sensation of hopeless melancholy coming back. "No happiness left … no home," he said. "Hanged for a crime I didn't commit." He was starting to resign himself to the inevitable.

The three lawmen left the table and huddled near the door to hold a conference. Rawley was still observing Plummer's every action. "There's a mystery about him all right," he mumbled under his breath, "very well could have some dark secrets."

Rawley took his eyes off the Sheriff just in time to see both deputies indicating toward him. Then they leaned in toward Plummer and began speaking to him very earnestly, as though they were trying to convince him of something. He heard Stinson say, "Reckon he ain't in cahoots with th' Mormons?"

Plummer seemed to be considering the notion. Then he looked over at Rawley and shook his head.

"Bless him, Lord," Rawley breathed, "for knowing an honest man when he sees one."

Caroline had busied herself covering the body again and as the huddle broke up, Ray walked over and bent down to her ear.

"Sugar," he said. The tone was so intimate Rawley felt embarrassed to be listening. Caroline didn't answer. She seemed to think Ray was going to ask some favor she didn't want to give.

"Sugar," Ray said again, "we want you to keep the body for a while. You do that for us?"

She didn't seem very pleased about the assignment but she nodded and Ray turned to Rawley. "Go ahead with the coffin," he said. He stood staring at Rawley for several moments and the suspicion in his eyes was evident. Then he added, "But hold up on the burial till I say so."

The three officers left by the rear exit. Rawley watched Plummer and Ray head in the direction of the stable and Stinson turned the other way. As the three of them disappeared from sight, he heaved a deep sigh and released his hold on the table but his legs were still wobbly and his left eye was jerked by an occasional twitch.

"Say," one of Caroline's girls called from behind the screens, "can't we come in and pay our respects to the deceased too?" It was the same girl who had bobbed her head in before.

She parted the screens and two other girls and a few male customers stuck their heads in and gaped at the covered body. Then the group brushed past Rawley as if he didn't exist and surrounded the gambling table.

"Hey, that mop o' white hair looks like Old Turk," one man

said. "Helluva nice feller. Give you the shirt off his back."

"Yep, just a nice old grampa," another man agreed. "One time I run into him buyin' meat at the butcher shop and he was boastin' about his forty-four grandchildren back in the States, swearin' he wasn't goin' home till he could make every last one of 'em rich."

Rawley would have liked to hear what else they had to say about the deceased but he couldn't stay any longer. The Lord had been gracious enough to deliver him from the fiery furnace and the lion's den and now he had to show his gratitude by keeping his promise. He had a coffin to build for a kind old grandfather who had been murdered by somebody.

And also he'd taken pay for the grandfather's burial, so he'd have to scout out Xavier Beidler and hire him to dig a grave up on cemetery hill.

CHAPTER THREE

It was dusk by the time the grandfather's pine box was finished. Rawley's back ached from bending over so long so he walked to the open front doors and began massaging his spine against the frame. While he rubbed the strained muscles, he caressed his beard and gazed out at the Sunday evening traffic. He was still nursing the sore back when Sheriff Plummer and Deputy Ray crossed the creek on horseback and rode onto main street with a prisoner in tow.

As they passed in front of the carpenter shop, Rawley got a good view of the teenage boy riding between the two officers. He was slender and had a face that was as pretty and delicate as a girl's. Underneath his slouch hat, his pale brown hair fringed out in a ragged border, as if he'd trimmed his own hair with a knife. He was astride a scrawny gray mule, and a cloth bundle was strung from its crude wooden saddle.

Tied behind Deputy Ray's horse was another scrawny mule, a white one. Rawley supposed the white mule and the pathetically few items loaded on its back were the estate of the deceased grandfather. As the weary little animal trudged by, he could see it was packed with a pick, a shovel, a buffalo robe, and some envelopes and a Bible which were strapped together with a rawhide thong.

On both sides of main street, customers and merchants began pouring from business houses and jostling each other out of the way so they could maneuver for a position directly behind the arrest party. While the rowdy parade advanced, it kept growing wider and longer. Rawley was exhausted but he couldn't resist running to join in. He wanted to see how Plummer and Ray handled their prisoner. "It could have been me," he said as he hurried to the center of the street.

Because of his small size, he was eventually able to work his way directly behind the prisoner. It wasn't until after he was in position that he realized he'd squeezed between Xavier Beidler and butcher Hank Crawford. Being sandwiched between two Stranglers wasn't a pleasant sensation, but he had no intentions of giving up this prize place for observing what was about to happen. It was every bit as good as the high barber chair.

He noticed the young prisoner was wearing a red flannel shirt that was too big for him and buckskin trousers that were so baggy they had to be cinched to his waist with a rope. It didn't take much imagination to see the clothes would have fit the dead grandfather a lot better than the thin boy.

Excited citizens were now pressing in on all sides of the arrest party and some of the wilder ones started hooting at the murder suspect. The boy began twisting his head around from side to side and trying to answer every tormentor who yelled at him.

"I didn't kill Old Turk," he insisted in a high-pitched voice. "I wouldn't never kill him. He was my onlyest friend."

Hearing him deny the awful crime outraged the crowd even more.

"String 'im up rycheer!" Beidler screamed at the top of his lungs.

The boy let out a long moan and dropped the mule's reins so he could cover up his ears. But the catcalls continued from all sides.

"Why'd ya slice out his tongue?" Hank Crawford bellowed over the other shouts, "so he couldn't tell on ya?"

Beside Rawley, Beidler began hopping up and down and swinging his arms over his head like he was completely crazed. "Do what he done t' ole Keeler!" he yelled. "Poke out 'is eyes! Cut off 'is tongue!"

From behind, a group of latecomers jolted against the mass of bodies that were already jammed into the pack and propelled them forward like dominoes. The impact sent Rawley sprawling headlong into the mule's rump. Fortunately the weak old animal ignored the bump, but the prisoner whirled around in his wooden saddle and gaped down at Rawley like he thought he'd struck the mule on purpose. The boy's hazel-colored eyes were big with fear.

Rawley quickly squirmed out of the mule's kicking range, just in case the animal had a change of heart, and fell in with the pace of the moving crowd again. "The boy's right to be afraid," he said. "I shouldn't have joined in. Too dangerous ... could turn into a lynch mob." But there was no way to extract himself now. All he could do was keep moving with the flow and hope things didn't turn any uglier than they already were.

Rawley was especially worried because he'd heard that before the miners convinced Plummer to take over as Sheriff, lynching had been standard practice at the mines. In fact some citizens had objected when the Sheriff had a jail built. They informed him they didn't like the idea of a delay between the arrest and the hanging.

The sturdy little log jail stood on the bank of the Grasshopper directly behind Chrisman's general store. That made it convenient for the lawmen because Plummer kept an office at the back of the store. As the riders passed Chrisman's and turned up the narrow alley toward the jail, there was another mighty surge forward and Rawley and some of the other lightweights were violently shoved aside and back onto main street. During the mad rush to fill in the gaps, Rawley was swept off his feet. As he went tumbling into the maze of bodies around him, he caught a fleeting glimpse of Plummer. The Sheriff had turned back in his saddle and was glancing down at the stampeding crowd behind him.

"Very calm," Rawley marveled, "Plummer looks very calm." Then the collection of bodies Rawley was leaning on collapsed like cards and he felt himself splashing into the ankle-deep dust of main street.

* * *

Stinson wasn't expecting Plummer and Ray back till morning so he'd gone home to put on his Sunday suit and take Sadie to services. There wasn't a real church in town but on the Sabbath a preacher of sorts delivered a long sermon in a big log hogan on

Yankee Flat.

Sadie was pregnant with their first child and she was feeling rather sick, so they had to board with the Tolands. That way Sadie didn't have to do any cleaning or cooking. She spent most of her time sitting in a straight-backed chair and keeping her plump little fingers busy at stitching baby clothes while she chatted with Mama Toland. The only time Sadie got out of the house was when Stinson took her to church on Sunday. She looked forward to it all week.

He stood in front of a small mirror hung on the rough-log wall of their bedroom and knotted his tie. Next he dipped a comb in the water basin he'd just washed in and slicked back his long hair. He was the only barber in town and he was too busy with his customers and the deputy work to give himself a haircut. Of course the deputy job didn't pay any money. The only reason he bothered with it was because it made Sadie so proud to see him on the right side of the law.

She was sitting on the edge of the bed with her face tilted up to him, like she was admiring his solid frame in a go-to-meeting outfit.

"Plain" was how most people described Sadie. Stinson knew that. And most people thought she was bossy too. But he owed her everything. In his eyes she was beautiful and loving. He'd been a hard case before she got hold of him, but she goaded him into giving up gambling and drinking and cussing and then gradually forced him around to religion. She was always bragging to the Tolands about what a fine man her Buck was, how he was the best-ever lawman and how she just knew he'd make the best-ever father too.

The Tolands were already dressed for church. They were waiting on the other side of the curtain that separated their front room from the Stinson quarters.

"Aintcha 'bout ready yet, Buck?" Mama Toland asked impatiently.

Before he could answer, the sound of angry shouts came echoing from across the creek. Stinson grabbed his hat and slapped it on his head and one by one the four of them hurried out the front door of the cabin. They could see a huge noisy crowd swarming around the little jail. It reminded Stinson of a bunch of mean old red ants that had been stirred out of their hill with a stick.

"Reckon it's a howlin' lynch mob," he muttered. "Gotta run."

Sadie bit her lip to keep from crying. "Now you take care, Buck," she said. Her voice was sharp and stern. "I don't want you comin' home in no pine box. In my condition I just couldn't stand that."

"Amen, Ma," Stinson answered. He gave her plump little arm a good-bye pinch.

He didn't take time to run down to the bridge. He just splashed through the creek even if it did soak his boots and the legs of his suit trousers. It wasn't till he reached the fringes of the mob and spotted the jailer standing in the jail doorway and holding a shotgun on the rowdy bunch that Stinson grabbed for his revolver and discovered he'd left it at the cabin. It was too late to go back for it now. He began elbowing his way through the mass of half-drunk miners so he could get to the panicky boy on top of the gray mule.

Above and ahead of him he could see Sheriff Plummer and Deputy Ray sitting on their tall horses. Plummer looked as coolheaded as always. And Ray seemed almost too casual, like he was foolish enough to expect that his luck at the gambling tables would carry over into his work.

Stinson couldn't help it if he wasn't like them. He was a born worrier. His mind always raced ahead to some awful ending and his muscles tensed and his eyes and nose and ears went on double-duty. Every hoot and catcall around him seemed magnified at least ten times.

With the uproar hammering against his eardrums, he kept on trying to force his way to the prisoner sitting on the mule. But he wasn't making much progress. Finally Ray caught sight of him and drew his revolver and fired in the air. The crowd froze where they were.

In the silence, Plummer spoke out. "Return to your Sunday recreation, Gentlemen," he said. "Justice will be served, you have my word on it."

The crowd hovered in their positions for a short time. Then they reluctantly began breaking up. Stinson noticed the dark-complected little carpenter with the bushy black beard standing over on main street. He was brushing dust off his clothes, like he'd just taken a spill. He looked almost as nervous as he had at the Bluebird but there wasn't any reason for it now. The Salt Lake freighters had told the same story about the body that he did so he was in the clear. Stinson watched him pull off his spectacles and wipe them with his handkerchief, then he smoothed down his suit and followed the stream flooding back toward the Elkhorn.

Stinson headed toward the new murder suspect so he could drag him off the mule and rush him inside the jail, but Ray came riding over and cut him off.

"Let the jailers handle that, Reb," he said. "Get on over to the Elkhorn and pick us a jury panel."

Stinson was anxious to get a closer look at the monster who'd carved up Old Turk, but he knew Ray was right. It was Sunday evening and he had to catch the miners before they started drifting back to their claims. He gave the skinny boy on the half-starved gray mule a quick once-over and felt himself shiver. Then he headed for the saloon, trailing on the heels of the crowd. They didn't seem quite so upset any more, but he still was. He'd felt that way ever since Miss Caroline came running to the Sheriff's office and told them about the queer little carpenter showing up at the Bluebird with a naked corpse whose clothes didn't fit him. Just remembering it made the smell of burning candles, mixed in with the scent of the perfumed water Miss Caroline had smeared all over the corpse, shoot up his nostrils and almost drown his brain, just like it had at the Bluebird in the afternoon. Something was wrong about the whole thing. It just wasn't natural to kill a man and then undress him. Stinson felt in his bones that it was a very bad omen.

He crossed the street and started down the boardwalk and it gave out its familiar creaks and snaps under his wet boots. The further he got from the jail, the better he was feeling. If they were lucky, the boy would confess and then they could get it over with right away and maybe forget it. Passing down main street and seeing the miners get back to enjoying their day off made his heart feel lighter too. And it made him know he was worth something because he was in charge of what went on in main street. It was the way he used to feel before Miss Caroline snatched that dainty little blue-flowered handkerchief off the dead man's face and he saw it didn't have any eyes and its mouth gaped open.

And speaking of gaping mouths, he was thinking how in another week or so there'd be another mouth for him to feed. So after he chose the panel, he probably should take time to settle a few customers in his barber chair and snip some shaggy heads and scrape off a few whiskers ... collect a little gold dust in his own pouch.

He looked up at the Elkhorn just ahead. It was the typical main street building, just a long narrow log cabin, but its false front was the fanciest in town and Stinson was proud to have his barber chair there. Cyrus Skinner bragged that the front of the building was a perfect copy of a Greek temple. Of course Sadie claimed a hateful old saloon had no business whatsoever copying a sacred temple, and to keep peace in the family Stinson didn't argue with her. But to be honest about it, he couldn't see the harm.

He admired those six square columns that pretended to be holding the building up and he thought the row of squiggles that ran all the way across the top of the false front was especially pretty. There was some fancy carving above the two front doors also, and each door had a big pane of glass. On each side of the double doors were more windows, and their glass had lots of small panes that reached up almost six feet high.

The doors were standing open and he stepped in and looked around. The long oak bar that stretched down the entire left-hand wall was truly a sight to behold. It had a design chiseled into it too, and Cyrus kept it polished till it fairly shone. But the back wall wasn't much to brag about. It was lined with bunks and dried-grass mattresses that Cyrus rented out like a hotel.

When Stinson first made arrangements to barber inside the saloon, he'd insisted his chair be as far away from the bunks as possible. He hadn't minced words either, he'd just told Cyrus straight out, "T' be right honest, Cy, that whole back wall stinks o' stale armpits an' dried piss an' I ain't fixin' t' have no payin' customer o' mine tolerate such stench!"

So Cyrus agreed to let him have the right front corner near the windows and that worked out fine. While Stinson snipped away, his customers could get a whiff of fresh air from the open front doors and at the same time entertain themselves watching what was going on in the main street. And there was always something going on. There were plenty of expert horsemen, like Plummer and Ray, passing by and showing off their riding skills and their tall glossy mounts. And there were long strings of oxen teams tugging lines of wagons that were linked together, and also shorter strings of single-file pack-jacks, braying like banshees from the minute they set hoof in town because they were so tired and hungry and thirsty.

Stinson sauntered over to the empty wall on the right side of the Elkhorn and leaned up against it and began taking stock of who was there. He wanted to survey the whole bunch before he began choosing. He noticed the little carpenter was perched up in the barber chair but he didn't see any harm in that. He wasn't ready to start taking customers yet anyway.

The bartender still hadn't shown up so Cyrus had to take over himself. He was a burly man with a red face and coarse homely features. He never bothered to slick down his mousey-brown hair and it stood up in rooster-tails all over his head. There was nothing Stinson hated more than trying to give him a haircut. And it wasn't just because of his unruly hair. It didn't matter whether Cyrus was talking or just laughing at his own jokes, he was always too loud. Stinson watched him standing in the light from the front windows and rolling up his shirt sleeves high enough to show off his big muscles. From wrist to shoulder, both of his thick arms were covered with red and blue ink tattoos. Stinson admired the colored tattoos almost as much as he admired the columns and carvings out front. His favorite tattoo was a picture of a blue mother holding a blue baby, and he also liked the red anchor. Cyrus was an ex-con. His crime had been stealing a mule. He always passed off his months on the prison brig at San Quentin as being in the navy. That's why he had the anchor tattoo, he said, because he'd weathered the storm and was in port now. He shoved his sleeves up past his bulging muscles and hustled behind the bar and announced he was ready for business.

Hank Crawford was first in line. He'd bullied his way to the front by pushing meeker men aside and he began calling for a double of the usual. The butcher made good money supplying the town with meat and he could afford to drink whatever he wanted. He didn't dress like a man who spent his time slaughtering animals and chopping them up in pieces. After Hank took off his bloody apron and turned the shop over to his assistant Conrad Kohrs, he washed every splatter of blood off his face and arms and then flattened his hair down with scented pomade and put on some spiffy clothes. Stinson thought Hank could easily have passed for a gambler ... brocade vest and stickpin and all, except that his big-knuckled scarred hands gave him away.

There was so much commotion over who was next in line for a drink that Stinson decided he'd just have to stand there and wait till things settled down before he could size up the crowd. He lifted one foot up and rested the sole of his boot against the wall to make himself more comfortable. It took lots of willpower for him to stand there without any glass in his hand and remember how fine it used to feel when a slug of sweet whiskey gently burned a track down his gullet. And then how smooth and easy life suddenly turned after only one swallow. Took lots of willpower all right ... only not his. All the willpower was on Sadie's part. She wouldn't put up with any backsliding from him. He watched Hank squeeze his tall glass and then flop down at his usual card table. Hank took a few gulps from his drink and fastened his deep-set hawkish eyes on Stinson.

"Personally," he said, and his voice rumbled in his narrow chest like he was a fire-and-brimstone revival preacher instead of a sharp-eyed rawboned frontiersman, "I'm agin Plummer's ways." Then he turned his sharp eyes on Stinson and studied his face to see if he'd got his goat.

Xavier Beidler glanced at Stinson's face too and then settled into a chair at the same table with Hank. He always broke the rules and brought his own liquor with him so he began searching in his pocket for his flask. In the oversized black coat he looked puny, but Stinson knew that underneath the layers of clothes, X. wasn't any sissy. He was strong in the arms and every bit as wiry as Hank.

"Hey!" Beidler announced, "ole X. here stan's with Hank." Then he looked around the room to see what kind of stir he'd caused.

But nobody seemed the least bit surprised. What Beidler lacked in height and weight he made up for in big talk. His favorite pastime was bragging how he was working night and day for the U.S. government. If anybody took the bait and asked him what his job was, he'd laugh and say he was exterminating red and yellow varmints. Nobody knew how much truth there was to his claims about the number of Indians and Chinamen he'd killed. But it was common knowledge he enjoyed lynching white men. Every chance he got he clamored for an instant hanging and he always volunteered to be the nooser.

After the exciting part was over and everybody else had left, Beidler'd hang around the beef scaffold or corral gate for an hour or so to be sure the victim was dead. Then he'd dig a grave and put the lynched man in it and demand payment from the victim's estate. Stinson figured Beidler must have a fascination for digging graves for folks. And he'd also noticed Beidler usually managed to end up with something off the corpse. Once it was an ivory-handled pocket knife, and another time it was a pair of fancy beaded leggings.

Beidler looked disappointed that he and Crawford hadn't been able to get Stinson riled up. He narrowed his eyes and studied Stinson for a while and then made a second stab at it.

He wasn't very original so he just repeated his first line. "Hey! ole X. here stan's with Hank."

Stinson knew Beidler was just fishing for a quarrel with him. That's exactly why he wasn't snapping at the worm.

But Beidler got lucky and landed an even bigger catch. From across the room Harry Percival Adams Smith called out, "Well, 'ole' X., ... old H. P. A. Smith here don't stand with Hank! How ya like them apples?"

The stout gray-haired lawyer was a known toper, but everybody agreed he was the best defense attorney this side of the mountains. Some time ago he'd gotten Stinson himself off the hook for one of his past shooting scrapes. Smith picked up his drink and strolled over to Crawford's table and stood there smiling down at Beidler and examining him from head to toe.

"Say ya noosin' little s.o.b.," he said, "what brings ya t' town? Lookin' for a grave t' dig?"

"Hopin' fer th' job o' diggin' yers," Beidler came back. He spoke with his usual nasal twang, like his nose was permanently plugged up.

Stinson thought for a man who couldn't read or write, Beidler was doing a pretty good job of holding his own against a book-reading lawyer. But Smith only chuckled. "Opium dream, my little man, just an opium dream."

Beidler busied himself shuffling the cards and didn't say any more. Stinson could see the little Strangler wasn't too pleased he'd hooked a fish that had more brains than he did.

But Smith didn't seem inclined to leave. He just stood there and kept on examining Beidler. It made Stinson a little nervous because he was afraid he might have to step in. And that could mean trouble since he'd rushed out of the cabin so fast he'd forgotten his revolver.

"Say, X.," Smith said, "that overcoat's so damn long it covers up your fancy beaded leggin's."

When Beidler let that remark slide by too, Smith gave up and shuffled back to his own table.

While Stinson leaned against the wall and observed the lot of them with an eagle eye, the men got their card games going. But it was obvious the mutilated miner and his boy partner were the only thing that was really on their minds, just like the young murderer and his victim were still at the back of Stinson's head. In fact he didn't even have to remind himself that's why he was here. He ignored the banter around him and started taking a serious look at who was there and trying to decide which ones he ought to select. He wanted to get the best men in the community so tomorrow morning when they were trying to get the trial going, the two lawyers wouldn't waste a lot of time fussing at each other while they picked eight men out of his panel.

As he slowly covered each table for likely candidates he noticed that no matter what new topic anybody brought up, the talk gradually drifted back to Old Turk and the boy. Then one tipsy Irish miner hopped up and began capering around and taking bets in his slouch hat on how soon Beidler would get soused and scramble up on the table and start calling for a necktie party over at the jail.

Stinson decided the time had come to remind the saloon crowd who was boss. Otherwise things might get out of hand and he had no gun on him.

He pulled his hat down over his bad forehead and threw his shoulders back and began weaving his way through the card tables. The crowded hall suddenly got quiet. He tapped the first man on the shoulder and then moved on. Then he wound around the tables and tapped the second man and then sauntered back toward the bunks. He didn't have to explain. Everybody knew what it meant.

It made Stinson recollect a game they used to play when he was a boy. It was called "I Had a Little Doggie." The lucky one who got to be "it" ran outside a circle of players holding hands and facing in toward the center. While "it" ran outside the ring he chanted, "I had a little doggie, an' it wouldn't bite y'all, an' it wouldn't bite y'all, an' it wouldn't bite y'all ... but it would bite ... !" Then "it" pecked the chosen player on the shoulder and took off running at top speed. The one who was doggie-bit got to chase "it" around the outside of the circle.

Stinson felt very lucky he just happened to be wearing his Sunday suit when it was his turn to be the big "it" at the Elkhorn tonight and he didn't mind dragging the suspense out a bit.

When he finally finished tapping the last man on the shoulder, he was about to ask the little carpenter to vacate the barber chair so he could get started at his real job. But all of a sudden he remembered Sadie waiting for him back at the cabin. With all the hoopla brought on by the boy's arrest, and then Sheriff having to break up the mob, and then his assignment of picking a jury panel, he'd completely forgotten about church.

Sadie would be twisting and squirming in the straight-backed chair. She'd be too worked up to keep her mind on sewing baby clothes so she'd just be sitting there staring out the door and watching for him and by now she'd probably be madder than a wet hen. He gave up the idea of barbering and headed straight for the open front doors on the run. Maybe if he hurried fast enough, they still might be able to catch the tail end of the sermon.

"Y'all be prompt now," he yelled back. "Jury selection at nine in th' mornin'."

CHAPTER FOUR

They buried the murder victim early Monday morning. The prosecutor was very disappointed because he'd been counting on displaying the corpse at the trial. But the Judge told him he couldn't do that. The crowd was going to be hard enough to handle as it was. And Deputy Stinson agreed.

Not many people showed up for the early-morning burial at the cemetery but the trial drew a big crowd. Miners and merchants began gathering on main street right after breakfast. Sheriff Plummer could see there were too many of them to fit into a building so he decided to hold the trial outdoors. He had the deputies and jail guards haul two freight wagons to a flat just past the stable and set up court there. One wagon was for the Judge and it had a table and chair in it, and the other wagon was for a witness stand so all it needed was a short wooden bench. Since the two freight wagons had such tall wheels, everybody standing in the audience could have a good view of the action.

They also set up two tables at ground level. One was for Sheriff Plummer and the prosecutor, and the other was for the defendant and his attorney, plus an armed jailer to protect them both. The crippled jailer had volunteered for the job so he wouldn't have to stand up like the rest of the lawmen on duty. To make a jury box, Stinson borrowed two long benches from the hurdy-gurdy house. As usual he had to do the biggest share of the grunting and heaving himself but he didn't mind because he knew a little hard work never hurt anybody.

All the time the deputies were getting things ready, the all-male audience that was gathering on the flat kept spreading out bigger and bigger. Stinson was relieved they had good weather for the big event. Since last night he'd been worried it might rain.

But the sky was a clear bright blue and there wasn't a single cloud overhead. There wasn't any wind either and the scent of sagebrush hung in the still air. The temperature was just crisp enough to make a light coat feel cozy.

As soon as the Judge climbed into his wagon, Stinson and Ray and two of the jailers took up their shotguns and stationed themselves at the four corners of the court's imaginary boundaries. Stinson hurried to grab the post right next to the witness wagon because he was anxious to hear the testimony.

Because the Stranglers were on the prowl, just before midnight Sheriff Plummer had ordered Deputy Ray to secretly move the prisoner out of the little log jail. They left two guards at the jail and kept a light burning inside just like they were keeping vigil over a prisoner, but under cover of darkness Ray's men eased the boy out the door and up the back alley and then across the street to the stable. They'd kept him hidden in the loft the rest of the night and he was still there.

When everybody in court was in place, four guards towed the boy over in a little cart. He was in chains so it would have taken too long for him to walk. They seated him at the defense table, right in between his lawyer H. P. A. Smith and the crippled jailer with a shotgun in hand.

It was Stinson's first chance to take a good hard look at the awful monster and he didn't waste the opportunity. He noticed right off that the skinny little murderer was shifty-eyed. The problem was that lawyer Smith had the boy's face shined up and his hair trimmed and wetted down till he looked like he was on his way to Sunday school. The only thing missing was a Bible in his hands.

Yesterday when Sheriff Plummer and Deputy Ray had brought the captured prisoner into town, Stinson had taken it for granted the boy was guilty. Otherwise Sheriff wouldn't have arrested him. Because as Stinson had figured out some time ago, Plummer was a man who could read minds. At least that's what Stinson always supposed Plummer was doing when his eyes bored into you that way.

So last night after the sermon at church, Stinson had walked

Sadie back to the cabin and then gone over to the jail. It was about ten o'clock when he arrived and Deputy Ray had just left to eat a late supper.

"Want me a look-see at th' monster," he told the guards.

The head guard unlocked the door and Stinson stepped inside. There was a candle burning and he could see the crippled jailer sitting on a bench and snoozing, only when the cripple heard the guard slam the door, he started and jumped out of his chair and stood up like a regular sentinel. Stinson began scolding him for sleeping on the job but in between his own words, he heard a strange sound in the cell beside them.

Standing there in the dim wavering light and listening to the muffled wailing coming out of the dark little cell next to them made goose pimples pop out all over Stinson's body. It brought to mind a night that still haunted him, a night he'd like to forget altogether except he couldn't. It was years and years ago but he still remembered it like yesterday. Everybody in the house was asleep except for him and Grandpappy, and the two of them were sitting together on the bear rug in front of the fireplace. Poor old Grandpappy was blind so he couldn't watch the orange flames dancing up out of the burning log and lighting up the sooty fireplace. But even though he couldn't see, Grandpappy could still hear as good as any hound dog.

"Listen at it, Bucky," Grandpappy whispered.

Buck listened and from a long ways off he could hear the faint warbling of a wolf. Grandpappy twisted the ends of his scraggly long white beard between his thumb and crookedy fingers and sat there taking in the wolf song like he was able to understand it. Then he closed his blind eyes and shook his head like it was more than he could stand.

"Bucky," he said, "that ole lone wolf's a singin' a awful sad piece."

"What's it sayin'?" Buck asked.

Grandpappy hesitated like he hated to tell. Finally he sort of groaned and said, "Well, t' tell th' awful truth, it's a wailin' 'bout how somebody's a goin' t' die."

That nearly scared the life out of Buck because the sweet old

Granny he loved with all his heart had been ailing for over a week and he was already worried sick about her. Ever since Buck could remember she'd been there to tell him stories and croon songs to him. And every time he was crying with the bellyache, she'd rock him to sleep.

That old lone wolf turned out to be telling the truth. That very night Granny died in her sleep. And with Granny gone, Grandpappy acted like he didn't give a hang about being alive either. Within a few weeks they lost him too. Ever since then, Buck couldn't stand to hear a wolf howl because it reminded him of Granny and Grandpappy's passing.

Stinson and the crippled jailer stood still and listened to the faint wailing in the dark tight little cell right beside them. The mournful sound kept on coming and coming and finally Stinson couldn't stand it any longer. It reminded him too much of the wolf howl on the night Granny died. He changed his mind. He decided it must be getting close to midnight and he didn't care to have a look-see at any werewolf. Instead he told the jailer to keep his rump off that danged bench and stomp around the best he could on his lame foot and try to stay awake in case he needed to fight off a pack of Stranglers.

Then Stinson hurried home as fast as his legs would trot and shed his clothes and hopped into bed and cuddled up to Sadie.

Deputy Stinson pulled his eyes off the frightful monster who'd been making the awful wailing in the dark the night before and began to check the crowd he was facing. He looked them over very carefully but as far as he could see, nobody had any weapons, at least none in view.

In spite of all the hard work of setting up the outside court, the trial didn't get off to a very good start. Stinson took that as another bad omen. Of course it was all old Justice Edgerton's fault. He was standing in the front row of the crowd wearing a flowing black cape and a black stovepipe hat that had most of the silk rubbed raw. The way his shoulders were hunched and the way his long nose curved down toward his sharp chin made Stinson think of Old Nick himself. As soon as the Judge pounded his gavel and called, "Order in the court," the old Justice jabbed his nephew and sent him scurrying up to the bench.

Stinson felt a little sorry for Wilbur. First of all, the unlucky fellow was bony and awkward and also he had a sort of clammy look about him, like he wasn't healthy. That was what made Stinson feel for him, because he understood all too well that life wasn't any picnic when you weren't handsome. And poor Wilbur had traveled West to be his Uncle's secretary for only one reason. He was crazy to become a famous man on the frontier. But that dream was spoiled because Edgerton was afraid to get on a horse. There wasn't any other way except horseback for Edgerton to get over the mountain trail to Lewiston to be sworn in as Chief Justice of the Territory, so that left Wilbur out in the cold. There wasn't any Chief Justice for him to be a secretary to. And what else could he do besides be a secretary? he didn't know the first thing about what really counted on the frontier, important things like shooting guns or riding horses or mining gold, so everybody poked fun of him. All poor Wilbur knew how to do was run errands for the crabby old uncle who never had a good word to say about anybody, especially the Bannack lawmen.

Wilbur was dressed in the same black get-up as his Uncle and looked as whey-faced as usual. As soon as he was standing just below the Judge's wagon, he slipped one long pale hand out of his black cape and pulled off his tall black hat.

"I want to lodge a protest," he said. "You see this court is not legal. It should be under jurisdiction of Justice Edgerton."

Wilbur stood fidgeting with his worn high hat and twisting his neck in his limp white collar while he waited for a response from the Judge.

The delay annoyed Stinson because he wanted to get the trial over as soon as possible so his own life could get back to normal. And of course the Judge wasn't going to be any help. The miners had elected him because he looked good on the bench. He had a stern face and his hair was streaked with silver, but he didn't know anything about the law. Naturally he didn't have the faintest idea how to handle Wilbur's protest but he didn't want to lose face so he just said, "Damn it to hell, Wilbur, your Uncle's no Justice! We just call him that to be polite."

Wilbur's face got red and he turned-tail and hurried back beside his Uncle. If that episode wasn't shameful enough, he got a second scolding from old Edgerton too. The two muddle-headed greenhorns were standing right in front of Stinson and he could hear every word.

"Damn it, Wilbur," Edgerton said, "you didn't handle it right!"

"I clearly made my point, Uncle Sid, but the Judge doesn't understand law and so he changed the ..."

"Oh hush up," Edgerton muttered without even looking over at Wilbur. "I'm trying to follow this farce."

It took only twenty minutes to select jurors from the panel Stinson had summoned. That made him proud because he knew he'd done a good job. After the eight men were seated on the hurdy-gurdy benches, the Judge said, "Well Billy, go ahead and get on with it."

The prosecutor was still miffed with the Judge for not letting him exhibit the corpse at the trial. He refused to even look up at his friend. Earlier, Stinson had heard the Prosecutor boasting to Plummer how it was an open and shut case so he didn't intend to waste any time on frills. Everybody knew that if a trial went on too long, several of the jurors would claim they had to get back and work their claims or else they'd lose them, and then it'd be a mistrial and they'd have to start all over again. And during the delay, the Stranglers would be out and around harping about swift justice and threatening to take over themselves.

In fact the prosecutor was in such a hurry to get the murderer convicted, he didn't waste time getting out of his chair. He just sat beside the Sheriff at their table and beckoned Doctor Glick to the witness bench. Then the court clerk brought a Bible and did the swearing in and they were ready to go. The prosecutor still hadn't stood up.

"Now Doc," he said from his chair, "just cause I'm in an all-fired hurry to rush these miners back to their claims so they can carry on with gettin' rich, don't mean you can't take your own sweet time. You just tell us everything you can about the wounds on Old Turk's body and since we ain't no doctors, you tell us what it all means."

The prosecutor wasn't normally that accommodating and that wasn't the way he usually talked either. But Stinson had been at enough trials to know Billy was trying to act like he was just common folk. That was because he was hoping to get on the good side of the jury.

On the witness stand Glick looked every bit as respectable as the day he'd showed up at the mines. He was stone-sober and his suit and shirt collar looked like they'd been ironed that very morning. But unfortunately he was also his usual windy self. He began lecturing about changes in the body after death and five minutes later he still hadn't gotten around to mentioning the wounds on Old Turk. In fact he really didn't say much of anything in those five minutes because he paused after every few words and let the men in the front rows relay his remarks to the men at the back who couldn't hear. On top of that, he began throwing in explanations about how the human body functions during life and how people should improve their health habits.

Stinson didn't see any reason why he should listen. He'd already read the report about the two revolver wounds that Doc wrote down on the paper. But that was when Doc was in a hurry to get back to his drink and card game, so he'd made it short. Stinson was beginning to get a little annoyed again at the waste of everybody's time. Besides, he'd never cared much for Doc. The man was snooty and he charged too much for his services. Even when he was so drunk he couldn't tie a bandage on straight he'd take a patient's very last pinch of gold dust. Stinson didn't want his legs getting stiff while Doc rambled on so he began marching along the imaginary line of the court and then turning and marching back just to get some exercise. The two jailers saw him and began doing the same thing but Deputy Ray just leaned back on the Judge's wagon and lounged where he was.

Most of the audience had visited Keeler while he was laid out at the Bluebird so they'd examined the wounds for themselves and were getting restless because of Doc's meanderings. That only created more worry for Stinson because it was hard to tell what restless miners might do. Just that morning he'd heard X.

Beidler saying how they ought to hang H. P. A. Smith on the gallows right alongside the boy ... for trying to get a murderer off the hook.

But Glick droned on and on. The audience began to shift around and hunt for a view of the prisoner instead of the witness and Stinson had to watch them every time they moved. Then after a while, some of them began drifting down the street to the business houses. Later they'd wander back to see if Glick was off the stand yet.

Sheriff Plummer wasn't one to sit still for very long either. He leaned over and said something to the prosecutor. Then he got up and left too. Stinson guessed Sheriff was going to make the rounds of main street because there were so many people down there by now.

The prosecutor was losing his audience and that didn't look good for him at all, but Stinson could understand his predicament. Billy had already made the mistake of announcing that Glick could take his sweet time, and if he was to jump in now and cut Doc off, that'd be breaking his word. If Billy was to win the case he couldn't show himself to be an out and out liar right in front of the whole town. So of course he had to let Glick ramble on.

Stinson kept on marching and resting, and then marching and resting again. In between, he'd study the horrible monster for a while and then scan the crowd again to be sure nobody had pulled out a weapon. He noticed it was the same bunch that somehow managed to make it to the front row wherever they were. Facing him was Justice Edgerton, wrapped up in his wrinkled black cape like an old woman in a shawl, and his nephew was jutting up beside him like a black bean-pole. The two of them stuck out like sore thumbs in the crowd. To Stinson they were bad omens themselves, they looked like two big old hunchbacked crows that'd come down to earth and perched among a bunch of humans. He doubted that either of the two greenhorns had enough common sense between them to pound sand in a rat hole. So he figured the only way they could have got the front row in a crowd that numbered in the hundreds was by coming early.

Hank Crawford, he'd probably bullied his way in. He had his rawboned frame decked out like a slick gambler, but his runty sidekick Beidler was in the same faded black overcoat he'd been wearing all day Sunday. The two of them and a few of their Strangler cronies were milling around in a little knot, probably trying to cook up some way to cause trouble for Stinson. And the little bushy-headed carpenter, he was in the front row too. He'd probably been able to worm his way up there because he was so little and delicate. When he saw Stinson watching him, he started to fidget and then pulled off his spectacles and began cleaning them with a white pocket handkerchief. Stinson decided he was the kind of man who looked guilty even when he wasn't.

As far as Stinson could tell, not one of the entire bunch had a weapon on them, or as he'd told himself before, at least not in sight.

By the time Sheriff Plummer came back, Glick was still going strong. He kept on pausing for the audience to relay his comments even though they'd stopped doing that some time ago. Finally Doc got down to brass tacks and said he believed a gun ball had entered the throat from inside the mouth and passed out the back of the head, causing almost instant death.

"It's impossible to say the exact hour Keeler died," he said. "but I'd guess some time Sunday morning."

That bright remark almost made Stinson laugh out loud. Because the Salt Lake freighters claimed they found Old Turk before noon on Sunday and at that time they calculated he hadn't been dead very long. So yes that would make the time he died some time Sunday morning all right. Any lamebrain could figure that out for himself.

Glick went on to list all the reasons it was so difficult to put his finger on the exact time of death. That sounded pretty silly to Stinson too. The real reason Doc couldn't say the exact time Old Turk died was because he wasn't there! He was at the saloon drinking hard liquor and losing at cards. Stinson had seen him with his own eyes.

Plummer didn't bother to go back to the prosecution table. Instead he hovered around the edge of the crowd. Stinson supposed Sheriff wanted to be free to come and go as he pleased like the rest of the audience. But that left the prosecutor without any support at the table. He kept shooting desperate glances at Plummer, but after about the third one, Plummer just turned away and headed back toward main street. He probably figured a man in his high position didn't need to waste time listening to a windbag like Doc.

The prosecutor looked over his shoulder to watch Plummer leave and saw about half the spectators had also deserted. That brought him right to his feet.

"We get the picture, Doc," he said. "You can step down now."

The men who'd been dogged enough to stick it out through Doc's boring testimony sighed with relief, and within several seconds Plummer suddenly reappeared at the prosecution table. But Stinson knew the trouble was far from over. The prosecutor was going to have to find some way to fire up the audience. Otherwise the whole bunch would eventually desert and go back to main street, and the worrisome problem was that with Sheriff back at the prosecution table there wasn't anybody downtown to keep order.

"Judge," the prosecutor announced, "I'd like to depart from procedure if you don't mind. I'd like to call the defendant, Peter Herron, to the stand at this time."

That unexpected announcement snapped the whole crowd to attention. After listening to Doc for so long they'd slipped into the notion of thinking the trial wasn't going to have any fireworks.

"Well that's a bit unusual, Your Honor," H. P. A. Smith said. He rested his head in his hands and thought it over for a while.

"Well," he finally said, "if Billy's got no case of his own, I guess I'll have to loan him mine."

He turned to the boy wedged in between him and the crippled jailer. "Peter," he said, "you go on and get up in the witness wagon there."

As the terrible monster rose to his feet, Stinson recalled the strange wailing noise he'd heard him making in his cell last night, and it made him so unstrung he felt his heart start to race. He scanned the crowd and saw they were standing so still they looked like they were stunned. Then several of them broke away from the bunch and dashed back toward main street, probably to find the wanderers and warn them they were about to miss the best part.

The ones who stayed behind craned their necks to watch young Peter Herron shuffle his way toward the wagon in short halting steps. Because of the heavy logging chains wrapped around his ankles, he had to slide one foot forward until it stopped with a jerk, and then he slid the other foot till the chains jerked it to a stop too. It was a slow process.

And all the way, the chains on his ankles jangled and clanked. Stinson could see how skittish the prisoner was but he could also tell things weren't right with himself either because the jangles and clanks got loud in his ears and echoed inside his head.

When the boy finally got to the wagon, he stopped and looked helplessly back at his lawyer. Stinson and a jailer had to lay down their guns and go over and pick up the murderer and lift him into the bed. It made Stinson feel creepy all over just to touch a monster. He felt like he needed to go somewhere and wash his hands afterwards but he couldn't leave his post. He stayed by the wagon and watched while the boy stuck his skinny hand out and laid it on the Bible. Even after he rested it on the Good Book his fingers were still trembling. And when he sank onto the witness bench it looked like he was fainting instead of sitting down.

For the first time since the trial started, the prosecutor approached the witness wagon. He was a small white-haired man with a puffed-out chest and belly that made his lower legs and feet look too small for the rest of him. Stinson had never taken much to Billy because he was almost as uppity as Doc.

The prosecutor stationed himself in front of the defendant and folded his arms across his bulging chest and leaned back at the waist. Then he stared the spindly youngster square in the eye.

"Whose red flannel shirt you a wearin' there, boy?" he asked roughly.

Peter Herron looked down at his shirt. "It's Old Turk Keeler's," he whispered.

"Speak up, boy!" the prosecutor ordered.

"Old Turk Keeler's shirt," he said. His voice was a little bit louder but it was quavery.

"An' whose buckskin pantaloons you got on?"

Peter Herron looked down at his clothes again. "Them's Old Turk's too."

The prosecutor turned and glanced over his shoulder and saw he was performing for a full audience and the relay system was in operation again.

"All right, an' them shoes?"

"Old Turk's."

"Mmm hmmm." The prosecutor turned to the jury and shook his head sadly. Stinson agreed with Billy that it was a sad case all right.

"How 'bout the Bible? Whose Bible might that be you had stowed under your bunk out there at the cabin on your claim?"

"That was Old Turk's Bible."

Stinson was amazed at the amount of evidence the prosecutor had gathered against the murderer and he supposed the jury had to feel the same way.

"Okay, the Bible was Old Turk's too," the prosecutor said. "That old white mule you tied out behind your cabin, it Old Turk's too?"

"Yes Sir," the boy answered, "my mule was the gray one. The white mule belonged to Old Turk."

The prosecutor gave the jury another sad shake of the head and Stinson caught himself shaking his head too. He had to stiffen his neck so his head wouldn't wobble every time Billy's did.

"But you just happened to have that old white mule in your possession ... along with Old Turk's shirt, an' his pantaloons, an' his shoes, an' his Bible. Right? Old Turk's things ... but he was dead an' you had 'em."

"Yes Sir, that's right," the boy agreed.

The prosecutor turned to the jury and shrugged his shoulders and held out his hands and turned both palms up. "Gentlemen," he said, "there's nothing more to be said here today so I won't waste your time. You can see the truth just as plain as I can.

This defendant shoved a revolver in his partner's mouth and shot him. Then he was still so angry at the old man that he mutilated the body. Then he stole clothes off a dead man's back ... and cold-bloodedly put them on his own."

Stinson wanted to warn Billy he'd slipped and wasn't talking like common folks anymore, except there was no way to do it without the jury seeing.

"And then he stole his partner's mule and all the possessions packed on it and rode down the trail till he came to a badger hole. He stuffed his old clothes in there to get rid of the evidence."

The miners' court had a rule that the lawyers weren't supposed to say anything that might sway the jury, but Billy always broke the rule and the Judge always let him get away with it.

"You can see the truth just as plain as I can, Gentlemen," he said. "A horrible murder's been committed ... and the cold-blooded murderer is sitting right here in front of you."

By now Stinson was so convinced he expected H. P. A. Smith would just have to give up the case and throw in the towel. He watched as Smith tilted back in his chair and stretched, like he was maybe considering it. But then he hefted himself to his feet.

"You done so quick, Billy?" he asked.

He waited for the prosecutor to sit down and then slowly made his way up to the witness stand and stood examining the boy's face.

"I see your lips tremblin', Son," he said. "Now you don't need to be scared, you hear? You just tell us the truth and we'll believe you. All right?"

Peter Herron blinked back tears and nodded. Smith smiled up at him reassuringly and then began strolling back and forth in front of the witness wagon. It reminded Stinson how at his own trial some time back, lawyer Smith had put his arm around his shoulders and patted him once and told him not to be nervous. Afterwards, Beidler had asked Smith how it felt to hug a murderer.

"Don't know, X.," Smith had said, "and probably never will. You ain't very huggable."

But H. P. A. didn't look near as confident now as he had

then. He appeared to be trying to think of his first question and it was keeping Stinson on pins and needles waiting to hear if he could come up with one.

Finally he said, "Son, why don't you tell us about the last time you saw Old Turk Keeler."

"Well it was last Sunday," the boy said. He was speaking out louder now and his voice didn't seem to be quavering so much. "I remember Old Turk got up while it was still dark and lit himself a candle and I was layin' in my bunk and I seen him put on his good suit and his old black overcoat on top of it. Then he turned and looked at me and said how he always preferred to travel light ..."

"Travel where?" Smith asked.

"Back to the States. We wasn't makin' much money at the mine and he wanted to get back to his wife cause she was sick. He said I could have the claim and cabin and all his things, even the Bible and so ..."

Smith raised one hand to interrupt. "The letters too? Old Turk said you could have the letters from his wife?"

"No. I believe he just forgot them letters was tied to the Bible."

Smith hadn't stopped pacing during his questions, but during the boy's answers he'd pause and lift his head up and gaze thoughtfully at the sagebrush hills rising just behind the court. It made Stinson wish he was more like Plummer so he'd know what thoughts were rolling around inside H. P. A.'s head and not have to go through the suspense of waiting every time.

"Did you watch Old Turk leave?" Smith asked.

"Yes, Sir. I got up and held the candle for him while he saddled his mule. And then he shook my hand and told me goodbye and rode away and I went back to bed."

"Ever see Old Turk again?"

"Never did ... they ..." The boy's voice broke and he hung his head and wiped his eyes. "They wouldn't let me go to the buryin'."

"By the way, Son, you or Turk own any kind of revolver?"

"Neither one of us did."

"All right, Son. Back to Sunday morning," Smith said. "What clothes did you put on when you got up?"

"His. Them ones Old Turk left me. Then I went outside and seen Old Turk's mule had come back."

Smith walked over to the Judge's table and asked him to please hand over the clothes the bullwhacker had found stuffed in the badger hole. Then he carefully spread them out on the defendant's table.

"Now how about these clothes spread out here?" he asked. One by one he displayed the tattered trousers, the ragged shirt, the pair of almost soleless shoes, and the muddy stockings for the jury.

"These here clothes from the badger hole belong to you?"

"No, Sir. Them ain't mine. I bundled up all my clothes and brought'm along when the Sheriff arrested me."

Smith walked back to the Judge and this time he returned with a cloth bundle. Stinson recognized it as the one the boy'd had slung from his saddle when he was sitting on the gray mule in front of the jail.

Smith stood next to the jury and worked out the knot and then pulled out a worn shirt and draped it over his left arm. Then one by one he pulled out a pair of trousers, two stockings, and a pair of long underwear and draped them on his left arm too. Next he took out a pair of brown shoes that were scuffed almost white and with his right hand held them up by their high tops. With short steps he paraded past the jury benches, displaying the items in front of the eight men's eyes. Stinson could see the clothes every bit as plain as the jurors only he was starting to get a little puzzled.

"All right, Son," Smith said, "now how about these things from the bundle on your saddle? They belong to you?"

"Yes, Sir, them's my clothes."

"All right, let's wrap your clothes back up in the cloth and give them back to the Judge. We'll forget about them for now."

When Smith came back from the bench, he rested both hands on the edge of the witness wagon and leaned forward and gazed up into the boy's eyes.

"You wouldn't lie to us about those clothes in the badger hole would you, Son? ... Remember you're under oath to tell the God's truth."

The boy shook his head. "I ain't about to tell no lies after I swore on the Bible."

"You're tellin' the honest to God's truth when you say the bundle of clothes I gave back to the Judge were yours, but the clothes the bullwhacker found in a badger hole on the trail ..." he turned and jabbed his pointer finger at the defense table, "those clothes the whacker found in the badger hole and I got spread out over there on our table, they don't belong to you?"

"Yes, Sir, that's right."

Smith spun away from the witness and stuffed his hands in his trouser pockets. He had a rather pleased look on his face but he began pacing with his eyes fixed on the ground. Stinson could tell the lawyer was wrestling with a hard decision. Occasionally Smith would pause and look over at the badger-hole clothes on the table. Finally he drew in a deep breath and sauntered over and looked down at the clothes. Then he snatched up the ragged shirt and headed back to the witness wagon.

"You wouldn't take offense would you, Son, if I asked you to put on this shirt from the badger hole? prove to us you're tellin' the God's truth? ... Go ahead and put on this shirt that you say don't belong to you ... go ahead ... right here in front of the jury."

The monster sat studying the shirt he claimed wasn't his. Only by now, Stinson was beginning to wonder if he really was a monster. Actually more than anything, he looked like an innocent boy who was scared out of his wits.

While they were all waiting for Peter Herron to answer, the crowd broke into a buzz of excited comments and Stinson had to forget watching the witness stand and go on the alert. While he was rapidly running his eyes over the crowd, the Judge pounded his gavel and the audience came to order. Then the Judge looked over at the witness and so did everybody else.

For just a second, the boy met the Judge's stern gaze. Then he reached down and grabbed the shirt from his lawyer.

Every eye in the court and audience was glued on him. Without unfastening Keeler's red flannel shirt, he yanked it over his head. Then he eased each skinny arm into a sleeve of the already unfastened shirt from the badger hole. When he tried to pull the two sides together to join them, they wouldn't meet. There were so many oohs and aahs coming from the crowd that Stinson had to raise his shotgun to the ready position and the Judge had to pound again.

But through it all Smith just calmly stood there and leaned against the wagon and pondered the unfastened shirt. Then he reached out his hand.

"That shirt from the badger hole is too small for you, Son," he said. "Give it back to me."

Stinson watched Smith amble over to the table and ease onto his chair. It was upsetting to him to see how cool H. P. A. was after the way he'd boggled Stinson's mind, making him wonder who it really was who stole Keeler's clothes and then stuck his own clothes in a badger hole way out there in the middle of nowhere. It was a sickening shock to believe it might be so, but Stinson was afraid maybe they'd pinned the blame on the wrong suspect. Quite naturally, his mind bounced back to the first suspect, the little carpenter who was standing in the front row and following the trial like his life depended on it, and all the while looking so guilty.

The prosecutor came back with cross-examination and asked Peter Herron if he and Old Turk hadn't gotten into an argument over their claim that Sunday morning, but the boy staunchly denied it.

Then the prosecutor asked, "You're still a growin' boy ain't ya? Ever have to wear a shirt that was too small?"

"No, Sir, not one I couldn't get fastened."

The answer got the prosecutor's dander up. He pounded one fist against the side of the wagon and the boy jumped like he'd been shot.

"Didn't you send a ball through Old Turk Keeler's mouth?" the prosecutor shouted, "just when he had his mouth open and was begging you not to shoot him didn't you shove the revolver in his mouth and fire? And then you poked out his eyes and you cut out his tongue too, didn't you? Huh, didn't you?" He pounded the side of the wagon again.

Tears flooded the boy's eyes and his reply came out more like a moan than words.

"No Sir, I didn't ... I didn't ... Old Turk was good to me. He was my onlyest friend."

Stinson thought it was a poor way for Billy to close the questioning because seeing the boy cry about his dead friend like that was a pitiful sight, and he knew the last thing Billy wanted was for the jury to feel any pity for the suspect. Evidently Billy was afraid it might get even worse if he tried to go on. He didn't offer another word. He just strode back to his table on his short little legs and plopped his top-heavy frame onto his chair and sat there and steamed.

The cross-examination was so short Lawyer Smith barely had time to catch his breath but he stood up and faced the Judge's bench.

"I know you're thinkin' 'bout a dinner break, Your Honor," he said, "but I can finish up here in two minutes if you'll let me. Just need to call Doc back for a quick question. I promise, only two minutes, and I know Doc'll cooperate and keep it short."

It was obvious to Stinson that H. P. A. had learned a lesson from the prosecutor's troubles with Glick. Before the doctor could even get seated on the witness bench, he asked his question.

"Let's us get down to business here, Doc," he said. "Isn't it likely the ball that was shot in the victim's mouth caused some bleedin'?"

Glick sat down and started to comment, but Smith didn't give him time.

"Wouldn't blood in an open mouth attract a scavenger bird ... say some hawk or magpie or just some big old black crow that happened to be flyin' over?"

Again Glick started to answer, but Smith went right on.

"And yes or no, Doc, could a big old black crow peck out a man's bloody tongue and peck his eyes clean out of their sockets too? Just yes or no, could it?"

"Well, I suppose so ..."

"Thanks, Doc. That'll be all."

Glick looked a little surly at being dismissed before he got a chance to go into any explanations but he stood up and began climbing out of the witness wagon.

"Say, Doc," Smith added a little apologetically, "I forgot to thank you for comin' here to court today." He'd caught Glick straddling the side of the wagon and dangling one foot down to reach the top of the high wheel.

"And, Doc, just one more quick yes or no since you're still on the stand, or at least halfways there. Anything at all on that poor old grandfather's body that told you who the heartless criminal was that stuck a gun in his mouth and shot him? ... Yes or no?"

Glick thought for a while and when he started to shake his head, Smith took over again.

"No? That's what I figured, Doc. Thanks for your expert opinion."

* * *

After dinner Stinson grabbed the sentinel post by the witness stand again. Now the crowd had some hot food in their bellies they were fairly sluggish and were behaving pretty well. First off the prosecution commenced its closing argument. It was just a repeat of what Billy had said before about the truth being plain to see, only this time he remembered to be folksy. It was a good speech but it wasn't so pleasant being outdoors now as it had been in the morning. The sun was high in the sky and with no breeze blowing, the heat trapped in the narrow valley was stifling, even with your jacket pulled off.

As Billy preached to the jury about the horrible murder and the plain truth, Stinson noticed the jurors were beginning to wiggle on their benches and fan themselves with their hats. Evidently Billy noticed too because he soon gave up.

And with the jury so restless, H. P. A. Smith cut his remarks short and let the eight men hurry down to the hurdy-gurdy house to start deliberating. The crowd began breaking up too. Most of them appeared quiet and thoughtful, like they didn't quite know what to make of the case.

After the very last one of them was gone, Deputy Ray and four guards carted the prisoner over to the stable to wait for the verdict and the rest of the jailers hurried down to patrol main street. All the bigwigs, that is Sheriff Plummer and the Judge and the two lawyers, went to wait in the shade of the Judge's wagon.

They were all educated men and Stinson knew he had no business trying to mix in and jaw with them. But still he was curious to know what they had to say about the trial so he casually strolled over and squatted down in the wagon shade and listened to them talking. None of them paid him any mind. But that didn't bother him. He knew his place.

Right away the two lawyers and the Judge began hashing over the testimony. Everything the Judge said riled up the lawyers and the three of them were going at it hot and heavy, but Sheriff Plummer didn't enter the conversation. As usual he was keeping his thoughts to himself. He leaned against the wagon and gazed off at the sagebrush hills, just like Lawyer Smith had done when he was considering something important.

The arguing going on between the lawyers and the Judge was making Stinson feel uneasy so he turned away from them and began studying Sheriff's face. He couldn't help wondering how a man as smart as Plummer could have made such a bad mistake while he was trying to read Peter Herron's mind.

CHAPTER FIVE

Stinson knew he should get back to main street and help out. It wasn't fair to ask the jailers to try to handle the big downtown crowd all by themselves. And the argument in the shade of the Judge's wagon was getting so hot he was thinking he should make a hasty exit before it broke out in a free-for-all. But he'd been on his feet since sunup so he decided he'd squat there a little bit longer and rest his weary legs.

Billy and H. P. A. were both too irritable to stand still. In between trials they were good friends but this afternoon, feelings were running so high they were keeping a safe distance between them. And Plummer didn't seem interested in having anything to do with either one of them. Stinson thought Sheriff appeared rather melancholy but that wasn't particularly unusual for him because he was prone to be a little moody.

The Judge took off his suit coat and folded it neatly and then draped it over the side of the wagon. Then he took out his handkerchief and wiped the sweat off his handsome face.

"Well, what you think, Plummer?" he asked. His voice sounded cross and that made Stinson think he must be miffed at Sheriff for not trying to cool things down between the two lawyers.

Sheriff shrugged his shoulders and continued to gaze off at the hills, like he thought there was some kind of answer to be found up there in the sagebrush.

"Difficult case," he finally said.

H. P. A. was pacing at one end of the wagon, but being careful to keep his hefty frame in range of the shade. He raked his thick fingers through his stiff gray hair.

"Well, boys," he said, "if the jurors are lookin' for good hard evidence, they'll have to acquit." He said it like he was trying to be friendly again but Stinson knew he was just trying to keep things stirred up.

"Since when did a jury ever care about evidence?" Billy came back. At the other end of the wagon, his feet that were too small for his puffy body were trampling out his own path in the loose dust. He kept patting his bulging chest with one hand, like he had heartburn, and with the other hand he tried to smooth a few strands of his shock of white hair over a little pink bald spot in the back of his head.

The Judge frowned and eyed one lawyer and then the other. Stinson had never seen him get so agitated about a case before.

"You two should've dug deeper," he said angrily. "Instead, the both of you left the damn gate wide open!"

By the way the two lawyers stepped up their pace and stirred up more dust, Stinson could tell the Judge's remark was definitely the wrong thing to say. Billy landed a fierce kick on a rock in his path, and then H. P. A. stopped walking and began pounding a hole in the dust with the heel of his right shoe.

"Billy could of dug a well to China and not found anything," he said indignantly. "Cause the boy's tellin' the truth."

"You don't know that," Billy called from his end of the wagon. He looked like he was mad enough to chew nails and then spit out the pieces right in H. P. A.'s face.

"I beg to differ with you, Billy," H. P. A. called back. He was trying to act like he was more calm and polite than Billy but his voice was so sharp he wasn't fooling anybody. "After all these years I can tell when a client's lyin' to me."

"Not if he's a good enough liar you can't," Billy insisted. This time he used both hands to try to push down the heartburn. "Besides, I didn't see you bring up any evidence somebody else killed Keeler."

"Did you say evidence? You-ou-ou, Billy? You-ou-ou?" H. P. A. laughed like it was a big joke. "Well, Billy, you were in the Elkhorn last night same as me. You saw Beidler struttin' around in an overcoat made for a real man instead of a noosin' little weasel and ..."

"Just what I said," the Judge interrupted. "You two didn't finish this thing off! And that leaves me in a bind.... Jury finds the boy guilty, I got to give the death sentence." He sighed and leaned back against the wagon and buried his face in both hands.

In the space the two lawyers were purposely leaving between them, Plummer began to pace around a little. Only now he was studying the dust instead of the hills. He still wasn't offering any opinions. When he lifted his face, he had a troubled look in his eyes. Stinson supposed Sheriff was kicking himself for the bad job of mind-reading he'd done on Peter Herron.

The Judge flopped his hands down to his sides and begin to swirl the toe of one high-top black shoe in the dust, tracing a circle that kept growing bigger and bigger. Stinson got the impression the Judge was seriously considering making an announcement, probably something about how he wanted out of the whole mess.

Finally he looked over at the Sheriff.

"How the hell we gonna handle this, Plummer?" he asked. "I don't believe you want to hang an innocent boy."

Plummer answered so quick it made Stinson think he'd just been waiting for the Judge to ask him.

"You could postpone the hanging till the priest comes on Wednesday," he said. "The boy's been asking to see a priest."

Billy shook his white head so hard the merged bulge made by his chest and belly jiggled like jelly. "O-o-h no!" he said. "O-o-h no! We can't sit on our thumbs and wait till Wednesday! The town wouldn't put up with it."

"And what good would it do?" the Judge asked. "It wouldn't help any."

"It might," Plummer said.

Billy leaned back at the waist and stuck his chest out and it looked like the buttons on his vest were about ready to explode. He glared over at Plummer.

"Like how?" he asked, "help like how?"

"If the boy's guilty," Plummer said, he sounded like he was patiently explaining to a spoiled child who wasn't old enough to have any sense yet, "he might confess to the priest."

H. P. A. was trying hard to act like he was as hard to ruffle as usual, but Stinson could see the trial had him almost turned inside-out. Plummer's suggestion seemed to upset him even more than it did Billy.

"Everybody's talkin' like the verdict's already in," H. P. A. barked out, "and it ain't! Just cause Peter wants to talk to a priest don't mean he's guilty of murder. We all got our little sins, now don't we, Billy. Billy knows all about that. Besides, the priest wouldn't tell us anything the boy confessed to anyhow."

"No," Plummer said, only this time his voice wasn't quite so patient, "but if the boy confesses to murder, the priest probably won't object to the hanging."

Stinson was wishing he'd left when he first thought of it. But his legs had felt lazy and he'd waited and now everybody was so vexed he didn't want to shift their attention onto himself by moving. Considering the ugly mood they were in, they were apt to blame him for something.

"And what if Peter don't confess to murder?" H. P. A. asked.

"Fairly obvious," Plummer answered. The others were raising their voices more and more but Stinson had noticed a long time ago that when Plummer was at the end of his patience, his voice got more hushed. "If the priest thinks the boy's innocent," he said quietly, "he might feel obligated to try to save his life."

"Well, maybe" the Judge said. He used the toe of his shoe to rub out the circles he'd been tracing. "I'd need to mull it over though before I do any serious postponing."

"Now just a damn minute," Billy said, "you better be mulling over another point too. You try to postpone a hanging in this town ... we'll have a mob on our hands."

Billy walked out of the shade and craned his fat little neck down toward the hurdy-gurdy house.

"Oh my God," he said, "here they come already ... and on the trot."

Stinson looked at his pocket watch and saw the eight men had reached their decision in only nine minutes. That was shameful but there was one advantage. The audience was scattered throughout the business houses, and maybe the court could get the rest of the trial over before most of them heard the jury was in.

If the crowd wasn't there, that would be one less problem for the deputies to worry about.

The Judge must have had the same thought in mind because he began scrambling up in his wagon. By the time he got his suit coat on and was seated at his table, the jury foreman was already climbing up behind him to hand over the verdict. Stinson wanted to watch the Judge's face when he read the slip of paper, but he didn't have time. He had to dash over to the stable to notify Ray.

Then when he got there he decided he should stay and help the guards tug the prisoner across the flat in the little wooden cart. By the time Stinson and Ray got to their sentinel posts, the news had leaked out and hundreds of men were already streaming out of the business houses and rushing up main street.

The foreman and the Judge put their heads together for a few minutes and discussed the verdict written on the paper, and that gave the crowd time to reach the flat and lump together in a solid mass in front of the court.

The foreman straightened up and threw back his shoulders and looked out over the audience. Then he took the slip of paper back from the Judge. Stinson didn't want to miss anything but he knew he better give the crowd a quick once-over. He saw they were standing as still as if they were posing to have their picture taken.

There was no sound at all in the still hot air and that was very unusual for any mining camp Stinson had ever lived in. Then from the direction of the Indian wickiups down creek came a high-pitched whining chant. Stinson supposed the Indians were every bit as good as the wolves when it came to knowing that somebody was going to die.

The foreman cleared his throat before he read from the paper. "We the jury find the defendant guilty of murder in the first degree."

Peter Herron broke into tears.

The Judge looked over at the boy and winced. Then he managed to get the severe look back on his face again.

"Young man," he said, "a jury of your mining peers has found you guilty of murder in the first degree. It's my duty to sentence you to be hanged by the neck until dead."

A raucous cheer went up from the crowd and echoed up and down the long narrow valley. Stinson slipped his shotgun between his knees and gripped it there so his hands would be free to cover his ears. Then he saw the audience begin to shush each other so they could make out the Judge's instructions, and he took his hands off his ears so he could hear too.

"The ... execution ..." the Judge said very slowly. Then he paused and pulled in a deep breath and looked down at Sheriff Plummer. When he started again he was speaking much faster.

"The execution will take place at sundown this Wednesday."

The audience had been prepared for the usual delay of one hour. They could put up with one hour, that just whetted the suspense. Besides, everybody agreed it was very civilized of the miners' court to give a condemned man sixty minutes to settle his business and write home. That was an accepted rule, but a postponement of more than forty-eight hours shocked the crowd. As it gradually sunk into their heads they weren't going to see a hanging that day after all, they began carrying on like a bunch of maniacs. It was obvious Billy had been right. Stinson pulled his shotgun out from between his legs and aimed it at the knot of Stranglers fuming in the front row.

Beidler was hopping up and down and waving a clenched fist in the air.

"Now!" he screamed. "Now! String 'im up now! Don't give 'im no more time 'n he give ole Keeler!"

That was all it took to drive the rest of the crowd completely wild. Then Beidler started swinging his arms in the direction of the Judge's wagon and hollering about stringing him up too. A panicky look came on the Judge's face and he began banging his gavel as loud as he could. But the crowd couldn't hear him. There was complete pandemonium on the flat and so much noise in Stinson's head he couldn't think straight. He just stood there gripping his shotgun and hoping it was pointed in the general direction of X. and his cronies. But they didn't even seem to notice his gun, or else maybe they thought he didn't really have the gumption to fire at them.

Stinson felt his muscles beginning to lock up on him and he was so stiff he could barely turn his head. He guessed that any minute X. would see the shotgun aimed at him and then fish inside his long overcoat and pull out a revolver and fire at Stinson. And X. was a good shot.

Suddenly a gun went off somewhere. It was followed by two more quick shots but Stinson was so rattled he couldn't tell where they were coming from. He felt sure somebody had plugged the Judge right between the eyes, and he managed to swivel his neck around toward the wagon. But the Judge was still seated at his table and he didn't seem to be hit. Then Stinson spotted Deputy Ray. He was the one making all the noise. He'd laid his shotgun on the ground and was firing his revolver in the air.

After the fourth shot, Ray swung the handgun down and leveled it on the crowd. First X.'s jaw dropped, and then his mouth clamped shut like a snapping turtle and he lowered both arms to his sides and held perfectly still.

The Judge stood up to let the crowd know the trial was over and everybody turned to look at him.

"Now Gentlemen," he said, "we WILL wait for a priest for this boy. If anybody ever needed to see a priest, it's surely a convicted murderer."

The crowd broke out in a some loud surly grumbles but at the same time they were keeping a wary eye on Deputy Ray's handgun. Everybody had always figured he was just hard-nosed and cold-blooded enough to fire right into a crowd. They had no intentions of testing him. Gradually the little clumps of men began breaking up and heading back toward main street. The Judge wasn't taking any chances on another close call so he jumped over the side of his wagon and hurried to mix inside the cordon the lawmen and lawyers were forming around the prisoner. Then the guards raised the condemned boy into the cart and the whole lot of them bunched together and began rumbling him back toward the log jail.

Stinson was trying hard to keep his place in the cordon but he had a sharp cramp in his gut and couldn't straighten all the way up. He kept on stepping it out alongside the others but he was bent over like a humpback.

'"What the hell's wrong with you, Reb?" Ray asked.

"Nothin'," Stinson answered, "just a bellyache."

He was so embarrassed he straightened up whether it hurt or not and kept on trucking till they reached the stable.

That night and the next two days were pure hell because some of the miners were so worked up they didn't bother to go back to their claims. After dark the lawmen moved the convicted murderer back to the jail and Sheriff Plummer beefed up the guard as best he could. The problem was there weren't very many sober men in town who were good shots and liked working for free.

All the while, Beidler and Crawford were hovering around main street and ogling the jail alley, like they were waiting for the first slip-up. Ray and Stinson wanted to send the two Stranglers packing but Plummer said he'd rather have them exactly where they were so he could keep an eye on them.

By Wednesday morning, Stinson's nerves were frazzled. But still he had to admit that the lawmen had several things to be grateful for. So far the Stranglers hadn't gotten to the prisoner, and the little carpenter had the boy's coffin built, and Beidler had the grave dug on cemetery hill. That meant they were all set for the ceremony that was scheduled for sundown.

But by noon the priest still hadn't arrived. That was very unusual because every Wednesday he rode in on his little mule early in the morning. The whole town was on the lookout for him and his little mule but by four in the afternoon, they still hadn't come.

This time the Judge didn't risk his neck by making any announcements. Instead he quietly slipped a notice in the window of Chrisman's store:

EXECUTION RESCHEDULED FOR DAWN TOMORROW

The sign in the store window let the news leak out gradually, so there wasn't any big uproar. And the delay left time so somebody could ride north and see what was holding up the priest. Sheriff Plummer explained to the two deputies that because of the Stranglers it was critical he remain in town, and he didn't want Ray to leave either because he needed him to be in charge of guarding the prisoner. Stinson seemed to be the logical one to go for the priest, Plummer said.

Stinson agreed with him on every count but he screwed up his courage and said he'd have to beg off.

"It's gettin' close t' Sadie's time," he said. "I daresn't go. But I'll stay at th' jail an' back up Deputy Ray."

So Plummer said he guessed he'd have to make the ride himself.

The minute Sheriff and his big bay disappeared over the top of cemetery hill, Beidler and Crawford began spreading a rumor that the miners' court was stalling and had no intentions of hanging the boy. They claimed Plummer wasn't coming back, that he'd got out of town while the getting was good.

The two Stranglers rounded up as many supporters as they could find and coaxed them over to the alley leading up to the jail. Ray claimed he wasn't one whit afraid of them and ordered Stinson to just let them be. He said he'd blow the head off the first man that stepped within ten yards of the jail, and that would give the rest of them something to think about all right.

While the deputies were discussing the problem, they knew the prisoner was sitting in the cell next to them and listening. Only the boy didn't make a peep.

Finally Stinson got so jumpy he completely lost his head and rushed out the door with his shotgun and ordered the whole bunch out of the alley. They all left. But within the hour Beidler and Crawford and a new crowd began slowly drifting back.

When Stinson started to dash out and chase them away too, Ray stopped him. He told Stinson all he was doing was playing into the Stranglers' hands. Beidler and Crawford were just baiting him, Ray said. Then he told Stinson to get out and patrol main street for a while.

"Leave your shotgun here," Ray said. "We might need it. Might have to give it to the boy."

Stinson found the town packed. Miners from some of the

distant claims hadn't gotten wind of the postponement so they kept on flocking into town in droves, expecting to see a hanging at sundown. When Stinson got to the Elkhorn, he saw the place was almost empty. Cyrus was standing behind the long polished bar displaying his red and blue tattoos only there was nobody lined up to admire them. He told Stinson the flood of customers had drunk him completely dry. There wasn't a single drop of alcohol left in the saloon. He said he had a rush order in at the brewery for anything they could whomp up. But in the meantime, things were getting shaky.

"Thirsty s.o.b.'s is as apt t' start a damn riot as not," Cyrus warned.

Stinson hurried over to the bakery to see if they had any liquor left but he found the front door locked. When he rattled it, the baker came out from the kitchen and yelled through the window glass that he was completely sold out of liquor and everything else too. Right now, he said, he was heating up the ovens so he could bake a new batch of bread and pies. "Figure the boys's about ready to start shootin' windows out," he added, "just t' amuse themselves."

Stinson could see Cyrus was wrong. Things were more than just shaky. With the two main businesses in town out of food and drink, the streets were crawling with hungry and thirsty men. And they were already sorely provoked because the hanging wasn't going to come off at sundown like the Judge had promised. All around him Stinson was being jostled and bumped by roughs who were so heated up they were ready to swing a fist at the drop of a hat.

But he wasn't fretting about a few petty brawls. It was a lynch mob he was worried about, and as he surveyed the streets he noticed that excited men were beginning to clot together all up and down the boardwalks. His bones told him this ungodly tension was coming to a peak. He slapped one hand over his gun holster to be sure his revolver didn't jounce out and circled behind the buildings and ran back to the jail as fast as he could go.

"Yank," he said the very second the guards let him inside, "th' boys's fixin' t' rush th' jail most any minute."

Ray scrunched his eyes shut and bit at his lower lip. He thought it over for a while and then said that in light of the emergency, he'd better send a guard over to the Edgerton cabin and ask for help. Everybody knew the old Justice kept a little cannon stashed under his bed and Ray said they just might have to use it to defend the jail.

Within less than five minutes the guard was back with the reply.

"The miners' court got themselves into this mess," Edgerton had said, "and they can damn well get themselves out."

Stinson began to pace around inside the jail and stew so much that after about ten minutes Ray told him to get back on the streets again and try to cool things down out there. Stinson knew he was just trying to get rid of him.

Before he could work his way out of the crowded alley, he ran into Edgerton and his nephew. He couldn't believe they were foolish enough to try patrolling the streets on their own but there was no doubt that's what they were up to. Stinson groaned. Then he told himself there was one good side to it. At least the two ignorant greenhorns weren't got up in their black capes and silk hats.

"I can't support the miners' court," old Edgerton said when he saw Stinson, "but I can tackle the problem myself. Just my presence on the streets will restore order."

"Y'all reckon that's th' case, Justice?" Stinson asked. The idea was so ridiculous he couldn't keep his mouth from curving into a grin. It felt good because it was the first time he'd had anything to grin about since last Sunday morning.

"Of course it's the case," Edgerton said. "These roughs know a figure of authority when they see one."

Then Edgerton brought up his bold record in Congress and also that he had his trusty Henry rifle to rely on and how earlier he'd had the foresight to send his secretary out to buy himself a revolver. Stinson could see Wilbur was carrying the new gun in his overcoat pocket. At least that's where Stinson supposed it was because every few seconds Wilbur would whip one long pale hand into his overcoat pocket and then fumble around like he was trying to get the feel of the new weapon.

Stinson had never liked Abraham Lincoln anyway because the man was a warty-faced warmonger, but at this moment he could gladly have throttled the president for turning this pair of looneys loose on the Territory. At any time either one of them could shoot himself in the foot, or worse yet, shoot somebody else. But Stinson didn't have time to worry about that now. He had to get back to main street.

There was one ray of hope, he thought, as he turned away and stepped up to the boardwalk. The two dumbbell greenhorns looked so danged pathetic the ugly old roughs might take pity and decide there wouldn't be any sport in tormenting the likes of them.

By dark, the town was as close to complete chaos as Stinson had seen it since the first stampede, way back in the days when the miners were arriving in flocks and fighting to stake claims along the Grasshopper.

As he patrolled he saw the Elkhorn was still almost empty and the bakery was still closed and the streets were even more jammed. And there was still no sign of the priest. And there was no sign of Plummer either. Stinson couldn't help wondering why the Stranglers were so sure Sheriff wasn't coming back. He was afraid they might know something he didn't.

For hours he did his best to quieten things down, walking the streets and chatting with the miners and assuring them there was going to be an execution all right, they didn't need to worry about that.

Then just before midnight the Judge showed up and ordered Stinson to go over to the jail and inform Deputy Ray the hanging would have to take place right on schedule, whether Plummer and the priest got there or not.

Stinson considered kicking up a protest about the order, but he knew the Judge was right. The miners were keyed up to see a hanging. And one way or another they were going to be sure they saw one. In their condition, they most likely didn't care who they got to watch swing on the gallows ... the boy ... or the Judge ... or Deputy Ray ... or himself!

Stinson decided it would be wiser to give in to the Judge without any argument whatsoever.

"First off in th' mornin'?" he asked.

The Judge nodded. "At dawn."

CHAPTER SIX

Deputy Stinson could see the sun wasn't in any hurry to rise this gloomy Thursday morning. Instead it just hung up there behind the hills like it had intentions of leaving Bannack in a gray haze all day.

"More'n likely Sheriff's a corpse by now." Stinson said it the second time because he wanted to be sure Deputy Ray and the jailers had heard him.

Out of respect for the boy that was going to die, Stinson wasn't wearing his hat and everybody in the crowd that was gathered in front of the gallows could see his bad forehead. Trickles of nervous sweat were oozing down to his eyebrows but he couldn't let go of his shotgun to wipe them away. His gun was stuck on Beidler.

"Y'all hang a innocent boy an' somethin' bad's fixin' t' happen," he reminded them again. The jailers had stopped trying to persuade Deputy Ray he shouldn't delay the hanging. And they'd also stopped saying they didn't have to follow his orders because he wasn't the sheriff. And when Stinson quit talking everything was still. The skinny boy standing on the tall dry-goods box with his legs bound together and his hands tied behind his back looked like he was frozen in place.

From the very instant Stinson had grabbed his shotgun off the ground and aimed it at Beidler, the hundreds of men jammed together to witness the hanging had quit moving and talking. Everybody knew there was a crisis at hand. Even the wind had given up its sighing and moaning and the gulch was quiet as a tomb. It seemed to Stinson like the whole world was waiting to see what was going to happen next.

Then Deputy Ray stepped out in front of the gallows and

faced the crowd. Before he could announce he was going to postpone the hanging and wait for Sheriff Plummer, old Justice Edgerton hurried over to the makeshift platform where the condemned boy was standing unguarded. He had a wild look in his squinty faded eyes and he began sweeping his Henry rifle from one end of the front semicircle of spectators and across to the other. The little carpenter was in the line of fire and he tried to back up but he couldn't squeeze his way through the pack behind him and had to duck to keep from getting hit in the face with the rifle barrel.

Wilbur saw his Uncle was trying to protect the boy on the box from the Stranglers so he hurried to help him. Just before he got there, he rammed one hand in his overcoat pocket. At first it wasn't clear where the explosion came from.

Then Wilbur tumbled to the ground and began rolling in the dust with his long legs kicking in the air. Edgerton was desperately searching the crowd to see who had fired the shot. He didn't seem to notice his nephew had fallen, but the carpenter and a few others saw and they ran to help the wounded man.

When they reached Wilbur they discovered his overcoat was on fire. Apparently he'd accidentally set off the revolver he was carrying in his pocket. Stinson stayed where he was and watched the men beat out the flames. Then they helped Wilbur to his feet and examined him for a wound but they couldn't find any.

Wilbur was too embarrassed to say thank you. Instead he grappled inside the pocket of the scorched overcoat and pulled out the revolver he'd been reaching for. Then he took a military stance beside his Uncle.

When the crowd realized nobody had been hit by the ball, they burst out in loud peals of laughter. Deputy Ray waited till the laughing died down and then began making his announcement. Stinson couldn't help noticing how hard Ray was trying to make his voice sound casual and disinterested.

"We'll have to wait for Sheriff Plummer," he said, "an execution wouldn't be legal without him."

"Ain't fer no deputy t' say!" Beidler yelled angrily. He began easing his stubby hand inside his overcoat and right away both Edgerton and Wilbur noticed and drew a bead on him.

The miners' Judge was standing in the front row also and evidently he decided it was time for him to show some backbone. He stepped up to the gallows and clambered onto the platform and stood beside the boy.

"It's for me to say," he shouted. "And this execution will proceed as scheduled."

Then he hopped down and hooked one hand around Edgerton's elbow and led him away from the gallows. Wilbur followed along after them.

"Writin's on th' wall," Stinson sighed.

He could see there was no use trying to resist the awful fate waiting for them. He gently deposited his shotgun at the jailers' feet and slowly walked back to the dry-goods box. First he wiped the sweat off his brow with the black bandana and then he mounted the box. He stretched to his tiptoes and snatched the dangling noose in his right hand and used his left hand to try to cover the condemned boy's face with the bandana. But the boy shook his head in refusal. He had his eyes shifted to the side and fastened on the trail winding down cemetery hill.

Stinson stuffed the sweaty bandana back in his pocket so he could use both hands to slip the noose over the boy's head. Then he cinched the coarse rope tight around the skinny neck. Just when he was ready to jump down, he saw somebody in the crowd jut a hand into the air and begin wildly motioning toward something behind him. Stinson wheeled around carefully so he wouldn't fall off the box. Just cresting cemetery hill he saw the silhouette of a long-legged horse and a lean rider.

"I was prayin' he'd make it," Peter Herron breathed in Stinson's ear, "just prayin' with all my soul Sheriff Plummer'd make it."

There was complete silence as every eye watched for the second silhouette to appear ... the familiar figure of the black-robed priest mounted on his little mule. But the Sheriff was almost halfway down the hill and there still wasn't a second figure on the horizon.

Plummer didn't ride all the way to the gallows. At the bottom of cemetery hill he reined up his horse and sat there with his head down. There was an unusual droop to his shoulders. Then he straightened up and raised his right hand. Stinson knew it was a signal to proceed and he wanted to get the horrible nightmare over with as fast as he possibly could. Quick as a wink he hopped to the ground and together he and Ray and the jailers grasped the rope fixed to the tall dry-goods box and gave it a hard yank.

They watched as the frail body fell freely and then suddenly jerked to a neck-snapping halt. For long moments the slim arms and legs covered by the oversized red flannel shirt and baggy buckskin pantaloons flailed against their bonds. Then as the torso and limbs gradually relaxed in death, the limp body began to rotate slowly at the end of the rope.

It seemed to Stinson like the dead boy wanted to give the hungry crowd a view of the awful thing that had been done to him. The thin suntanned face that was tilted down toward them was now turning a dark blue and the eyeballs bulged from their sockets. From the open mouth, the tongue hung down almost to the delicate chin.

When Wilbur had accidentally fired his revolver in his coat pocket, a group of Indians had come running to join the crowd and now one of them who was standing off to Stinson's right stared up at the boy's distorted features and then vomited down the front of his shirt and onto the ground. Stinson could make out chunks of meat and some dark colored roots. It made him glad he hadn't tried to eat any breakfast.

When the boy's tortured face rotated into Deputy Ray's vision, he quickly shoved the box back under the gallows and hoisted himself up and draped his bandana over the bowed head. Now that the results of the boy's death agony were hidden from view, the crowd began to dissolve. They'd seen what they came for. Miners were anxious to get back to their neglected claims and merchants were anxious to get their stores open.

While Ray was still standing on the box top next to the twisting corpse, Sheriff Plummer rode up beside a gallows post. He didn't say anything but he glanced over at Ray and caught his eye and then nodded his head toward his own cabin and kept on going. Ray didn't say anything either, but Stinson hurried to catch up to Plummer's horse and began walking alongside.

"Sheriff," he said, "th' Stranglers come near takin' over while y'all was gone."

"I'll take care of it." Plummer answered so quietly Stinson could barely make out the words.

Stinson stopped and stood watching Plummer weave his tall horse through the departing crowd. When the horse and rider turned onto main street and disappeared from sight, Stinson ambled back to the gallows to stand guard with Ray.

"Reckon Sheriff's ole consumption's actin' up," Stinson grumbled. "Stan' here for 'n hour … then see t' th' buryin' too." He took a quick look up at Peter Herron's dangling body and shivered and jerked his head away. "Yeah that ole consumption acts up an' …"

"Listen at the Reb," Ray said. He was also avoiding any more glances up at the boy's corpse only he was just being less obvious about it than Stinson. "Yeah, Reb," he said, "I saw you up there on the box … quaking like a damned leaf…. So don't try to let on to me you don't know what's up with Plummer."

"Y'all mistaken there, Yank," Stinson answered. "Ba-a-ad mistaken. Don't nobody ever know what's up with Plummer."

CHAPTER SEVEN

As soon as Plummer crossed the log slung across Grasshopper Creek and entered Yankee Flat, he could see Electa sitting on their doorsill watching for him. She spotted him at the same time he saw her and jumped up and began hurrying toward him. From the distance she looked like a child. She was small and fragile and quick in her movements.

As she came closer, he was surprised to see she had on the dress she'd worn when the priest had married them at Sun River. She'd begun sewing the gray calico dress several days before the wedding, and he'd arrived at the mission in time to watch her trim the neck and sleeves with white lace and gray satin ribbon. She'd told him it broke her heart that she couldn't wear white. That was how she'd always imagined it, she said, a white dress. But there were no supplies closer than Fort Benton, and that was sixty miles away.

Ordinarily she kept the wedding dress stored in her steamer trunk, but he supposed she'd put it on this morning to make a special occasion out of his safe return.

He waved and she quickened her pace till she was almost running. Watching her hurry toward him made his heart flood with a love so strong it was almost painful. When she reached him, she grabbed his arm and swung on it to stop herself. She was all smiles now but he could see her eyes were red from crying.

It made him feel guilty that she worried about him so much. Every time he had to leave the valley she was afraid he'd be killed. Instead of going to bed, she stayed awake all night and kept a candle lit and prayed for him. She was so devout she made everybody else in the entire world seem like a heathen.

"I waited up for you all night," she said.

"You shouldn't have."

"Only I slept part of the time," she added, "in the chair."

They hadn't seen each other since yesterday but that was all she said. She'd always been quiet and shy, even around him, and usually he had to try to guess what was in her mind. As they walked, he bent his head and brushed his cheek against her hair, just for the feel of it.

Being with her made it impossible to think about what had just happened. The execution at the gallows seemed like a bad dream ... a terrible nightmare that he'd had to kill a boy. But now she was with him, and he was awake, and everything was as it should be.

It was always the same when he was with her ... except for those few times when they had quarreled. The bad times came mainly because she didn't love the frontier the same way he did. The sense of freedom and opportunity in the West was so real to him he could breathe it in along with the sharp odor of sagebrush and the scent of fresh-turned earth at a gold claim. But when she was in one of her moods, she had a habit of whining like a spoiled child about how wicked Bannack was, and how much she missed the farm in Ohio ... the long straight rows of tall green corn and the fields of golden wheat that bent and rolled with every breeze.

And she said that for the life of her she couldn't understand why he wanted to be a Sheriff anyway since there wasn't any pay for the work. He was excited by the phenomenal amount of gold his workers were extracting daily from his mines, but she wasn't interested in the mines either. She claimed they were tainted by the love of money, just like the town. That was why she rarely left their cabin. Every time he invited her to walk along with him and visit a nearby claim, or ride horseback with him to one of the remote camps, she always refused. Then she pouted about being alone so much and complained about the hours he spent at the mines and on the job. And she threw a tantrum any time she found out he'd done the smallest favor for some miner's family. As best he could understand, she was unhappy any time she wasn't the center of his attention. It was his own fault of course for being so charmed by her innocence, that was why he allowed her to behave like a child. When she complained or pouted, he tried to put her in a better mood by distracting her.

"Let's settle down in front of the fire and watch the flames," he'd say.

Sometimes it worked and sometimes it didn't. Occasionally she continued to carry on until he couldn't stand it and had to leave the cabin.

But when she was happy they seemed to be transported to a different world, just the way they were now. As they walked, he looked up at the high gray hills penning them in on each side and saw they were just as dry and barren as before. The creek winding off to their right was as muddy as usual from miners gouging out the banks. And the pale-blue sky above them was just as empty and just as endless as it had been when he'd ridden north to find the priest. But with her next to him, it was a breathtaking world glowing with excitement and hope. He felt that every one of his dreams and ambitions, no matter how lofty, could come true. The two of them would have a large family of healthy intelligent children. And when the Territory became a state, he would undoubtedly be elected a senator, ... or governor, whichever one he chose. The Democrats had already spoken to him about it. The party was already predicting they could win and they wanted him to decide which office he preferred.

She'd left the door ajar and as they stepped into the cabin, the odor of fresh-baked bread was in the air. And a fire was burning on the hearth. It was only a crude mud-and-stick fireplace but it gave the cabin a homey feeling. He could see he'd been right about the special occasion. The rough plank table was covered with a blue-checked cloth, and for a centerpiece she'd put a sprig of dried blue lupine in an empty medicine bottle. The water waiting for him in the porcelain basin had been warmed, and while he was washing, she spread a blanket over the wooden cot they used as a divan. Apparently she guessed he'd ridden most of the night and would be very tired.

They didn't need to say how much they'd missed each other, or speak about anything at all for that matter. The table was set with the blue willow dishware he'd ordered for her from Salt Lake City. He'd told her many times to use it every day, but instead she saved it for special occasions, like this morning. They sat side by side on a bench, so close her shoulder was brushing against his arm, and ate a breakfast of tea and warm bread.

Afterwards he lay down on the divan to rest. Instead of clearing the table and washing the dishes like she usually did, she came and sat on the floor beside him and rested her head on his chest. After only a few minutes, he felt her falling asleep. As he was drifting off himself, he rubbed his fingertips over the gray calico of her dress and then felt the satin ribbon. The smoothness of the satin brought peaceful images to his mind.

They were kneeling before the priest, and the folds of his long black robe nearly touched the floor. The wide front doors of the Sun River mission had been thrown open, and a panel of gentle sunlight flooded over the three of them. He remembered the sun had felt warm on his face and hands. Then the priest ... for just a moment the priest brought to mind a vision of a thin boy standing on a platform with his legs and hands bound ... but Plummer reached for her soft thick hair and worked his fingers into the swirl of braids wound at the back of her neck, and then they were back at Sun River again, kneeling together before the priest in the patch of warm sunlight.

It was afternoon when he woke. She was standing above him. She'd unpinned the wound braids and was now carefully unweaving them with a comb. Her face and body were so delicate that the mane of glossy pale-brown hair seemed to dominate her. The long waves hung past her waist and were so thick she had to comb them in sections. Watching her reminded him of their wedding night, that had been the first time he'd seen her with her hair down.

After the ceremony at Sun River they'd driven as far as the Dearborn River and then stopped to make camp. When he came back from staking out the horses, she was sitting by the camp fire in a white nightdress and brushing her hair. He recalled how the light from the low flames reflected off her hair and lit it up like spun gold. Her face was tilted away from the heat, and the darkness made her eyes look black instead of gray.

Suddenly she stopped combing and glanced down and saw that his eyes were open and he was watching her. She smiled at him, but rather anxiously he thought. He supposed she'd been awake for some time and was impatient for him to wake up too.

"Where did you find the priest?" she asked.

At first he thought she was talking about their wedding, but there was an uneasy tone to her voice that bothered him.

"The priest?" he asked.

"How far did you have to ride to find him?"

He couldn't believe she was betraying him, purposely leading him out of their private world and back into a terrible reality before he was ready to go.

"What's wrong?" she asked. She dropped the comb onto the small table next to the divan and knelt beside him.

Her hair was draped on his shoulder and he wanted to touch it but he didn't. Instead he turned his face away from her and studied the rough log wall. The bark was peeling off the logs and the dry mud chinked between them was beginning to crack.

"I didn't find the priest," he said. To his own ears his voice sounded flat and dead, like the voice of a sick man. "The priest went to Fort Benton."

He felt her rise to her feet, and turned his face to look up at her. Sometimes it was easy for him to read what she was thinking. Without warning she'd taken them back to what she should have guessed he was trying to forget, and now she was afraid to ask the next question because she wasn't sure she could bear to hear the answer.

Finally she said, "You got them to wait. You saved the boy."

"No, I didn't," he said quietly.

"That's why you rode to get the priest," she went on. She was looking down at him very intently and nodding her head like she expected him to nod in agreement, "... so you could save the boy. You said so."

"Only it didn't turn out that way," he answered. "I raised my hand and gave the signal to hang the boy."

"No ... no!" She stamped her foot and shook her head and

the mane of shiny hair trembled all the way to her waist. "You were going to save him. You told me so!"

He got up from the divan and walked past her to the only window in the cabin. The curtains she'd sewn for it were made from the same bolt of fabric she'd used for her wedding dress. He touched the ruffled gray calico and then pulled it back and gazed out through the small panes. The backs of the false-fronted log cabins lining this side of main street blocked his view of the pine gallows but he could see the tops of the gray hills that rose on each side of Gallows Gulch.

"I gave the signal to hang the boy," he repeated. "The boy is dead. By now he's buried. While I was sleeping, they were burying him on cemetery hill."

Behind him, he could hear her hurrying to the other room and when he turned back, he saw her lying on the bed, hiding her face in a pillow and sobbing. It was very painful for him to watch her cry. In spite of her possessive nature, he always thought of her as pure ... incredibly pure and innocent. He felt a sudden contempt for himself.

He was trying to place the blame on her, hoping to blame her for making his nightmare the reality it was. And actually it was just the other way around. He'd let her down. He hadn't lived up to what she thought he was.

He wanted very badly to go in and comfort her but he was afraid if he tried to touch her, she might push him away. She had never done that and he didn't want it to ever happen, especially not at this difficult time. When he started to speak, he intended to say how sorry he was, how sick he felt about what he'd had to do, but a new wave of the hurt he'd just pushed deep inside him suddenly surged up again, and he felt completely out of patience with her.

"You're a child," he said quietly, "living in a child's world."

She kept on sobbing. She was trying to stifle the sound in the pillow but he could still hear it, and he couldn't stand to hear it, so he left.

He walked rapidly across Yankee Flat and hurried on to main street, the center of his domain. Perhaps he could piece his crumbling world back together by seeing familiar places, places that had been trusted to his care, first the sprawling stable yards and then the assay office. "Will," the miners' president had said to him, "you're the only one this side of the mountains who can take on the Stranglers." At the time he'd believed it. He'd accepted the position as his civic duty.

He passed the carpenter shop and noticed Professor Rawley leaning against the empty workbench where he'd built the boy's coffin and staring idly out the window. And there was no activity on main street either. The miners had returned to their claims and the boardwalks and streets were nearly empty. He was glad the miners were gone because he didn't feel like seeing them now. It was the miners who had brought him to this nightmare. He passed the Elkhorn and approached the Goodrich hotel. It was a two-story building with an ornate balcony above a square-columned porch, and as he reached the front doors, a blur of faces and voices from both stories greeted him. He was too absorbed in his own thoughts and feelings to recognize who they were or what they were saying, but he managed to nod in response.

At the lane that led to the gallows, he paused but he could not bring himself to turn his head and look up the gulch. Quickly he walked on, past the hurdy-gurdy house and the restaurant, and even before he got to it, the stench of the butcher shop sickened him. It was surrounded by frames covered with green hides, and scattered behind it were thickets of tangled antelope horns and deer antlers. Beside the log building there was also a beef scaffold, and dangling from it were two skinned deer with the legs sawed off at the first joint. Evidently Crawford had just finished dressing the carcasses because both of them were still twisting slowly at the end of their ropes. Plummer turned his head away and hurried by.

At the last block of town, he stopped walking and took a deep breath and then tilted his face up to contemplate the cemetery. They were plainly visible, the two fresh graves ... side by side on the hill ... the upturned earth heaped loosely over the two mounds.

He was thinking that every morning when he made his

rounds of town, the two graves would be there on the hill, gazing down at him and reminding him of what he'd done at dawn today. And every night when he went home to the cabin, she'd be there to remind him.

He crossed the street and continued walking till he reached the Grasshopper and then turned left and followed its meandering course downstream. Ahead of him a raggedly dressed red-bearded miner wearing gum boots waded into the creek and then squatted and filled the pan he was gripping. When he recognized Plummer, the miner let go of the pan with one hand and tipped his black slouch hat, uncovering a head of shaggy deep-red hair.

"Afternoon, Sheriff Plummer," he said. Then he put on his hat and expertly swirled the water in the pan.

Plummer didn't know the miner well. But he was better acquainted with the miner's wife. In fact he'd had a relationship with Vera for several weeks and it had brought some pleasant moments. The only drawback was the constant worry that Electa might find out. It had all come about in the most casual and natural way. The red-headed miner had set his family up in housekeeping in a bend of the creek, not far from one of Plummer's richest mining claims. But the miner hadn't been nearly so lucky. His family's only shelter was a wheelless wagon bed with a pole and canvas lean-to attached at the front. When Plummer walked down creek to talk to the foreman at his lucky claim—it was averaging over $2,000 for each day's crushing—he had to pass the unfortunate family camped in the bend.

The first time he saw Vera, she was standing under the canvas awning and jogging a whimpering baby in her arms. The baby had it's father's red hair, only much paler in color, and a little redheaded boy was clinging to his mother's skirt.

"Afternoon, Sheriff," Vera said.

She had a haggard face and was tall and bony-framed, and her dress was loose-fitting and faded. But in spite of her rather dreary appearance, he sensed a quiet strength about her, as though she could survive all the suffering that came her way. Her hands looked strong and clean and she held her back erect and had an almost proud tilt to her angular chin. Apparently she was getting ready to serve dinner on the ground. She'd spread out a blanket and set it with three tin bowls and cups, and there was a pot of stew bubbling over an open fire.

As soon as he got back to the office, he'd asked Deputy Stinson to borrow a wooden box from Chrisman and deliver it to the miner's wife camped in the bend. "She's probably too proud to take anything else," he explained.

"Y'all mean Miss Vera?" Stinson asked. "Reckon she's th' most neediest soul hereabouts." Then he went to hunt up a dry-goods box.

That had been the beginning of the rather strange relationship. The next time Plummer walked to his claim, he noticed that Vera was using the box as a table, just as he'd intended, and that pleased him.

On his return trip, she was waiting for him. She had the same grim expression on her face, but as he passed, she reached out with a tin plate of warm biscuits in her hands. She didn't have an oven and must have baked them on hot rocks. As he accepted the plate, he noticed it gave off the pleasant scent of wood smoke.

He thanked her and left. He couldn't take the biscuits home because Electa would be upset, so he took them to the office. He and Stinson and Ray and Chrisman gathered around his desk and ate every crumb of the warm bread.

Afterwards they felt bad about taking food out of the mouths of the two little redheaded children, so Plummer bought a bag of flour and a crock of lard from Chrisman and asked Stinson to deliver them to Vera along with the empty tin plate.

The next time Plummer passed the bend, Vera gave him what he concluded must be a smile. It was only the slightest upturn at the corners of her mouth, but it did brighten her face a little. She said the usual "Afternoon, Sheriff" but she didn't mention the flour and lard, and he was wondering if Stinson had forgotten to make the delivery.

Then on his return trip, he caught sight of her pressed against one side of the wagon, as if she were hiding. She stayed in the shadow until he was just even with her and then stepped out quickly and slipped something into his coat pocket. Her movements had been so sudden that when she touched his coat, it startled him. But he managed to hide his surprise. He thanked her with a nod and walked on.

He supposed it was food again but he thought she might still be watching him, and it would appear greedy to dip into his pocket immediately. So he waited till he was inside the office.

As soon as his fingers touched the gift he could feel it wasn't food. It was something made from cloth. He pulled it out of his pocket and saw a neatly folded white handkerchief. The fabric was worn but it had been scrubbed to a gleaming white and then ironed and every stitch in the hem was small and perfectly even. With dark blue thread, she'd embroidered the initials WP on one corner. Because of Electa he couldn't take the handkerchief home either so he kept it in his desk. Each time he walked down to check on his claim, he'd bring the embroidered cloth out of its little drawer and tuck it into his suit pocket with the blue initials showing.

Vera never said anything other than "Afternoon, Sheriff," but every time she saw the blue initials showing above his pocket, her thin lips would curl up in a little smile.

As thanks he sent her a bag of sugar, and one day later she came back with a sugar pie. He and Chrisman each ate a small slice but when they came back for seconds, they discovered that some of Chrisman's customers had already finished off the entire pie.

But all of that was in better days. All of those pleasant little exchanges were before the arrest and the trial and the execution of a young miner named Peter Herron. Now it would all change. The attentions and gifts and honors he'd once enjoyed as a respected miners' sheriff would come to an end. They would be only bittersweet memories.

Plummer nodded to the redheaded miner squatting in the creek and continued on toward the bend. He had half a mind to turn back because he didn't feel like encountering Vera. In his desk at the office he had several hanks of blue yarn for her, but he'd been too upset to think about bringing it. He hoped she wouldn't hide beside the wagon and then dart out and slip another gift in his pocket because he was so depressed he might appear ungrateful, and that would hurt her needlessly. Besides, he didn't see how he could look her in the eye. She couldn't have any true respect left for him after he'd just executed a mere boy.

He kept his eyes on the path and didn't glance up until he was beside the wagon bed. To his relief, he could see her moving around inside. She seemed to be putting the baby down for a nap, and he hurried by before she noticed him.

Oh, the miners' wives and their children, ... those uprooted struggling families. Who could help but feel for them. But it was because of the miners that his own life was now in shambles. He'd let them persuade him to be the "law of the country." To him it had seemed to be something a Plummer could and should do ... bring a civilized justice system to the wilderness. His ancestors had done it in the Maine wilderness. And he'd tried to do it here in the Western wilderness, but he no longer felt any pride in his accomplishments. At dawn, he'd given the signal to hang a boy who might have been innocent, and he didn't see how anything in his life could ever be the same again.

It was after midnight when he returned to the cabin and he was tired from the long walk. He'd hoped Electa would be asleep but a light was still burning in the bedroom. It wasn't till he lit the candle in the front room that he noticed the steamer trunk. It was sitting next to the divan with the lid propped open. The trunk was packed, and on top of her things was a quilt she'd been piecing together for their bed. Folded neatly beside the unfinished quilt was the gray calico wedding dress.

At first he refused to believe what it meant. He began groping in his mind for some other explanation, ... she wanted to go up to Sun River for a short visit with her sister, and the separation would only be a few weeks. But his common sense told him she was leaving him for good. She didn't love him anymore. It was another reality he'd have to accept.

He didn't think he could live without her, but if she wanted to leave him why should he try to force her to stay. That wouldn't make her love him again. The light in the bedroom went out. It was as though she'd stayed up long enough to be sure he saw the trunk.

He supposed she wanted to go to sleep, but suddenly she appeared in the bedroom doorway. She was wearing her white nightdress and stood there looking at him and not saying anything.

"Guess I'm not fit to live with," he said.

She didn't answer.

He tried to think of what he could say to let her know how deeply he loved her and how much he wanted her to stay. But he felt so diminished in her eyes that he didn't blame her for wanting to leave him. She disappeared from the doorway and he could hear her getting into bed. While he was wondering what he should do, there was a loud pounding on the front door.

He knew it had to be serious trouble for anyone to come by his home so late. Before he could get to the front door, it swung open and the ragged red-haired miner stuck his head into the room. He was breathing hard, as though he'd been running.

"Sheriff," he said, "can ya' help me? Baby's sick unto dyin'. I went after Doc, he promised he'd stop by the wagon only then he didn't and I ain't got no idee where he's at."

Plummer sent the miner back to his family and then hurried to locate the doctor. Glick had fallen asleep in one of the bunks at the back of the Elkhorn, and Plummer shook him awake and found his black bag for him, and then guided him outside. They cut directly across to the creek and followed its winding bank. The moonlight reflecting off the water lit their way. They were walking fast and he could hear Glick breathing hard beside him. To their right, the hillside was burrowed with dugouts, and a miner suddenly swung open his door and let a patch of light twinkle in the darkness like a bright star. And then just as quickly the door swung shut and the light was extinguished.

Ahead of them was the bend and the canvas awning, glowing white from the candle burning beneath it. As he and Glick approached, they could see the parents watching for them. The father was holding the older boy on one arm, and Vera was cradling the baby's limp form.

Plummer didn't go all the way to the camp. He stood and watched till he saw Glick set his bag on the ground and take the baby in his arms. Then he turned and walked slowly back to the cabin.

Electa appeared to be asleep and he didn't disturb her.

CHAPTER EIGHT

Early Friday morning Rawley left the carpenter shop and headed down the street toward Chrisman's store. It was a gloomy overcast day, with gray clouds hanging so low they merged with the tops of the gray hills. "The weather fits the occasion," Rawley said as he walked. He stopped and tilted his head up and saw that some of the clouds directly overhead were beginning to turn black.

"Oh dear Lord," he said, "please don't send rain down on a child's funeral."

The front doors of Chrisman's store were standing open and a few shoppers were mulling about inside. Others were seated at the fireplace. Rawley was searching for some sort of decoration to soften the appearance of the little coffin he was building. As he browsed through the few items carefully arranged in colorful patterns on the shelves and counters, he could hear Justice Edgerton and his nephew heatedly discussing politics at their fireplace seats.

"Damn Democrats," Wilbur Sanders said.

"Damn Copperheads!" Edgerton muttered. "Damn ignorant Copperheads! Sit around and yammer about peace, when anybody with half a brain can see it's war this country needs!"

From across the street a harsh voice shouted, "Giddeeyap there! Giddeeyap!" Wilbur twisted his neck and looked in the direction of the shout and then reared out of his chair and strode toward the front doors, taking long swinging steps and brushing against Rawley as he passed.

"Ichabod Crane," Rawley murmured to himself. "A regular Ichabod Crane."

Wilbur stepped out onto the boardwalk and stood gaping

across the street at the Goodrich Hotel.

"I thought so," he said triumphantly. "It's her! That's Mrs. Plummer!"

"The farm girl?" Edgerton asked disinterestedly from his chair.

"She's leaving on the Salt Lake stage!" Wilbur said gleefully. "And the miners' great minister of justice is just sitting there on his horse and watching her go." Wilbur slapped his long palms together and shifted from one foot to the other, as if the boardwalk were hot.

"She's leaving him, Uncle Sid. She's leaving him! Come see for yourself."

Edgerton took another puff on his cigar and then slowly lifted himself out of his chair and stiffly walked over to the front windows and pulled back the curtain. Out of curiosity Rawley went to the windows on the other side of the door and looked out himself.

The stage bound for Salt Lake was just pulling away from the hotel. It wasn't a real stage, just a springless wagon drawn by six mules. Its bed was loaded with a steamer trunk and several other bundles. The driver who was calling "Giddeeyap" was an unkempt heavily bearded man with a sullen expression that seemed permanently set on his face.

There was only one passenger, a thin girl sitting on the bench beside the driver, but keeping as far away from him as possible. She was wearing a dark blue traveling outfit and matching hat that both had a homemade out-of-fashion look, and on her lap she was holding a bag made from the same blue fabric. From time to time she took a white handkerchief out of the blue bag and dabbed at her eyes.

Plummer sat on his horse watching as the stage lurched and jolted toward the center of the street. As it settled into the main ruts, its tall wheels sank in deep and then began spurting up clouds of dust behind them. Last Sunday when Rawley had met Plummer at the Bluebird, it had been almost impossible to read his thoughts or emotions, but now the shock and pain in his face were obvious.

"Lord," Rawley whispered, "we don't need any more sadness in this day."

As the heavy wagon lumbered up main street, Plummer nudged his horse forward and caught up to it. When he was directly beside his wife, he slowed the horse to the same pace as the mules and continued riding alongside. His wife kept her eyes straight ahead, as though she weren't aware of her husband's presence. The stage wagon turned left to cross the creek, and Plummer's horse also turned left.

"Oh dear Lord," Rawley whispered, "oh dear Lord, ... he's giving her escort. All the way to Salt Lake. All the way to Salt Lake, he's going to ride alongside the wife who's leaving him."

* * *

The rain fell steadily all afternoon and Rawley had to work steadily to get the coffin ready in time. The mother was nearly out of her mind with grief and the father had said he wanted to get the burial over while he could still pry the dead infant out of Vera's arms. There hadn't been any suitable decoration at Chrisman's store, so Rawley had used his pocket knife to carve a sleeping lamb on the lid of the coffin. He was no artist and the figure turned out rather crude.

As he stepped back to look at the finished product, he regretted having attempted the carving.

"I've spoiled the entire thing," he said.

But it was too late to prepare a new lid.

"Well, anyway," he said, "by the long drooping ears you can tell it's a lamb, and you can tell it's sleeping peacefully. Maybe that will be some comfort to the mother."

It was doubtful there'd be any pay for the expensive lumber he'd used, let alone all of his work. The red-haired miner who'd placed the order appeared to be penniless. That was evident from his ragged clothing.

Late in the afternoon the rain stopped, but still the sun refused to show its face. "The weather fits the occasion," Rawley said again. The father of the dead child had told him they were going to have the burial at dusk, that was what Vera wanted.

When the miner returned to the shop, he gazed down at the little coffin and ran his fingers over the carving of the lamb. Rawley was afraid he was disgusted by the poor artistry, but he made no comment. He just lifted the box in his arms and headed for the front door.

"Pay soon as I can," he said.

"Certainly," Rawley answered.

As the miner left, Beidler entered. He was carrying a shotgun that was an inch or two taller than he was and wearing the dingy black overcoat and a slouch hat that had once been white. Evidently he'd been hovering outside and waiting for the miner to pay his bill so he could come in and collect wages for digging the grave.

"Is the grave ready?" Rawley asked before he offered the pay.

"It's ready, ya bet!" Beidler said. He extended a small leather pouch that already had the mouth gaping open and jabbed his forefinger at it. "Rycheer! Put 'er rycheer!"

Rawley went behind the curtain at the back, where he slept and where he also hid the precious hoard that would take him home some day soon, and came back with ten dollars from the currency the freighters had paid him and stuffed it in the open purse.

As Beidler tightened the drawstrings and pocketed the pouch he had nothing to say. But just as he was going out the door, he hesitated and turned back.

"Ya ain't got no frien's," he said, "so ya ain't no frien' t' Plummer neither, I guess."

Rawley found the small man's harsh nasal twang irritating, and he was offended by the slur. Besides, he still hadn't forgotten how Beidler had called him the "ejycated li'l fool."

"Of course I'm not a friend to Plummer," he answered. "I scarcely know the man."

Beidler squinted his eyes and stared hard at Rawley, as if he were trying to make up his mind about something.

"Well," he finally said, "there's a meetin' after dark. Ya got a invite."

"What sort of meeting?"

"Business meetin'. Business folk gonna hitch up t'gether n' hep out th' town."

Rawley was all for progress but he doubted he'd be around long enough to participate in any civic activities. He stroked his beard and considered his duty in the matter.

"I'll try to make it," he said.

Beidler leaned back into the shop and said in a low voice, "Butcher shop. Roun' back ... after dark." Then he swaggered out onto the boardwalk and headed in the direction of the Elkhorn.

"Avoid the strangling little illiterate like a rattlesnake," Rawley advised himself.

But evening came and he had nothing to do. He didn't want to spend the night next door at Skinner's saloon like he usually did. That would deplete his hoard of currency even further. After a long debate with himself, he closed the front doors. Then he lit a candle and washed his face and hands and trimmed his mustache and beard and put on a shirt with a freshly starched collar and bosom. While he was knotting his tie he began to feel nervous about his decision to attend the meeting. He kept remembering how Beidler's eyes had narrowed while he studied him. "Could Beidler possibly have the notion I killed Keeler?" he asked. "Maybe the meeting's a necktie party for me." He glanced nervously at the front doors. He wasn't sure he'd remembered to lock them. He started toward them, but just before he got there a face pressed against the window. He jumped back and heard himself give a sharp cry.

"It's me," a deep voice said.

Rawley was torn between taking one more step forward and locking the front doors, or dashing for the back door.

"My wife, she says many thanks for the lamb."

The image of the crude carving he'd cut into the coffin lid flashed into Rawley's mind and he shamefacedly opened one door. Without being invited, the miner stepped inside. Rawley hardly recognized the large man without his ragged work clothes. He was wearing a suit and tie, and his bushy red beard had been trimmed down to a goatee.

"Well, we got the buryin' over with," he said sadly, "and then Vera she sent me ... wants me t' say many thanks for the lamb."

The sorrow that was so evident in the miner's face and voice tore at Rawley's heart. He remembered all too well how it felt to lose a small daughter. His and Angeline's only child had died when she was three years old. He remembered how on the day they had buried her, it had rained from dawn till dusk.

"Would you like a cup of coffee?" Rawley asked. "Maybe a slice of pie. It's fresh from the bakery." He'd planned to have it for his breakfast, but he had nothing else to offer the miner.

"I'll take my piece home t' the boy," the miner answered.

Rawley had no real kitchen, just a table and cupboard and small stove at the back of the shop. The miner trailed after him and watched him open the cupboard and take out the slice of dried-peach pie and then wrap it in a sheet from an old newspaper he'd been rereading earlier.

"The boy'll be right pleased with that," the miner said.

He stretched out his hand and took the wrapped slice but he didn't turn back toward the front doors. He stood holding the slice of pie and looking intently at Rawley like there was something else he wanted to say. Finally he cleared his throat and begin drawling out words in a melancholy voice.

"I was born back in Missouri in eighteen and thirty-five ... piece o' land there north o' Jump Creek ya know ..."

When Rawley realized the miner was relating his life story, he brought him a stool and then took one opposite. Rawley didn't interrupt with questions, and the miner perched himself on the edge of the stool with the wrapped pie balanced on one knee and kept on talking in a grave monotone. Occasionally he'd raise his head and gravely eye Rawley, as if he wanted to remind him to pay close attention, but most of the time the miner kept his eyes on the dirt floor. The gist of the meandering account seemed to be that he was sorry he'd left his fertile farm in Missouri and come West to try to get rich at the gold mines. It had caused his family too much suffering. When he got to the part where his baby daughter took sick, he covered his face and began to cry.

"Blaming himself for the child's death," Rawley whispered. He could hardly keep from crying himself.

By the time the miner finished his life story, it had been dark for over an hour. Rawley saw his guest to the door. He was half afraid to ask a question because it might set off another long story. But this was the first real offer of friendship he'd had since he arrived at the mines and he couldn't help feeling grateful for the company.

"By the way," he said, "I didn't catch your name."

"Grizzert," the miner said, "Freddie Junior Grizzert."

"Goodnight, Mr. Grizzert," Rawley said quickly. Then he grabbed the miner's hand and gave it a quick shake, and Grizzert left.

"Too late to go to the civic meeting, now," Rawley sighed. Still, he wasn't sleepy and he'd already read his only newspaper at least twenty times. "Wouldn't hurt to stroll down to the butcher shop and see if the meeting is still going on."

He heated the flat iron on his small stove and then spread out his best trousers on the table and gave them a quick press. "Wouldn't do to go to a civic meeting and not look neat," he said. After he put on the pressed trousers and tucked in the stiff-bosomed shirt, he combed his hair and beard. Then he doused the fire in the stove and blew out the candle and set out.

As he approached the butcher shop, its stench reached his nostrils. He was a little disappointed to see the entire building was dark. He walked behind a hide-drying frame and approached one window and could detect it had been covered. "Why cover the windows for a civic meeting?" he asked. He skirted the beef scaffold with its dangling carcasses and was heading toward the back door when he heard it creak open. Instinctively he stepped back to the wall and pressed against it.

In a moment a small figure swaggered out from behind the building, but instead of coming toward him to enter main street, it disappeared into the darkness behind the row of buildings. Rawley could feel the hair rise on the back of his neck. He had a panicky desire to hurry back to the safety of the carpenter shop, but he was afraid he'd be detected if he moved.

While he waited, the back door creaked again and seconds later another shadowy figure emerged and headed down the back alley. "Leaving one at a time," he whispered. "And meeting while Sheriff Plummer is out of town ... businessmen all right, except their business is strangling."

Moments later there was another creak and then another figure. Rawley was still afraid to move and kept on waiting but there was only silence. "Three," he said, "only three ... and maybe Crawford still inside, so that's four."

He continued waiting in the darkness until he was certain it was safe to leave. The odor of dried animal blood was making him sick to his stomach and his legs felt weak. He tugged at his beard and squinted his left eye shut because the tics were jerking it. "The lamb," he whispered, "the lamb saved me. If Grizzert hadn't come back to the shop, I'd have delivered myself right into the Strangler's hands."

Edging alongside the butcher shop and then stepping wide of the scaffold and also avoiding the drying frames, he gradually worked his way out to main street and then walked rapidly to his shop.

Though he locked both front and rear doors and stacked sawhorses in front of them, he could not go to sleep. It seemed to him he could sense another presence in the room with him. Finally he got up and groped his way to the workbench and found his hammer and carried it back and laid it on the floor beside his bunk. But even with the weapon at hand, he still wasn't able to sleep. Whoever or whatever was still there. He lay on his back, staring up into the darkness.

"It's so strong I can feel it," he whispered. "I can feel it, only I don't know what it is.... It recalls something from a long time ago, but I can't remember exactly what."

He turned on his right side for a while, then on his left. Finally he tried lying on his stomach. But in that position, he felt too vulnerable and quickly rolled over onto his back again. He decided to distract himself by thinking of Angeline.

"At this very minute she's sleeping in the bed we shared. No, ... maybe lying awake and thinking about me ... missing me

... reaching her soft little arm over to feel my empty place."

He thought he heard a noise at the front doors and raised to a sitting position on the bunk. At the same instant a flash of lightning lit up the windows. He couldn't see anyone on the boardwalk in front of the shop. Then there was darkness again and a roll of thunder.

In the instant of brightness, he'd clearly seen his plane and his saw lying on the workbench, and beside them was a pile of wood shavings he'd forgotten to sweep up. He groped for the candle beside the bunk and lit it and went to tidy the bench. It wasn't like him to forget to clean up after himself. He took the hammer with him for protection and kept it close at hand while he worked. It felt very odd to be working at the bench in his long underwear.

As he bent forward and brushed loose wood shavings into the palm of his left hand, he was struck by the sweetness of their odor. "Like Father's shop," he said. The lightning flashed again, nearly blinding him with its brightness. He felt dizzy, as though he'd been struck by the bolt, and staggered back and kept walking backwards until he reached the bunk. Then he sank onto it and closed his eyes. But the brightness was still dazzling them, and the smell of the wood shavings clutched in his left hand was strong in his nostrils.

"I remember," he said aloud. "I remember."

It had happened when he was only five. He'd never been fortunate enough to know a brother or sister. All of them had died before he was born. So he spent the lonely days playing beside a small stream that ran across their property. His favorite game was sailing a fleet of three small ships his father had built for him. They were exact replicas, with tiny cloth sails, and one by one he would launch them and then trot alongside while they floated downstream.

But on this particular day, a sudden thunderstorm erupted and he scooped the boats out of the water and ran to his father's carpenter shop. As he entered, he observed how old his father looked. He had gray hair and a long gray beard and was frail, but he was vigorously sawing a board in half, with sawdust spraying out in a fine mist on both sides.

As soon as his father saw him he laid down the saw. "Oh, it's you is it, Richard Charles," he said. He sank onto a plank laid across two sawhorses and for a few minutes sat watching the fierce rain storm going on outside. Then he commenced a story. It was his usual way of entertaining his son.

"When I was a very young man," his said, "I once fell in with a crowd of wicked friends."

While his father talked, Richard carefully dried the three ships with his handkerchief and arranged the fleet in a neat row. Then he settled himself on the floor beside them. Next to him was a heap of curled wood shavings left by the plane, and while his father went on with the story, Richard began hooking the shavings together to form a fragile chain.

A strong wind was driving the rain against the windows and it felt good to be inside where it was warm and dry. Richard was wearing the new sailor suit his mother had sewn for him, and he reached down and caressed the beautiful blue braiding on the square white collar.

Because he was his mother's only surviving child, she had insisted on keeping him in dresses until the day he turned four. On that birthday, she presented him with his first pair of trousers. Then before he went to bed that night, she lifted him to a high stool and cropped off the long black curls she'd set just that morning by first wetting his thick hair and then winding strands of it around one of her fingers.

His mother cried when she saw him with short hair, but he looked down from the stool and saw the mass of black ringlets spread out on the floor and felt proud to have finally graduated into manhood.

Since the day his mother had cut off his curls and cried about it, he and his father had been talking man talk, like they were now. The curled wood shavings he was carefully linking together smelled sweet to him, almost as sweet as taffy.

"After our parents went to sleep every night," his father was saying, "my wicked friends and I would sneak out of our houses and drink strong spirits and then carouse about town destroying decent people's property while they were asleep."

A clap of thunder startled both of them and his father stopped talking for a moment. When he went on, he didn't seem to be talking to Richard. He seemed completely caught up in the memory and Richard noticed with alarm that his father's voice took on an eerie tone.

"One night I came home late and was so worn out from all of our pranks and so full of strong spirits that I quickly dropped off to sleep. But I had a very strange dream."

His father stopped again, as though that were the end of the tale and he was going to keep the dream a secret. When he finally continued, his voice sounded faint and distant, like it was coming from somewhere above him.

"I dreamed that Satan entered my room and tiptoed to my bed and then bent over my pillow. I knew it was Satan because he had two little horns and a short pointy beard and was wearing a red suit. And he smelt of sulfur and brimstone. 'I've come for your soul,' he whispered in my ear. I was so frightened I woke up in a cold sweat. But the strangest part ... the strangest part of all ... even after I realized it was only a dream, I could still feel Satan's presence. Moonlight was flooding in from the window and it brightened my bedroom and I could see there was nobody there. But inside me, I could feel Satan inhaling and exhaling. I remember how regular the rhythm was and how my chest was moving with the same rhythm."

"Was he trying to suck your breath?" Richard asked.

"No," his father answered, "but the evil in the room was so strong I could feel it, and it frightened me nearly to death. After that terrible dream, I never again went carousing with my wicked friends."

Rawley reached his right hand to his left shoulder to caress the blue braiding on his white collar, but instead he found himself stroking the ribbed weave of his long underwear. Thoughtfully he got up and dropped the shavings still clutched in his left hand into the woodbin beside the little stove and then put out the candle. Then he lay back down on the bunk and closed his eyes.

"When evil is strong enough," he said, "you can feel it."

The marvelous insight seemed to give him peace. He wasn't sure why. For a moment he thought about the hammer he'd left on the workbench, but he decided he didn't need it. He rolled over onto his stomach and fell asleep.

CHAPTER NINE

As Plummer rode back toward Bannack, the steady wind turned into a near gale. Billowing white alkali dust blocked the sun and blurred the horizon of the dreary wasteland surrounding him. He lowered his head and hunched his shoulders and headed his horse due north. It was easy to stay on course. All he had to do was keep riding directly into the wind.

It was finally clear to him that he had to give up Electa, but it wasn't clear to him why he was going back to Bannack. From the time they'd left main street last week, he'd seriously considered putting Electa on the first Salt Lake stage heading toward Ohio, and then riding into the wilderness and shooting himself. To ride beside her through the long miles and know she didn't love him anymore had left him with no reason to live. Since they'd first met at Sun River, he'd told her he couldn't live without her. But now he knew that wasn't completely true. He could go on living. It was just that he didn't want to.

The north wind he was riding into was gradually letting up, and the white alkali dust in the air began to settle over the colorless landscape in a powdery cloud. For as far as he could see on all sides of him, there was no sign of life. The loneliness was almost unbearable and he felt a sudden anxiousness to be in Bannack. He pictured its main street–the boardwalks and the two facing rows of decorated fronts masking the log cabins, the merchant's attempts to bring a touch of civilization to the wilderness. He pictured the miners working along the creek and remembered how at night they opened the doors to their dugouts and lit up the black hillside with patches of light. It was suddenly clear to him why he was returning. Bannack was all that was left of his life. All he had now was the commitment he'd made to the miners a year ago.

So he could escort her through the wilderness, he'd left town hurriedly and there were several things he needed to do when he got back. First on the list was to give Hank Crawford a warning that the miners association wouldn't tolerate any more vigilance activity in the valley.

It was after midnight when he arrived. He left his horse at the stable and without thinking started to head across the creek to the cabin. Then he remembered that she wouldn't be there, so he walked down to the Goodrich Hotel. Bill Goodrich was polite enough not to ask any questions. He just assigned Plummer his old room, the one he'd lived in while he was still single.

It felt good to lie down but after he was in bed, he was too tired to fall asleep. In the darkness he lay on the cot thinking about the last time he'd been in the room. He hadn't been able to sleep that night either, because the next morning he'd be leaving for Sun River to marry Electa and bring her back with him.

On the ride from Salt Lake, he'd promised himself not to think about her again. But now he had, and memories of her filled his mind. After he quit trying to fight them, they began to give him a rather peaceful feeling, and occasionally he'd even doze off. Then he'd wake with a start. But whether he was awake or dozing, he was reliving the autumn they'd spent together at the Sun River mission.

It was a perfect Indian summer and they were walking under the cottonwood trees lining the river bank. The current was lazy and the water was a mirror, reflecting back the yellow leaves of the tall trees and the blue sky and the white clouds above them. In the distance, large buttes jutted into the landscape, and beyond the scattering of buttes were purple mountains that faded into even higher mountains, blue mountains with snow-covered peaks.

Electa, he was thinking as he walked beside her, had all the naturalness and beauty of everything around them. He'd known many women but none had loved him the way she did. And when autumn ended and he rode away from Sun River, he could feel her waiting for him, waiting for him to come back and keep his promise to marry her in the Spring.

Being in the hotel room again gave him the strange sensation that he'd gone back in time and Electa was still waiting for him at Sun River. Finally he fell into a deep sleep.

At dawn he woke with the same feeling, that the wedding at the mission was still ahead of them. He didn't try to shake off the sense of false happiness. As he washed and dressed in the small cold room, he let the image of Electa waiting for him at Sun River play on his mind.

As always, he started his patrol of town on the north side of main street, beginning at the stable. The rim of the sun barely brightened the fog hanging over Gallows Gulch, and flurries of snowflakes gave the valley and the town lining it a hazy appearance. As he passed each business, he checked to be sure there'd been no break-ins during the night and then walked on. It was a weekday and as far as he could tell, he was the only person in town who was up and stirring. The emptiness and quiet of the streets gave him the eerie feeling of patrolling an abandoned settlement.

At the lane leading up the gulch, the mist was so thick he couldn't see the gallows, and above him cemetery hill was also completely shrouded in fog. As he approached the butcher shop, the odor of animal slaughter brought the first touch of reality to the scene. Then a light flickered inside the log building and he knew there was at least one other person in town who was awake.

He continued on to the end of main street and started up the south side, past the Peabody Saloon and the Durand Saloon and Kustar's Bakery. From across the street he heard a door creak open and turned to look. Apparently Crawford had just come out the back door of the butcher shop. In his arms he was carrying a bulky hide, and he walked to the side of the building and began stretching the hide over an empty drying frame. When he finished, he disappeared behind the shop and there was the sound of the back door creaking open and then closing. For a moment, Plummer was tempted to cross the street and have it out with Crawford about the vigilante issue, but he decided he should complete his rounds first.

Automatically his fingers reached down and checked the

door of the bakery, but his mind was on Electa waiting at Sun River. He was just approaching the Sears Hotel when the ball struck him from behind. The force of the shot knocked him to the ground and stunned him. He was lying on his left side and he could feel snowflakes falling on the right side of his face. He wasn't sure where he'd been hit. Then he heard the sound of someone running toward him and tried to reach for his revolver but his right arm was numb.

From the corner of his eye he saw a dark form bending over him and made another effort to use his right arm, but it still wouldn't move.

"What happened, Sheriff?"

The voice sounded familiar and he turned his head and saw the red-haired miner kneeling beside him.

"Some son of a bitch has shot me," Plummer answered. He pushed himself up with his left hand and then saw the blood spurting from his right arm.

* * *

Dr. Glick picked up a pair of tweezers and fished around in the incision he'd cut and pulled out more bone fragments. He deposited them on the table beside the others and blotted the bleeding wound with a towel that was already saturated.

"Has to come off," he said, "has to be amputated."

Plummer raised his head and looked down at his right arm. It was swollen and streaked with blood.

"Find the ball," he told Glick.

"That's what I've been trying to do for the past hour," Glick answered. "I've got the arm slashed open from the elbow to the wrist and I still can't find the damn ball!"

"Can't you trace the path?" Plummer asked. He reached down with his left hand and took another drink from the bottle of whiskey he was using as an anesthesia.

"I followed the damn path," Glick insisted, "chips of broken bone all the way. Bone chips everywhere, but no ball. Can't find it." He reached his hand toward the whiskey.

Instead of offering the bottle, Plummer held onto it. "That

won't help you find it," he said. He set the bottle down on the floor on the opposite side of the cot, where Glick couldn't reach it.

Glick grunted with disgust and picked up the scalpel lying on the table and made a second incision near the wrist and Plummer groaned and took another drink.

"Same thing here," Glick said, "bone chips everywhere ... no path you can follow." He grabbed the tweezers and plucked out more fragments and then sopped up more blood. "No two ways about it. That arm has to be amputated."

Glick stood up and put his hands on his hips and stretched his back and swivelled his neck a few times, as though he were limbering himself up for the surgery. Then he gazed down at Plummer.

"Ready?" he asked irritably.

"I'll keep the arm," Plummer said. He closed his eyes to show the discussion was over.

Glick cursed under his breath and then found his needle and thread and began stitching up the longer incision.

When both cuts had been sewn shut, he washed his hands at the basin and then cleaned his utensils and packed them in the black bag.

"You'll keep the arm?" he asked.

Plummer nodded.

"All right ... and you'll die," he said. "Already burning up with fever."

Glick rolled down his shirt sleeves and collected his suit coat from the row of pegs that served as the room's clothes closet. Then he grabbed his bag.

"Doesn't matter a whit to me," he said. "If that's what you want, then lie there and die."

"That's just what I'll do," Plummer answered.

The sound of the door closing behind Glick was muffled and Plummer knew the fever must be affecting his senses. But somehow his mind seemed keen and his thoughts were as clear as crystal. He recognized the fate that had been waiting for him for thirty-two years. In fact it seemed rather familiar to him. He would never leave Bannack. His dust would become part of

Bannack's dust.

After a while he opened his eyes and turned his face toward the tall narrow window of the hotel room. The fog had lifted and through the light snowfall he could see the top of cemetery hill. It was completely white but he could still make out the curve separating it from the gray sky.

They would probably bury him in the plot next to Vera's child. And on the other side of the child was Peter Herron, and then beyond him was Keeler. The four of them would sleep side by side on the hill rising above main street.

Looking back over his life, he felt many regrets about things he'd done, or hadn't done, but most of all he blamed himself for having lost the struggle with the Stranglers. It was his own fault for letting down his guard. He had no doubts they'd soon be in control of the entire Territory and that troubled him a great deal.

It was even more painful to think of Electa and his mother. His only consolation was that by the time they heard, he would have been dead for months, and that might make it easier for them. And Electa would find another husband. She would remember him, maybe even for the rest of her life, but she would find somebody else. With his mother it was different. She would never find another son to replace him. He closed his eyes and pictured her in his mind and tried to remember the sound of her voice and then he felt himself gradually slipping into unconsciousness.

To prevent it, he reached his left hand out to touch the log wall, but instead his fingers brushed against a soft textured surface. He opened his eyes and turned his head toward what should have been a rough log and watched the fingertips of his left hand caressing a velvety white flower flocked on cream-colored wallpaper. Then his hand moved on to feel the gloss of massive dark-stained woodwork. He was standing up now and he walked to a large glass-doored cupboard and stood looking in at the rows of shelves. They were filled with china tea sets and ivory figurines. As he examined them, he could recall each gift his father had brought back from the voyages and also which far country each gift had come from. And each of his father's gifts was still sitting exactly where his mother had carefully positioned it. A feeling of security so deep he had forgotten it ever existed flooded over him. He was home.

CHAPTER TEN

Home was the rugged seacoast of Maine. It was a different world in a far different time, and it was a completely different life. From as early as Will could remember, he used to imagine that he was already a captain, like his father and his older brothers. Each night while he was lying alone in his high bed and listening to the leaves of the red-maple tree brush against his windows and trying to fall asleep, he'd silently speak to his imaginary crew in a firm but kind voice, reassuring them he would see them through the crisis. Then he'd guide his graceful high-sailed clipper ship through a treacherous typhoon and put into a steamy tropical port. There he'd take time to buy a red silk fan painted in gold for his mother and also a silver necklace for Becky.

As a boy he'd never once doubted the notion that if he wanted something badly enough, it was bound to come true.

It was the summer when he turned nine years old that he learned otherwise. He remembered that it was an unusually warm summer. The last of the older children had just left home, and he and Becky had full run of the house and yard and fields. But with their new freedom came new responsibilities. One day his mother called Will to the library and told him that while his father was at sea, he was to be the man of the family. He was to tend the horses and cows and sheep and pigs and chickens, and also chop wood for the many fireplaces in the large house.

Becky always worked side by side with him. And since she was two years older, she actually did as much work as he did, but still Will felt the new duties lying heavy on his thin shoulders.

Each day after the chores were done, he walked to the pasture and caught the gentlest of the horses. Then he rode the gray mare back for Becky, and pulled her on behind him. She locked her arms around his waist, and with his heels he prodded the mare to a jouncing pace and they rode bareback into the cool pine forest beyond the Plummer fields. Honey, their big fawn-colored hound, loped alongside them with his long ears flopping and his mouth opened in a smile and his curled tongue lolling out.

On the way home, they always chose a path through the tall grasses of the salt marsh, where years earlier their father and their older brothers had built dikes to hold back the sea. Will would rein up the mare and gaze out at the endless expanse of clear blue sky meeting clear blue water that was to be his destiny.

One day they came back from their usual ride and found their father's sister at the house. When Aunt Mary left, she took Becky along with her for a visit with the cousins. It was the first time Will had been separated from his sister. She had been there from the first day of his life and quite naturally he'd taken it for granted she always would be.

Without Becky, the large house seemed empty and the yard was lifeless and the chores became a burden. And all the familiar things he saw around him no longer seemed to have any connection to him. He tried to ignore the strange feeling by keeping busy, but he soon discovered there was nothing he enjoyed doing by himself.

After he'd finished his chores, he trailed after his mother as she did the housework and cooking. For the first time he noticed that Elizabeth talked very little. She was cheerful and intelligent but in looking back over the nine years of his life, Will could see that unless Elizabeth was telling a story, she limited her communication with her children to offering bits of advice.

"Don't let the sun rise on your wrath," she'd say when he and Becky carried a quarrel over to the second day. Or when Will was a very small child and had complained that one of the older brothers had treated him unfairly, she'd say, "Turn the other cheek, Will." And later, after he'd entered school, if he happened to criticize any of his schoolmates, she'd say, "Live and let live, Will."

As he trailed her about the house, he wanted in the worst way to explain to his mother that he was desperate with loneliness, but he didn't know how to break the silence between them.

He stood at her elbow and watched as she grated spice into a bowl of gingersnap batter. After she put the cookies into the oven to bake, he sat on the high wooden stool and scraped the bowl with a spoon, licking off every drop of the sweet spicy batter.

He would have liked to help her clean the kitchen but he had learned better. Once when he was smaller, he'd climbed onto the same high stool to help Becky wash dishes. But just as he dipped his hands into the warm rinse water, his father appeared at the kitchen door. Jeremiah Plummer was a patient soft-spoken man, but when he was angry he could give a tongue lashing that would leave Will quivering with shame and fear. Jeremiah quickly lifted Will from the stool and then turned to his wife.

"Betsy," he said sharply, "I won't have you making the boy into a woman."

After that day, Will tried very hard to never again disappoint his father by doing woman's work. But only a short time later, another unfortunate incident occurred. Will and Becky were playing in the tree house and by accident he dropped one of her little green-glass teacups. As it struck the ground, it split in half. They were afraid to tell their father about the broken cup because he had brought the tea set to Becky on his last trip to Boston.

But the most shameful part was that Will had been handling dishes again, and clumsily at that.

The two of them buried the broken pieces of the little green cup in the barnyard. But from that day on, Will had to be on constant guard that Honey didn't dig up one of the pieces and unexpectedly appear at the front door of the house with half a tiny green-glass cup gripped between his big jaws.

The first meal without Becky at home was awkward. Elizabeth and Will sat alone at the long dining room table. Neither one of them spoke while they ate, and Will was conscious of the loud sound of his chewing.

When his mother finally excused him from the table, he grabbed a handful of ginger snaps and went out the back door and lay down on his back in the shade of the red-maple tree.

Not a breath of air stirred the drooping three-fingered leaves on the branches above him. Slowly he munched the gingersnaps and looked up through the maple leaves at the dancing specks of dull blue sky overhead. It was clear to him that by leaving him so alone, Becky had betrayed him. He remembered how happy she had looked as they rode away and he knew his relationship with her would never be quite the same. He would never be able to trust her like before. In fact he could not trust that she would even come back. She might decide to stay with the cousins. He saw nothing ahead of him but endless solitude ... solitude for the rest of his life.

The bees hovering over his mother's bright orange poppies droned a dry song that barely disturbed the silence, but lingered in his ears as though he were hearing the aching loneliness inside him. He watched the bees at work and realized how cut off he was from the rest of the world. He gazed hard at his mother's poppies–the petalled orange cups rising on thin leafless stems– and refused to admire their beauty. As he lay there marveling at his own hardness, a wonderful idea suddenly blossomed inside his head. He couldn't imagine why he hadn't thought of it sooner because he was sure it would restore his world to its proper happy state. He would ask to go with his father when he sailed to New York.

True, all of his brothers had been older when they made their first trips to sea, but he'd done several other things younger than his brothers had. He was only four when his oldest brother taught him to read. And both of his parents always gave the impression they thought he was special. Their "little man" they always called him. And since he would be a big help with the work aboard ship, he felt certain his father would be pleased that he wanted to go along to New York.

At first Elizabeth opposed the plan, but Will continued to press his case in a calm reasonable voice and finally she agreed. After that she seemed to be as enthusiastic as he was. Together they climbed the ladder to the attic and carried down the little sea chest stored there. It had belonged to William Henry Handy when he was a boy. He was Elizabeth's younger brother who had died at sea, and Will was his namesake: William Henry Handy Plummer. His mother often told him stories about Uncle William

Henry, how he'd gone to sea at age sixteen as a steward, and how by the time he was nineteen he was the captain of a beautiful clipper ship. Will's grandfather had built Uncle William Henry's ship for him and then named it for Will's grandmother.

Long ago Will had figured out without even asking anybody that all the clippers were women and all of their captains were in love with them. Quite naturally Uncle William Henry was in love with his clipper and he had picked a fine brave crew and the lot of them had sailed around the world.

But one day while they were in the Madeira Islands, the young captain contracted a disease. His crew sailed him safely home, but while they were mooring in the harbor at Boston, he died aboard his own ship. Elizabeth always closed her story by saying that Will had the same serious gray eyes as his Uncle William Henry.

Elizabeth had lots of experience packing sea chests so she helped Will select the things he would need for the trip. On top of his clothes she put the square brown bottle of medicine for his cough. She had bundled it in cloth so it wouldn't leak on his clothes and stain them.

As his mother closed the lid of the chest, Will was suddenly overwhelmed by the realization that the destiny he'd been dreaming of ever since he could remember was suddenly upon him. Since he hadn't expected it to come so soon, he really wasn't prepared and the prospects of the adventure that was suddenly so close at hand made him dizzy with excitement.

The next morning he and Elizabeth stood side by side on the widow's walk that crowned the large house, shading their eyes against the sun and looking down the lane. At last the tall bay horse came into sight and at first they could see only Jeremiah's lean frame, but then as he got closer, they could see his dark beard and his captain's hat.

For Will, the rest of the day was only a blur. He scarcely took time to examine the new pocket knife his father had brought him. Instead he ran upstairs and slipped it into the sea chest with his other things. While his mother prepared a feast of a supper, the two men rested on the cool back porch. Will sat on his father's knee and occasionally reached out for a taste from the glass of red wine Jeremiah was sipping to give himself a good appetite. Jeremiah had advised him it was all right because Will was too thin and needed a good appetite too.

Gradually a feeling of dreamy bliss settled over Will. It seemed to him he was actually part of his father, and together they were part of everything around them. He thought how the big red-maple tree that was shading them had been planted there by his grandfather, Moses the Third, and how his own father had built their grand three-story house on the very site where the first Moses Plummer had built his little home in the Maine wilderness, long, long ago when the land still belonged to the King of England.

But while they were eating supper, a rather worrisome incident occurred. Jeremiah laid down his fork and sat looking at the food on his plate. Then he picked up a crystal water glass by its delicate stem and slowly rotated it between his thumb and fingers, contemplating the pattern of colors it gave off in the light from the candle chandelier overhead.

"Betsy," he said rather sadly, "I'm not so sure it's wise to take the boy along."

Will held his breath while he waited for his mother to answer.

"I think it will work out all right," she said calmly.

Jeremiah nodded and seemed to forget the matter. He went back to talking about the voyage, how the ocean had been smooth as glass and how a school of dolphins had swum alongside the ship like an escort. Sometimes the dolphins would leap into the air, as though they wanted to have a better look at Jeremiah's crew, just to see if they approved of them. Will had heard such stories many times but it was the first time he'd been able to picture them so clearly in his mind.

After supper the three of them went upstairs to bed. Jeremiah was home only for the short time it would take to have his ship reloaded with lumber and father and son would be leaving at dawn. Will knew if he didn't wake up healthy, Jeremiah wouldn't want to take him, but because he was trying so hard, it took him a long time to fall asleep. He lay tossing and turning and listening to the leaves of the maple tree brushing against his windows and thinking how the next night he wouldn't be hearing the leaves at all. Instead he would be hearing waves lapping against the ship. It was a sound he'd never heard.

The sun woke him. It was flooding through the sheer white curtains over his high windows with a glare that was too strong for early morning light. He hopped out of bed and ran down the hall to his parents' bedroom. The door was open and his mother was standing alone at the bay windows. She turned and looked at him with the hard expression in her eyes that always came just after his father left.

"Did he go without me?" Will asked. Hearing his fear put into words brought a sharp pain to his stomach.

His mother nodded. "He was afraid ..." She took a deep breath and then let it out slowly. "Afraid you might get ill."

Ill ... ill. He hated the word. That was how she always referred to his consumption. Every time she said the word, it made him feel dirty and tainted.

Elizabeth looked directly into his eyes as if she were trying to get him to be reasonable and agree with her. "You know, Will, like you do sometimes."

"Is he really gone?" Will asked. He looked about him quickly, trying to catch sight of some of Jeremiah's possessions that would indicate he was still here–the captain's cap, or the pipe and tobacco pouch.

"Yes, he's gone." There was a coldness and a finality in his mother's voice that settled the matter. She turned back to the window and looked down the empty lane. "By now," she added a little crossly, "they've surely sailed."

Will heard a small choking sound and realized it must have come from his own throat. He pressed his hand over his mouth and ran out into the hall and back to his own room. Uncle William Henry's small chest sat waiting next to the bed, and he reached down and pushed both hands against it, hoping that would hold back the fierce ache that was spreading up to his throat and mouth, but the force was too strong for him. He sank to the floor and rested his head on the lid of the chest. The feeling of being left behind for a second time that week seemed more than he could bear. It was pressing the breath out of him. He thought of the others on the ship far out at sea, and the tears suddenly came and would not quit.

Then he felt his mother's hand on his shoulder. He was ashamed she'd seen him behaving like a child and immediately stopped his crying.

Elizabeth was a small thin woman, not much taller than he was, but she placed her hands firmly under his arms and raised him to her shoulder. He was too big for her and his feet hung nearly to the floor. With the heavy burden, she had to step slowly and carefully as they passed down the long hall. His body hung limp and awkward in her arms, and his bare feet dangled against her legs as she walked.

She sat down in the big rocking chair in front of the bay windows and pulled him onto her lap. Then she pressed his head to her shoulder and began to rock very slowly. They sat together without speaking, listening to the creak of the rocking chair. Both of them knew his disappointment was too great to be soothed by mere words.

He tried very hard, but he was unable to hold it back any longer. With his trembling fingers he clutched onto the sleeves of her dress and began to sob.

She waited until he had quieted a little and then said in a calm quiet voice, "There'll be another time, Will."

He wished he could accept her comfort but he knew he would never again in his entire life want anything as much as he had wanted to go to sea with his father that morning. But finally he stopped crying altogether and let go of her sleeves and sat staring listlessly out the window. He felt spent and dry inside.

After a while his mother began to hum. It was a rather happy tune and he had always liked the words. They told about a wonderful doe who licked a dead man's wounds and then took him up on her back and buried him in a lake. His mother began to sing very softly and when she got to the refrain, Will joined in.

Half-heartedly he whispered the words, "Down, derry, derry,

down, down."

But as he repeated the familiar syllables, he wasn't thinking of them. He was thinking that when the other time his mother had spoken of finally did come, he couldn't really be completely happy because some of this same feeling of sadness would still be there, locked deep inside him.

Of course his mother was right. There was another time. But on his first trip to sea, Will became "ill" and had to spend most of the time below deck. He lay on Jeremiah's bunk and coughed and spit up blood and fought for each breath and then took more medicine from the brown bottle he'd told his mother he was certain he wouldn't need.

It was only a few years after that disappointing trip when they received word that Jeremiah's ship had gone down in a storm. By then Will and his mother were the only ones left at home. And since their lives centered around Jeremiah's comings and goings, both of them took his death especially hard. The hope that some day he'd ride the tall bay horse up the lane did not die easily.

While the air in the big house was still heavy with mourning, Elizabeth came to Will's room early one morning and knelt beside the bed. She took his face in her hands and looked at him.

"You look like your Uncle William Henry," she said.

Before it had always seemed to make her happy that Will looked so much like his uncle. But now her voice sounded very worried. She kept looking at him as though she hadn't finished what she'd come to say, and Will realized she couldn't bring herself to ask. But he was sure she was hoping he'd give up his lifelong dream of going to sea. Silently he agreed. But he remembered how his father had always said that a man must be what he is born to, and so he felt by agreeing with what she wanted, he was giving up his very soul.

The next day he rode to town and made arrangements to commence studying law with an attorney who had been a close friend to Jeremiah. Will had never intended to abandon his mother, but he couldn't stand to see her living in poverty. She was accustomed to the good life Jeremiah had always given them.

The day Will sailed for the gold fields of California, he promised Elizabeth he'd be back just as soon as he was rich and he could tell she believed him.

While he was in California he always sent her money and he also wrote. He told her about his fabulously productive mines. And he wrote and told her when he was elected city manager and marshal of Nevada City. He also wrote and told her when he was nominated for the state legislature and how he was expected to win. He even wrote and explained to her why he lost the election, how the opposition party had carried out a massive smear campaign that had unfairly damaged his reputation, but when he was sent to San Quentin for second-degree murder, he didn't tell her about that.

On the day he entered prison he was suffering with consumption and he spent the entire six months he was at San Quentin in the sick ward. Then officials from two counties prepared a petition protesting his innocence. Days later the governor's pardon came. He was very glad his mother had been spared. She would never have to know that he'd brought shame to the Plummer name.

Elizabeth was still waiting for him to come home. And he could now see her face as clearly as that morning she'd come into his bedroom and silently asked for his promise.

Plummer woke with the vision of his mother and the big house clear in his mind, but as he opened his eyes he saw the mud-chinked log walls of the small dark hotel room. His pillow and blanket were damp with perspiration, but that was good news because it meant the fever had broken.

He sat up and swung his legs over the edge of the cot and raised to his feet and began walking, steadying himself against the wall with his left arm. He discovered he was so weak he couldn't stay on his feet without leaning against the wall, but he made his way to the light from the window and carefully examined his right arm. He still couldn't move his wrist or elbow, but he could see the swelling had gone down a little.

On the small table by the cot he noticed a bowl of soup and guessed that Vera had sent it. Shakily he made his way back and lowered himself to the cot and began drinking the cold liquid, tipping the tin bowl up to get the last drop. Evidently someone who had been nursing him during his delirium had also left some reading material on the table. He picked up the two tattered pamphlets and recognized them immediately. Both belonged to Deaf Dick. Due to the shortage of books during the first winter at Bannack, the pamphlets had been passed from hand to hand and now were almost as fragile as a butterfly wing. One was "The Travels of St. Paul" and the other was "A Marvelous Salve Developed by those Wonderful Japanese people to heal Syphilis Sores." That first winter he'd read both pamphlets many times, but never felt very enlightened by either one of them.

The soup gave him enough strength to make it back to the window again. He stood gazing out at the town below and remembering the morning before he'd left for Sun River. He was looking out this same window and had noticed a trailing flash of blue. He followed it with his eyes and watched a bluebird come to rest on a pole projecting from the top of one of the wickiups on Bachelor's Row. He'd taken the bluebird as a good omen for his coming marriage.

But today there were no bluebirds. The snow had melted off Cemetery Hill, and main street had turned to soggy muck. Still the sight below looked good to him. He guessed it was because he was glad to be alive.

It was now very clear to him what he wanted for the life that lay ahead. He wanted to be with the two people who meant more than anything in the world to him. It was his duty to stay in Bannack and keep the miners' courts going until Edgerton could set up the Territorial system. But in the Spring, he'd go to Ohio for Electa and take her back to Maine with him. She was still his wife and somehow he'd earn her love again. It wasn't like a Plummer to give up as easily as he had when he'd let her leave.

It brought him a feeling of great contentment to think that the children he and Electa would have would be born in the same house where he'd been born and that they would grow up on the land the Plummers had taken out of the wilderness. And just as he'd done as a child, they would ride horseback into the pine woods and then on to the salt marshes to gaze at the ocean where generations of Plummer captains had sailed away in their ships, and where his sons would also set sail. And he'd tell his sons stories about how he had joined the Gold Rush, but that it was good to be home again.

He glanced down at the empty poles sticking up from the wickiups on Bachelor's Row and suddenly couldn't help wondering if on that morning before he set out for Sun River he had only imagined seeing a bluebird, just as when he'd been delirious he had imagined he was finally home.

CHAPTER ELEVEN

Deputy Ray couldn't concentrate on the card game. He had something more important on his mind. He was determined that this time come hell or high water he was going to teach Caroline a lesson. While he absentmindedly considered which card to play, Deaf Dick drummed his thick fingers on the table. But Ray ignored the annoying rat-a-tat, rat-a-tat, rat-a-tat and for about the sixtieth time in the past hour laid down his cards and pulled out his pocket watch and checked the time. He knew that if he was going to succeed in teaching Caroline a lesson this time around, the timing was critical, lots more critical than how the card game turned out.

"Hey, Ed," Dick blared out in his whining monotone, "your turn!" Ray stuffed the gold watch Caroline had given him back inside his vest pocket and cupped both hands over his ears to let Dick know he was too loud.

If Ray had been playing a professional gambler, he'd have lost his shirt by now because of his lack of concentration. But Deaf Dick was easy. You could tell when he had a good hand even if you weren't paying close attention.

"Whatsa matter, Ed? Better half expectin' ya?" Cyrus Skinner asked. "That what's gotcha itchy?" Then he let out a loud laugh that made his belly bounce.

Ray ignored Cyrus too. He would have liked to put the saloon keeper in his place once and for all but there wouldn't be any satisfaction in that. Cyrus was just an ex-con, and besides that he had the poor taste to purposely roll up his sleeves to show off the cheap red and blue tattoos punched in his arms. Cyrus had been needling Ray about Caroline ever since the time she stuck her head in the doors of the Elkhorn and called out, "Say …

my Edward Ray in here?"

On their way home, Ray had warned her never to do that again.

"Edward Ray doesn't belong to anybody but himself," he told her, "and if you ever come down to the Elkhorn and do that again, I'm moving out of the cabin."

But the threat didn't do much good. Caroline only halfway listened and only halfway understood what he meant and the next time she came looking for him, she stepped in the Elkhorn doorway and called out, "Say ... my husband in here?"

Cyrus made lots of hay out of that line.

While Deaf Dick shuffled the cards, Ray looked at his watch one more time. There was no use trying to hold a conversation with a deaf man. The first day he'd met Dick, Ray had immediately stuck him in the "boring category." Ray considered himself an intelligent man, and as he saw it, there were two general classes of human beings: the ones who were boring, like Deaf Dick, and the ones who were crazy. Dick was boring mainly because he was too bashful to look anybody square in the face so he could try to read their lips. Since all Dick ever did was look down, he never had the foggiest idea what was going on around him. And he didn't even seem to have the wits to realize he couldn't hear. He was always cupping his hand behind one ear and muttering in his toneless whine, "What's that ya say?"

H. P. A. Smith sauntered over and flopped down at their table and Dick dealt him a hand too. Ray filed Smith in the crazy category. He was crazy enough to think he could reason with a jury and then they'd acquit his client. Educated as he was, he didn't seem able to get it through his head that jurors at the mines wanted to convict. They wanted to see a hanging.

But Ray didn't hold it against H. P. A. or anybody else for being crazy. He was crazy himself. He worked for the miners for nothing. The only pay the miners gave their lawmen was fifty cents for each arrest warrant issued. And then of course he was also crazy for getting mixed up with Caroline in the first place. He didn't even frequent the Bluebird and here he was living with its owner.

While Dick was still dealing, Doctor Glick sat down and wanted in the game too. Glick fit perfectly into the boring class. He was in love with the sound of his own voice and once he got started talking he didn't know how to quit and nothing he said was ever the slightest whit interesting, just endless mishmash. Ray was under enough pressure as it was without having to listen to Glick, so he tossed in his cards and then checked his watch again.

Caroline had told him to be back for breakfast at precisely nine and it was now ten, so he decided it would be all right to head for home. As he passed Chrisman's store, he stopped in and reminded Plummer he was taking the day off.

"Caroline wants to go on a picnic," he said.

Plummer was sitting at his desk with his right arm in a sling, and with his left hand he was trying to sign the papers from the sheriff's sales. He looked up at Ray.

"Looks like it might snow," he said.

"I'm counting on it," Ray answered.

Then he was on his way. It had only been three hours but he was anxious to see her. He'd missed spending time with her while Plummer was laid up with the gun wound in his arm. As head deputy Ray had to take over and that kept him busy day and night. First there was the manhunt for Crawford. They found the rifle still balanced on the hide frame where he'd steadied it to shoot Plummer from behind. The only thing that saved Plummer's life was Crawford was a poor shot. Instead of hitting the Sheriff in the center of the back, like he intended, he hit the right elbow and the ball entered the arm and traveled down to the wrist.

A few minutes after the shooting, Vera Grizzert noticed a man hiding behind the flour barrel in her wagon, but by the time she ran down to the creek and got her husband, the man had disappeared. Then the stableman reported a horse and saddle missing. Ray put two and two together and packed his gear and was going to try to pick up Crawford's trail but the miners' president was against it.

"Good riddance," he said, "let it go at that."

That meant Ray had to find somebody to take over the

butcher shop so the town would still have a good supply of meat. Crawford's employee, Conrad Kohrs, was glad to take on the responsibility. Then there were two sheriff's sales to conduct and three court cases over mining claim disputes. Since Ray didn't particularly like associating with the Reb, he'd done most of the work himself.

The first thing he did when Plummer showed up at the office again was ask for some time off to spend with Caroline, and this was the first day of the vacation. He couldn't wait to see her but at the same time he knew she might be looking out the window for him, so he ambled along at a snail's pace. He didn't know why he bothered trying to teach her anything. It was more or less useless. For months he'd been trying to get her to call him Ed. But when they were first introduced she somehow got it into her head that Edward Ray was his given name and she persisted in calling him that. What irritated him most about her though was the way she always had to control everything, including the weather and him.

"Bad day for a picnic," he'd told her.

"Now don't think that way, Edward Ray," she'd answered. "You'll go an' make it snow when I'm countin' on a picnic."

In the past months he'd tried to explain to her that the thoughts in his mind had absolutely no connection with what the elements decided to do. But every time he tried to prove it to her, Nature always took her side. He had to admit Caroline was not only lucky, but also shrewd at her business. But the woman had no common sense. And she was rich, but she didn't know the first thing about being polite. As for himself he was a stickler for politeness. His mother had drilled it into him since he was a little shaver because she claimed it was his nature to be critical of other people.

But when he tried to drill anything into Caroline it usually backfired on him. Since the day he moved in with her he'd tried to get her to stop saying "ain't" and "he don't" and "you was" but instead it went the other way. Lately more times than not he caught himself saying "ain't" and "he don't" and "you was." And that was the wrong impression for an educated man like himself to give.

Of course there were some things he liked about Caroline. There was absolutely nothing boring about her, that was for certain. In fact she'd showed him how to enjoy life. Every morning she poured brandy in his coffee without him even asking for it. And she approved of him earning his living by gambling. Or when he rode off on a manhunt after some dangerous desperado, she thought it was exciting. She was the one who'd talked him into wearing his hair long, and actually, he thought he looked better that way.

Naturally he hated how she made a living and it bothered him a lot how much she seemed to care about money, but still he couldn't help admiring the way she lived, all those luxuries she'd accumulated over the years. The two of them didn't have a serious life like he and Libby used to have. Instead they just let things kind of run on and squeezed all the pleasure out of them they could get. The two of them didn't bother about making any plans for the future. That was how he wanted it.

After Libby and the baby died of cholera, he'd lost interest in life. Looking back he could see that was why he gave up his civil engineering job in California and drifted from gold camp to gold camp. The last thing he wanted to do was get mixed up with another woman when he still loved Libby. But he felt comfortable with Caroline because he wasn't in love with her and he'd never told her he was. All he had to do was enjoy himself and keep his guard up when she tried to control him.

She saw him coming and threw the door open and stamped her foot on the sill.

"Damn you Edward Ray," she said, "you're more'n an hour late. I told you nine o'clock on th' dot."

"That's why I came at ten," he said. "You'd get lots more out of me, Caroline, if you'd learn to ask nicely instead of layin' down the law. I ain't one of your girls."

"Don't I know that!" she said. She laughed and wrapped her arms around his neck and gave him a long kiss on the lips.

She had the table spread with white linen and set with crystal wine glasses and china plates painted with dainty violets and twining green leaves. The food was waiting on the table: a plate of delicate little soda biscuits brushed with melted butter, a bowl of oysters, and a cut-glass decanter of red wine. Ray also noticed that the picnic basket was packed and waiting by the door.

It was a little chilly in the cabin so he put another log on the fire. Then he washed in the gold-rimmed basin she'd bought in San Francisco and dried his face and hands on a little embroidered hand towel she'd made during slow hours at the Bluebird. As he sat down on the bench beside her, he kissed her on the back of the neck.

"Missed the hell out of ya, Sugar," he whispered in her ear.

While she poured the wine, he began devouring biscuits and oysters.

"Only one thing you do better than cook," he said, "and that's ..."

She had her mouth full of biscuit but she interrupted anyway. "Never was much at cookin'."

That irritated him because at least a hundred times he'd warned her about interrupting. And at every meal they ate, he had to remind her at least once not to talk with her mouth full.

"As I was saying, Caroline, there's only one thing you do better ..." he paused to let another oyster slip down his throat and she leaned over with her linen napkin and swiped oyster juice off his chin.

"Go ahead an' say it. I'm waitin'. I ain't interruptin'."

"Well couldn't I just show you instead?" he asked.

"Wait a minute now," she said. "If I'm so damn good then how come you're th' one's gonna do th' showin'?"

"I didn't say I wasn't good too!"

She burst out laughing and squeezed his knee. "You are damn good, Edward Ray."

He stood up and pulled her off the bench too and grabbed her around the waist and swung her in a circle. Then he picked her up and carried her to the bedroom. It wasn't a separate room but she'd hung satin sheets around the bed to partition it off from the rest of the house.

While they were taking off their clothes, somebody knocked

at the door. Ray jerked his trousers back on and tucked in his shirt but didn't bother with his stockings and boots.

"I'll get rid of 'em," he said. "You go ahead and get ready."

When he opened the door he saw it was snowing, large flakes fluttering down and just beginning to whiten the ground.

"Hallelujah!" he whooped. "It's snowin'."

"Damn you Edward Ray," she yelled from behind the curtain, "now see what you gone an' done! You spoiled my picnic."

"I swear I had nothin' t' do with it, Sugar," he answered. He turned and saw Justice Edgerton hovering under the eaves next to the door. "Morning, Judge," he said. "Sheriff Plummer's back now ... any business you have, you can just take up with him. He'll be glad to help you."

He started to swing the door shut but Edgerton pushed by him and stepped into the room. As usual the old man was dressed all in black. He reminded Ray of a scruffy old raven. And as usual his wife hadn't bothered to press his trousers or stiffen his shirt collar. He took off his stovepipe hat and dusted the snowflakes on Caroline's Turkish rug and then brushed more flakes off the shoulders of his overcoat. It was all Ray could do to keep his mouth shut.

Since Ray was barefooted, Edgerton was as tall as he was and they were standing eye to eye. Ray looked him over and right away shoved him into the boring category. The old man slouched and that rounded his shoulders and make his back hunch a little. Ray felt like telling the old bird that if he'd just stand up straight and throw his shoulders back, he'd be a hell of a lot easier to look at. He did think though that the Justice looked better with the shock of shaggy white hair showing. It made him look distinguished and also distracted you from his long hooked nose and the puffy bags under his small eagle-like eyes.

"You're the man I need to see," Edgerton said decisively, "not Plummer. I'm headed over to advise the miners' president to dump our illustrious minister of justice."

Ray was too surprised to answer.

"You come along," Edgerton went on. "Lend some support."

He stood there slapping his tall black hat against his thigh as he waited for the answer.

Ray couldn't believe the old man was serious. "No—thank—you!" he answered. "Maybe you don't know it but Plummer's the miners' handpicked sheriff."

Edgerton scowled. "The man's a Copperhead! These damn stupid Copperheads sit around on their hands and yammer about peace when the country needs war! War's what'll hold this country together!"

When he raised his voice like he was giving a speech, Caroline grabbed the curtain and pulled it back and peeked her head around the corner to see what was going on. Ray was irked at her for being so nosy but he didn't want to let on in front of company.

"Judge Edgerton," he said, "I'd like you to meet my wife, Mrs. Ray. Mother, this is the gentleman that President Lincoln sent all the way out here to the Territory to take care of us."

Caroline grinned and said, "Howjadoo, Justice."

Ray could see she was eyeing old Edgerton as a potential customer for the Bluebird. But he could also see that Edgerton had strong opinions about women butting into men's affairs. In fact the old man appeared to be so offended he wouldn't even look in Caroline's direction.

"Ray," he went on, "you're the man for the job. I recollect how you called on me during that crisis at the jail, and you probably recollect how Wilbur and I bailed you out. I know you'll cooperate with the new system."

Ray couldn't help laughing. "No, Judge, afraid you got the wrong man. I'm not much on cooperation. Just ask Mrs. Ray there if you don't believe me."

Caroline leaned out further, exposing her bare shoulder and part of one hip. "You really know the President?" she asked.

Ray didn't like the gleam of admiration in her eyes. And her normally harsh voice had suddenly turned so syrupy that Edgerton swung his head and looked to see if there was a different woman in the room now. Caroline's shoulder and hip were still exposed and the satin sheet was draped around her body, flowing over every bulge and curve and dip.

Edgerton gaped at her and the corners of his thin lips turned down in disgust. "My God, man," he said to Ray, "I'll have to step outside."

"Not necessary, Judge," Ray said firmly. He decided it was time he took over in his own household. "Now, Mother," he said sternly, "you just step back behind the curtain there and get on with your housework. Just go on making the bed like you were doing when the Justice came."

"All right, Papa," Caroline answered meekly.

Ray was glad she showed enough sense to play along with the game. She disappeared from sight and they could hear a whoosh as she plopped down on the feather mattress. Ray had visions of her lying on the bed naked, waiting to wrap her long legs around him. He was tired of pussyfooting around with this pompous old ass just because he had some pull in Washington. He decided to lay it right on the line.

"Look," he said, "back in California, folks thought Plummer was presidential timber. I know because I was there."

Edgerton's eyes opened wide, like something had scared him. He chewed at his lip. Then he raised one hand and clawed at his scalp and his eyes narrowed down to slits. He leaned over close to Ray.

"Listen, " he said quietly, "when they split this Territory, I'm in line to be Governor. I could give you a nice appointment ... plum position ... not much work."

Ray was put out that anybody would insinuate he didn't like work. Let them sit up all day and half the night trying to wrangle gold coin out of some shark dealer. Let them try it and see if it wasn't work all right. A heck of a lot trickier than building a bridge.

"Not interested, not interested," he said brusquely. "Come spring, I'm taking Mrs. Ray back to New York."

He stepped to the door and held it open. Edgerton glowered at him and then swung his tall hat back to his head. "I'll have no trouble getting help elsewhere," he said as he stepped through the door. Then he turned back. "But I'm sorry for you, Ray. You'll regret the decision."

Ray felt like firing back an answer but in a way he was ashamed of himself. It wasn't right to rush a guest out the front door. He'd been brought up better. He even considered saying he was sorry but it had always been hard for him to apologize. And the more he thought about it, the more he resented the threat about how he'd somehow regret it. He had a strong urge to reach out and grab the pathetic old coot by his coat collar and say, "Go slow, Edgerton. Around me you just go slow!" He decided against it though because he always tried not to let anything throw him. He kept his mouth shut and closed the door quietly and pattered barefoot back to the bedroom.

While he was sitting on the edge of the bed pulling off his trousers again and halfway kicking himself for not firing back an answer and at the same time wondering if Caroline thought he was a yellowbelly, she raised up and gently touched his face.

"You really mean that, Edward Ray?"

"What's that?" he asked. He was so anxious to get his shirt off and jump in bed with her that he accidentally ripped one of the buttons off the front.

"Damn!" he said.

"You know ... th' part about ... about takin' me back t' ..." Her voice was soft and sweet again, like when she'd surprised Edgerton.

"I don't know, Sugar," he said. He was working at the cuff links and trying to be more careful this time. "Never really thought about it."

"You had t' think about it," she said. He could tell by the tone of her voice she'd turned argumentative again, back to her normal self. "You had t' think about it," she insisted, "cause you said it, so th' thought had t' be in your head before th' words could come out your mouth."

Ray could have shot old Edgerton right between his little eagle eyes for coming by and getting him into this mess. "I just said it to get rid of him, that's all."

From behind him he heard Caroline give a sob. He'd never seen her cry, never even thought she was capable of breaking down. But when he turned around and looked at her, her face was all twisted up and tears were carrying the black eye makeup around her eyes down her cheeks. It shocked him to see her that way and he grabbed her and hugged her to his chest.

"Hey, Sugar," he said, "quit that! I didn't mean any hurt. Last thing in the world I'd want to do is hurt you."

She kept on crying. "You don't appreciate nothin' I do."

He felt for her chin and tipped her face up to his. "That what you think? Huh? That what you think? ... Then you're dead wrong. You're dead wrong if that's how you think. I appreciate every time you raise a finger around this house. I do. I notice and I appreciate."

She quit sobbing but tears were still leaving black tracks on her pink cheeks, and her body convulsed every time a sob would have come out.

"Yeah," she said, "but you don't care nothin' for me."

He reached down to the floor where he'd dropped his trousers and hastily fumbled through them till he found the white handkerchief she'd ironed and stuffed in his pocket that morning before he went out the door for an early game of cards.

"You know that ain't true, Sugar. Why else'd I be here? Huh? I'm here ain't I?" He wiped her eyes and grinned at her to try and jolly her up a little but she didn't grin back.

"Oh, Edward Ray," she said and then heaved a long sigh. Her voice had been so soft he could hardly hear it, and it was a little sad too. She pulled away and sat looking past him. "You do have a way about you all right, Edward Ray."

"Say listen," he said, "if I made it snow—now I ain't sayin' I did, just sayin' if—if I did make it snow why then I'm sorry. I know you was countin' on that picnic. I saw the basket of little sandwiches and the champagne glasses and all. Soon as I stepped in the door I noticed the basket sittin' there all packed up and I was just as hungry for that picnic as you."

She looked up at him like she was surprised and he started to kiss her but there was another knock at the door.

She flung herself back on the bed. "Damn it t' hell," she said, "can't that old Justice leave us alone?"

Ray began pulling on his shirt and trousers again. "I'll take care of him this time," he said, "be right back."

She reached down and snatched her chemise off the floor and began pulling it over her head. "Ain't no hurry," she said. "I ain't in th' mood no more anyways."

When Ray opened the door and stuck his head out, it wasn't Edgerton. It was the little black-bearded carpenter. The first time Ray had seen him, he was perched in the high barber chair at the saloon and talking to himself about Prince Hamlet. There'd been no doubt in Ray's mind which of the two categories Rawley belonged in.

"Sorry to bother you, Deputy Ray," Rawley said, "but do you know a Mr. Frank Parrish?"

Ray noticed the carpenter's voice was anxious and one eye was twitching.

"Parrish owns Rattlesnake Ranch," he answered. He was anxious to get back to Caroline and wanted to make it as short as possible. "Virginia City stage leaves at dawn and Rattlesnake's the first station. Can't miss it." He began closing the door.

"If I hired a horse, could I get there tonight?" Rawley's voice sounded almost desperate.

Ray looked up at the steadily falling snow. "Hmm umm, don't try that, not in this weather. Just cool your heels overnight and take the stage."

As Rawley started to thank him, Ray held up his hand as a "your welcome" and slammed the door. Then he hurried back to Caroline. She was nearly dressed.

"Say I was just thinkin'," he said, "we could hike up the gulch. Have a snowball fight or somethin'. Then come back and sit on the bear rug in front of the fire and eat those little bitty sandwiches you made and drink champagne. Ain't that a picnic?"

She didn't answer.

"You get yourself bundled up," he said, "and we'll go."

She just sat there on the bed gazing down at her hands. Both of them were streaked black and pink from wiping tears off her face.

Finally she sighed, "All right, Papa."

But he could see she was still a little sulky with him for making it snow.

CHAPTER TWELVE

Rawley was afraid to wait till morning. He pulled out the note Frank Parrish had scrawled on the back of a used envelope and read it again.

Mister carpenter— dont now your name but if youre a good worker come on out to the ranch—im cripled up since my toes and fingers got frostbit so bad last winter—i got some build work out hear will last maybe a week—if you dont come rite away ill have to get some body else—yours truly—Frank Parrish

Rawley didn't want to lose the job. With what he'd already saved, a week's pay would give him enough money to leave for home. He looked up at the sky and watched big snowflakes slowly fluttering to the ground. "Think I'll chance it," he said.

He wasn't an expert rider, but the hired pony seemed gentle enough. And the cold didn't bother him. He'd wrapped himself in an overcoat and scarf and then put on a wool cap and a pair of gloves. And the heat from the pony's body warmed his legs. He took a deep breath and sucked the frosty air into his nostrils and felt clean and renewed.

The first hour was a peaceful ride. Lazy snowflakes continued to drift down around them until the hills on both sides were completely white and each scraggly sagebrush looked like it was draped with white lace. He and the sturdy little pony seemed to be the only living creatures in the world. The only sound was the pony's rhythmic breathing and the cushioned thud of the small hooves. The surrounding silence added to Rawley's inner peace. His terror of the Stranglers was gone now. "It was the Sheriff they wanted to kill," he said, "not me. If I'd known, I'd have warned Plummer."

He could hardly believe that in a week he'd be going home.

He'd soon be back where he belonged, back with Angeline. He'd never understood what such a beautiful woman had seen in him. His creole princess, he called her. Black hair and dark eyes and a complexion like smoothed ivory. Somehow she'd been fooled into thinking he was handsome and witty. "Wonder if she's sitting in the window seat," he said. He could picture her there snuggled into the green velvet cushions, holding back the lace curtains with one hand so she could watch the snow fall. And probably she was watching for him too.

The snow was coating his spectacles, and finally he had to take them off and put them in his pocket. He was glad the pony knew the way. But as they were descending a slope, the little animal slipped and almost fell. Rawley felt a moment of fear. "It's not like me," he said, "to try something this dangerous."

At times he was afraid they were lost, but the pony plodded on. Finally Rawley reined up, and put on the spectacles and took a good look around him. He'd only been on the trail once before but he thought he recognized Badger Pass. That stilled his fears and he slipped the spectacles back in his pocket and let the pony have free rein.

They were approaching a willow thicket on a creek bank when Rawley saw the vague outline of a deer. It appeared to be a large buck standing perfectly still and watching them as though it were transfixed. Suddenly it sprang from the brush and bounded across their trail. The pony shied and then reared on its hind legs. Rawley felt himself sliding off and then he landed on his back in the snow. It was a soft fall and he wasn't hurt but when he stood up, he noticed his feet were a little numb.

The pony had run as soon as it threw him and now was nowhere in sight. At first Rawley felt panicky but even without his spectacles he could see the hoofprints running parallel to the twisting creek. "The pony knows the trail," he said. "I'll follow his tracks."

He stomped his feet to wake them up and then began walking at a fast clip. At first it was invigorating, but after a while it became hard for him to get his breath. He also noticed he had almost no sensation at all in his feet. It was hard to keep his balance because he couldn't feel the ground he was stepping on. He took one tumble and then another. The falls frightened him. "Keep your head," he said firmly. "Otherwise you could die out here."

He pressed on, but his steps were very unsteady and he was gasping for breath. Finally he sat down and pulled off his gloves and then removed his shoes and stockings and very gently massaged his feet. As he rubbed, he noticed his fingers were also becoming numb. He had an urge to lie back in the snow and rest, but he knew better. He fumbled his stockings and shoes back onto his feet and put on his gloves and then hobbled on.

The flakes were falling faster now and a wind had come up. The blowing snow blurred his limited vision even more, and it was getting almost impossible for him to see the pony's tracks. "Just follow the creek," he said to calm himself. "And keep moving. Keep moving."

He wanted to pull out the gold watch Angeline had given him and see how long he'd been on the trail, but his fingers wouldn't work. The wind had turned fierce and was driving the cold right through his coat, and flakes swirling in front of his eyes made him so dizzy he could hardly keep his balance. He grabbed out for the willows with his right hand and held on to them as he walked. The twigs and branches were too close for him to see but they were scraping his face. Still he couldn't feel them. He could only hear them lashing against his almost frozen flesh. With his free hand he tried to brush away the snow that kept caking on his face, but his gloved hands were clumsy and sometimes he missed. He stumbled blindly ahead, gripping wildly at the willows on his right side for support.

He tried to say, "I'll be at the ranch soon." But his mouth and tongue seemed completely frozen, so he had to be satisfied with just thinking it. "Keep moving. Keep moving," he thought. "Be at the ranch soon."

It seemed to him that he fell asleep even before he finally lay down in the snow for a brief rest.

Some time later the sound of donkeys braying woke him. At least he thought he was awake but he wasn't sure his eyes were completely open. He was aware that something was looming just above him. It appeared to be a small man in a bulky overcoat. "Maybe Beidler," he thought. Then the man above him stooped and stuck his hand inside Rawley's coat like he was feeling for his heart. "I've been rescued," he thought. He fell back to sleep with that comforting thought.

When he woke again he was still alone, lying in the snow with the wind howling in his ears. He tried to get up but he couldn't move so he decided to rest a little longer. He eased onto his side and curled up and then heaped snow over him like a blanket and went back to sleep.

* * *

The first sensation Rawley was aware of was intense pain. The wind had died down and the sun had come out and the trail ahead of them was a brilliant flashing white. He was sitting on top of a tall horse, riding in the saddle with somebody sitting behind him and gripping him around the waist with one arm. With each motion of the horse's body, stabbing pains ran through Rawley's legs. He wanted to get down and lie in the snow again and go back to sleep, but for what seemed like endless hours they continued riding on.

There was another horse behind them and sometimes it caught up and rode alongside them and the two riders spoke to each other in low voices. He knew they were talking about him but he couldn't understand exactly what they were saying, and he didn't care. He only wished they would lay him down in the snow and let him go back to sleep.

He was in the embrace of a stranger, but what bothered him most was that he also seemed to be a stranger to himself. He couldn't remember who he was and he had no idea where they were headed and he didn't recognize any of the landscape around them. It was just a sparkling white that burned his eyes. Now the pains were shooting through his hands and arms as well as his legs, and he didn't think he could stand it any longer.

Then they left the valley and gradually wound up a steep hill. When they got to the top, he saw rows of wooden grave markers and then three snow-blanketed mounds that were unmarked. "Oh yes," he said, "oh yes." His lips and tongue were working, but not very well. "I know those mounds. The grandfather, Keeler ... and the boy, Peter Herron ... and the baby, the Grizzert's child. I built coffins for all three of them."

The other horse rode alongside them again. "I'll go on ahead and locate Glick." The voice had an upstate New York accent and as the rider pushed past them and started down the hill, Rawley recognized Ed Ray, the man who'd warned him not to ride to Rattlesnake Ranch during a snowstorm.

As their horse began descending the hill, Rawley looked down at one of his throbbing legs and noticed he was astride a big bay. At the same moment, he felt himself slumping forward and the man behind him gripped him harder and pulled him back against his chest. The chest he was leaning on heaved with a long sigh, and then a low and very gentle voice said, "We're home."

CHAPTER THIRTEEN

Rawley lay on the bunk in his carpenter shop and looked down at the bandages wrapped around the stumps of his legs and felt very sorry he was alive. He felt no gratitude to Ray and Plummer for coming to find him. In fact he blamed them. Now that his memory had returned, he vaguely recalled Ray waking him from his stupor and then lifting him onto the horse in front of Plummer. And he also remembered that the arm Plummer had kept around him had a bandage coming out of the coat sleeve.

The two lawmen had come to visit him after Glick amputated the feet, but Rawley had turned his face to the wall and refused to speak to them. In fact since the operation he had no desire to speak to anyone, not even himself. He knew he could never go home to Angeline and his parents in this condition. And without them, there was no reason for him to be alive. His problem was he didn't have the courage to take his own life.

From the other side of the curtain partition he could hear Vera Grizzert getting out of bed. He didn't mind having her here though because she was so tight-lipped. She rarely spoke to her son or husband, and she never spoke to him unless she absolutely had to. Twice a day she brought him a tin bowl of smelly gruel which he supposed was venison stew. And when Plummer sent flour and sugar, she baked biscuits and sugar pie in the little sheet-iron stove. She also did Rawley's laundry and pressed his shirts and trousers.

She worked quietly and since there was nothing else for him to do, he sometimes pulled back the curtain around his bed and watched her. He could tell by the hard look in her eyes that she didn't want to be alive any more than he did. The two of them made a good pair. Rawley wanted to be back in the snow sleeping the long sleep and she wanted to be up on the hill sleeping beside her baby. There wasn't a day went by when she didn't visit the cemetery.

It had been Plummer's idea that Grizzert move his family into the carpenter shop to get them out of the weather. Rawley had no objection. They paid their rent by taking care of him. And Plummer and Ray had also sent a carpenter named French to rent the shop and tools. The agreement was that Rawley and the Grizzerts could live in the back.

The other two members of the family were no more trouble than Vera. Grizzert didn't have time to tell any long stories. He left for his claim every morning before anybody else was awake. When he got home at dark, he slurped up the leftover stew and minutes later he would groan as his back hit the bed.

As for the little boy, he was very shy. In fact he'd only spoken to Rawley once. That was the day they moved in. While his mother was busy unpacking, he slipped behind the curtain and walked over to the bunk and stood examining Rawley's bandages for some time. Then he said quietly, "Do you have any more peach pie?"

While he waited for Rawley to answer, his eyes opened wide and his serious little face lit up. But Rawley was in too much pain to think about anybody but himself, so he just shook his head "no." The child's face fell and he swished back through the curtain. The only sound he ever made while he was playing was stacking pieces of wood on top of each other. French had made him a set of blocks and he spent most of the day sitting on the dirt floor and building houses that finally collapsed.

French was as untalkative as Vera Grizzert, but he seemed to be a kind enough man. On his second day at the shop, he walked back to Rawley's cot and bent over him and began carefully measuring his legs. Hours later, he brought a pair of crude artificial feet and set them beside the bunk and left without uttering a word.

Rawley looked down at the two oblong pegs. Each was about the size of a foot and had been attached to wooden braces which were intended to go all the way up to his knee. The braces had rawhide straps that evidently were supposed to be bound to his legs. But Rawley didn't feel up to strapping on the contraptions to see if he could stand or walk. In fact it turned his stomach just to look at them so he slid them under his bunk. There was no place he wanted to go anyway. He wasn't interested in Gold Rush society anymore. He'd learned more about it than he cared to know.

French never questioned him about the braces. Instead he went about his work as though he were the only person in the long narrow room. He concentrated only on the board he was sawing or planing. In the early afternoon he closed the shop and without saying good-bye went home to eat. He returned after dinner without greeting anybody and immediately bent over his work again.

When there was no building going on in the shop, Rawley lived in a world of near silence. Even Doctor Glick wasn't speaking to him anymore. In fact he'd paid few calls since Rawley exploded in a fit of anger over the high fee for the amputations. He'd called Glick a heartless butcher and a Shylock who'd gotten his pound of flesh. After that outburst, Rawley had to change his own bandages. He supposed Vera would have done it if he'd asked her, but he didn't like exposing his deformity to her.

There was only one regular visitor to the bunk at the back of the carpenter shop. During the years Rawley had been a professor he'd never imagined himself having an ex-convict with tattoos on his arms as a bosom comrade, a best friend who was intellectually stunted and whose world of cultural sensibilities was about the size of a walnut. But late every afternoon, Cyrus Skinner would come lumbering through the front doors with a jug hooked on one forefinger and a foolish grin stamped on his flushed face and his dun-colored hair sprouting out in cowlicks, like he'd slept on it wrong and hadn't bothered to comb it since he rolled out of bed.

The two of them had nothing in common so there was little conversation. Cyrus pulled up a stool and Rawley sat up in the bunk and they took turns drinking from the jug.

At the saloon, Cyrus was boisterous and foulmouthed, but at the carpenter shop he always tried to behave like a perfect gentleman. That was because he respected Vera Grizzert. During his talkative hours at the Elkhorn, Cyrus was always boasting that he had great respect for Christian ladies. He said he even respected his wife Nellie. Rawley could understand why he used the word "even." Nellie had the reputation of having been a loose woman before she married and settled down.

The daily visit made Rawley's life bearable, and he always drank as much as he possibly could. If Cyrus was in a good mood, he'd leave the unfinished jug. After he was gone, Rawley would heft it to estimate how much treasure he'd inherited and then ration it out to last till night. That made the evenings bearable too.

This morning he had his curtain pulled back and was watching as Vera chopped up venison for the day's stew. It must be about eight o'clock now. French would arrive at nine and go home about two and come back about three. From that point on, Rawley would have to guess what time it was and how soon Cyrus would arrive. That was because during the disastrous trip in the snow he'd somehow lost the watch Angeline had given him. At first he'd felt desperate without it, but then he realized that not having the watch pressed against his heart would help him forget his wife sooner.

Vera stepped past the open curtain and set a steaming bowl on the small table beside his bunk. The odor of the rancid bear grease in the stew turned his stomach and when she handed him a spoon, he shook his head. He decided he'd wait till afternoon and drink his breakfast with Cyrus. He longed for the gold watch to help him tick off the minutes till his comforter, that is the jug, would arrive. The little boy was clutching his mother's skirt while she walked, and as they left he turned back and looked hard at the surly patient. Rawley was surprised to see fear in the child's eyes.

It made him feel hatred for the bitter uncaring person he'd let himself become. But he didn't hate himself half as much as he hated the horrible mutilation of his body.

To pass the time he decided to take a morning nap. He was just drifting off when he heard the front doors open. It was too early for French, so he sat up and craned his neck to see who was entering. He was surprised to see it was Grizzert. The miner had a wild look in his eyes and he rushed to Vera and grabbed her by the arm and began shaking her.

"Ma," he said, "ya ain't payin' me no mind! I said keep them doors locked when French ain't here, and ya ain't payin' me no mind!" He shook her harder.

Rawley was angry at being waked out of his morning nap, and he had half a notion to tell Grizzert that if he was going to come home and raise a family ruckus, he'd have to move out.

"I won't have this in my house, Grizzert," he said. "What in God's name is wrong with you?"

The miner yanked off his slouch hat and then kicked the stool Cyrus sat on when he came by to drink. "Robbers!" he said. "That's what's wrong. This town ain't safe no more. They gone and robbed the stage this mornin'!" Grizzert usually spoke with a leisurely drawl but he was spitting out words so fast Rawley could hardly understand him. "Badger Pass. Two road agents come ridin' down a gully wavin' shotguns ...."

Rawley had pretty well lost interest in life but he remembered that he'd traveled alone in that very area and a shiver went down his spine.

"They was wearin' hoods and all and so was their horses and nobody knows who they was. Got almost five hunert dollars off'n the stage folks. Sheriff Plummer, I just seen him. He gone and rolled up a pack and headed out after 'em."

"Anybody killed?" Rawley asked. He was still thinking how he'd walked through the area alone and unarmed.

"Wasn't no shots fired." Grizzert had calmed down a little and he shamefacedly picked up the stool he'd kicked over. "Well, back t' work," he said. "Ma, I don't never want t' come home agin and find them doors unlocked! Mind what I say now!"

Vera dutifully locked the front doors behind her husband.

"No skin off my nose if the mines are infested with robbers," Rawley said. It was the first time he'd talked to himself since the surgery. It calmed him and he settled down again for his morning nap.

When he woke, French was working with a fine-toothed saw

at the bench and Beidler was standing beside him looking into his face and talking quietly.

"Any frien' t' Plummer?" he asked.

It occurred to Rawley it was the same question Beidler had asked him before the night meeting at the butcher shop. He was curious to know what Beidler was up to so he closed his eyes and pretended to be asleep.

He heard French lay the saw on the bench but he didn't answer for a while, as though he were considering the question.

Finally he said, "Ain't no particular friend to him, no. But I do believe he's the best lawman there is."

Nothing more was said and Rawley heard the small saw buzzing across wood again and then the front doors closed. He sat up and looked at Beidler through the front windows. He was standing outside the carpenter shop, flipping his head one way and then the other as though he were looking for somebody. Then he reached into his overcoat and pulled out a watch and checked the time and put it back and began scanning main street again. Rawley felt certain Beidler had another one of his secret meetings in mind. "Like last time Plummer left town," he said to himself. But gradually his curiosity began fading. Whatever went on in Bannack was of no concern to him.

He'd about decided to lie down and try to go back to sleep when he saw Beidler hop off the boardwalk and begin hurriedly worming his way through the traffic to reach the other side of the street. Rawley swung his feetless legs over the side of the bed and sat up as straight as he could so he could see better. It appeared the person Beidler was hurrying to intercept was Edgerton's nephew.

Wilbur was swinging along with his long stride in the direction of Chrisman's store, and when Beidler caught up to him, he gave Wilbur's sleeve a quick tug. Wilbur halted and flashed hasty glances on all sides of him. Then he brushed off Beidler's hold and rapidly walked on, and Beidler headed in another direction. But during the brief exchange it appeared to Rawley that both men's lips had moved.

"Another meeting at the butcher shop," Rawley murmured.

He'd thought he had no decency left in him, but his conscience was stirring a little, as though it had intentions of nagging at him the way it used to before his amputations. He lay back down and covered his feet so he could think about something else besides them. He had a difficult problem to wrestle with. The pros were he doubted he could just sit by while the Stranglers made another attempt to kill the Sheriff. He'd done it once already, only then he'd had an excuse because he thought they were after him instead. This time he was left with no excuse.

But the cons were he was angry at the Sheriff for interfering in his life rather than letting nature take its course in the snow. What turned him against Plummer more than anything was remembering how the Sheriff had decided to die rather than lose his own arm. While on the other hand, he'd sentenced Rawley to life without feet. Another con, there was no proof of anything and if he mentioned his suspicions, people might laugh at him and call him crazy.

While he was considering both sides of the issue, the image of Beidler checking his pocket watch suddenly popped back into his head. It was the first time he'd seen Beidler pull out a timepiece. He closed his eyes and tried to revive the memory of the small man bending over him while he slept in the snow. He'd heard donkeys braying and of course Beidler owned a string of pack-jacks. And he distinctly remembered thinking "Maybe Beidler" and then feeling a hand shoved inside his coat. It seemed quite likely that the small man who'd found him in the snow had thought he was dead and was robbing the corpse. And if it was Beidler, then a Strangler was walking around with Angeline's gold watch pressed to his heart. For the first time in his life, Rawley had the urge to kill.

He'd been so absorbed in his maze of thoughts that it hadn't occurred to him before how strange it was that Beidler had approached Wilbur. It didn't seem likely a Strangler would have any business with the secretary for the Chief Justice .... But of course it was all too clear. Ever since Crawford escaped, Beidler had been looking for a new leader. Evidently he'd finally found one.

Unlikely as it seemed, Rawley felt certain the Stranglers and President Lincoln's two men were joining forces, uniting against Plummer and the miners. "So Ichabod Crane and The Littlest Strangler have teamed up!" he marveled. "What a pair ... the Political Pimp and the Grave Robber." He knew he was on to something too big for him to handle alone. "But how could I persuade anyone else?" he asked. He'd kept silent about the meeting he'd seen breaking up behind the butcher shop, and now it was coming back to haunt him. He should have informed Plummer about the conspiracy.

He found it ironic that he of all people was the only one in town who was in a position to fit all the pieces together. He felt like a crippled Prince Hamlet. "Something is rotten in the town of Bannack," he said, "... the time is out of joint—O cursed spite, that ever I was born to set it right!"

The absurdity of his words almost made him laugh. He couldn't even set his own life right, let alone justice in the wilderness, and besides he'd been shorted when God passed out courage. He remembered that dark night when he'd stood beside the butcher shop and trembled as he watched the Stranglers stealthily ease out the back door one by one. And he remembered how even after he was home and in bed he had still felt the presence of evil. He reached for his watch and then remembered that it was probably in Beidler's pocket.

He could see his main problem. He was terrified of the Stranglers. And he was even more vulnerable now because he was tied to his bed. The only people he could turn to for help were the Grizzerts and French, and he didn't dare send them directly to Plummer. They'd be observed and that would be a death sentence for them too. And even if he sent them to Deputy Ray with a warning that Sheriff Plummer was a target, he'd still be endangering all their lives. "It has to be somebody who can talk to Ray in the normal course of business and not appear suspicious," he said. "Otherwise they'll all be strangled along with the Sheriff. And of course the trail would lead right back to me." He had a vision of waking up in the dark of night to find himself smothered by a mob of faceless Stranglers and wanting to spring off the bunk and run, but he couldn't, he had no feet. A sudden chill racked his body and he felt himself quaking like he'd been taken with a fit of ague.

The front doors swung open and against the background of light from the windows, Rawley watched Cyrus's burly form lumbering down the long room toward the bunk. Cyrus was carrying a large jug.

"The perfect man," Rawley breathed. "The perfect man. Cyrus could pass the warning to Ray while he's serving him a drink."

He had to tell Cyrus immediately. Rawley knew himself well and if he didn't speak up now—before he had time to ponder the danger involved—he'd lose his nerve and not be able to tell at all. He steeled himself and began preparing to blurt out the whole story.

Cyrus was beside the bunk now and Rawley gazed up into the dull narrow-set eyes and saw no glimmer of intelligence. "Have to tell him right away," he whispered, "before I lose my nerve."

As he tried to think of how he could simplify the message he wanted to send to Ray, so Cyrus could remember it, a wave of fear swept over him. For days he'd been wishing he was dead but now he wasn't sure he wanted to involve himself in another life-and-death situation. The last time he'd dared to try something dangerous, he'd ended up ruining his life.

Cyrus plopped onto the stool and popped the cork and sat grinning down at the open jug. Rawley didn't wait for an offer. He reached one trembling hand out and grabbed the jug and took a long swig and instead of passing it back, held onto it and took a second drink. Cyrus raised his eyebrows but he didn't say anything.

Rawley didn't say anything either.

CHAPTER FOURTEEN

Wilbur Sanders was so jittery he couldn't eat the Saturday night supper his wife Hattie put in front of him, even though she'd gone to the trouble of frying scones. She had to serve the meal herself because their hired girl was lame and usually spilled the food. Hattie didn't seem to notice he wasn't touching his antelope steak. She was chattering about some funny thing one of the little boys had said that afternoon, and how the hired girl had laughed till she got tears in her eyes.

Hattie wasn't pretty but she had a sweet disposition, and her continual patter made a comfortable backdrop for serious thoughts. What he liked most about her was that she didn't expect him to answer back. He pushed the plate away and stood up and walked over and put on his overcoat.

"Business meeting," he said. "Don't wait up."

When she saw she was losing her audience, Hattie turned her face toward the lame servant, even though the girl already knew the story, and went right on talking.

As Wilbur walked away from the cabin, a hazy moon barely lit his path. It was only a few blocks to his uncle's cabin, and with every long stride Wilbur was anticipating the rebuff. His face burned as he remembered what his uncle had said to him the last time they talked.

"So if Plummer's presidential timber, what's that make you, Wilbur? A sapling?" Then he'd laughed and left Wilbur flushing and squirming for an answer.

If his uncle had compared him to any other man besides Plummer, he wouldn't have minded so much. But he'd never hated a man as much as he loathed The Great Minister of Justice. Things came too easy to Plummer. He was very good looking, so quite naturally he was a regular ladies' man. He could ride a horse like an Indian, and he could fire a gun like a military sharpshooter. Now that his damaged right hand was so stiff he could hardly use it, he'd only turned to his left hand, and he seemed to be almost as good at everything with it. It wasn't hard to see why the ignorant miners had that annoying way of talking about their Sheriff as though he were half-god.

Part of the reason Wilbur hated the man so much was because his uncle never let up on the goading. "Plummer's your main obstacle, Wilbur. You say you want to be a senator? Well face it, you're outclassed. Better get rid of the stiff competition!"

Wilbur knew he wasn't outclassed by anybody, but his uncle had a way of making him feel bumbling and incompetent.

He was at the door of the Edgerton cabin now, even though he'd been warned to stay away on this particular night. It took him a while to work up enough nerve to knock. Finally he tapped quietly at the door and waited. When nobody answered, he raised his knuckles to the door and started to tap again. On second thought, he didn't want to irk his uncle even more so he waited.

Finally the door cracked open and Edgerton peered out. He was holding a candle in one hand so he could see who it was, and in the light his small puffy eyes looked bleary, like he'd been napping.

"What in damnation?" he muttered.

Wilbur was afraid his uncle would slam the door in his face so he said quickly, "I've got to talk to you, Uncle Sid. It's urgent!"

Edgerton opened the door a little wider and strained his eyes to survey the dark street.

"It's all right," Wilbur assured him. "Nobody's watching. I checked first."

Edgerton reached out and grabbed his nephew by the arm and tugged him into the room. Then he slammed the door and jerked in the latchstring. The rest of the family had gone to bed and the two of them had the front room to themselves. Edgerton blew out the candle so the only light was from the fireplace. Then he slowly lowered himself into a chair in front of the flames. His shoulders were hunched toward the fire and the shifting shadows on his gaunt face gave him a sinister look.

Wilbur pulled a bench next to his uncle and sat down and slung his right leg across his left knee and fiddled with his trouser cuffs. He knew there was nothing he could do but wait till the barrage was over.

Edgerton let out an exaggerated sigh and covered his face with his bony hands. "Wilbur," he said, "I specifically told you the Chief Justice cannot be involved in this matter. I told you to take care of everything and keep me out of it. Now here you are leaving a trail right to my doorstep." His words were muffled because his mouth was covered and he was talking in a low tone because the bedroom walls were only sheets. "Sometimes I wonder if you're fit to be a senator."

Wilbur hated playing the toady, but with his uncle there was no way except to plead like a child, either that or else use flattery. "Uncle Sid," he said, "I have to rely on your wisdom. I want your approval before we go ahead with the plan."

Edgerton dropped his hands to his scraggy knees and gazed into the fire and shook his head. "Damn it to hell, Wilbur," he said, "do you understand the English language? I can't know the plan. Don't you see?"

"I see, Uncle Sid, but nobody will ever know you're involved. I'll deny it. I swear I will. I just don't want to go ahead with the assassination if you're not satisfied with ..."

Edgerton clapped his hands back over his eyes and groaned. "Not assassination, Wilbur. I thought even you knew better than that. Execution! Execution of a criminal! Get it? Get the difference?"

Wilbur shifted on his bench. Then he jerked his right foot off his left knee and switched the left foot over to the right knee, but he couldn't seem to get comfortable. He felt certain his uncle wouldn't approve of the plan he and Beidler had worked out. In fact the old man rarely approved of anything that didn't come straight from his own head.

Wilbur had a sneaking suspicion his uncle was setting him up to take the blame in case the assassination turned out to be a fiasco and the federal government heard about it and brought a murder charge. But he was willing to take the risk. He was determined to rise to the top, and he realized there wasn't any easy and nice way to get there.

"Uncle Sid," he said quietly, "we're going to send a warning to Stinson that a lynch mob is after the three lawmen. Believe me, the ignorant Rebel is easy to spook." He was trying to get it out as fast as he could because he knew his uncle would try to stop him. "We'll say we have three saddled horses waiting at the stable so the officers can make their escape. Then we'll post three sharpshooters in the loft of the stable and when ..."

"My God, Wilbur! You miss the whole point! It—has—to—look—legal! Why can't you get that through your head? A hanging ... a hanging! not a damn ambush!"

Wilbur sighed with relief. He had what he'd come for, an idea right from the horse's mouth. "I get it, Uncle Sid," he said. He stood up and headed for the door. "I won't bother you any more. I've got a surefire speech ready for the butcher shop crew. The whole town's edgy over the stage robbery so now's the ideal time to ... "

Edgerton scowled and raised one hand to silence him.

"Goodnight, Uncle Sid," he said. It took courage but as he was at the door he added, "You can sleep well. YOUR plan is in good hands."

Behind him he could hear his uncle blustering, but he slammed the door and hurried away. It was the first time he'd ever bested the old man, and it felt very, very good.

He didn't want to go straight to the butcher shop because he needed to rehearse the speech one more time. It was the best thing he'd ever composed, a stroke of genius, and the delivery had to be perfect. On main street, the miners were raising the usual Saturday night ruckus so he stayed on Yankee Flat.

"Very disturbing news from the Florence mines, Gentlemen. Very disturbing news."

He wanted to get just the right timbre to his voice, very grave and very believable, and he needed more resonance. He started again, pacing about in the dark and experimenting with different tones and gestures. He remembered that his uncle wouldn't be there to criticize him afterwards and that gave him confidence. No matter how it went, he could tell his uncle he'd been a stunning success.

"Very disturbing news from the Florence mines, Gentlemen."

The darkness gave him confidence too and gradually he began to let out the first-rate orator he'd always known was trapped inside his gawky frame. He practiced till the last minute and then carefully edged his way across the log bridge to the business side of town. Then he pushed through the main street crowd.

He didn't intend to make his appearance until Beidler had the crowd ready. If Beidler had enough sense to remember, he was supposed to inform the audience that the speaker at this civic meeting would be Colonel Sanders of Union army fame. Then he was supposed to whip them into a frenzy about the stage robbery and point out how worrisome it was that Plummer hadn't caught the culprits yet, and how they should keep in mind that maybe Plummer was purposely trying to let the robbers get away.

While he waited for the signal Beidler was supposed to give, he wasn't able to stand still. He was nervous and shaky and his palms were so wet he had to keep swiping them dry on his trousers. He hated like the devil having to put any confidence in an ignorant and crude man like Beidler, but he seemed to be the shrewdest and the most fanatic of the Strangler lot.

Suddenly a candle lit up the shade covering the front window of the butcher shop and then disappeared, just as they'd agreed. Evidently Beidler was bright enough to follow the plan they'd worked out. The initial success sent a surge of excitement flooding through him and carried him around to the back door like he was treading on air. Cautiously he swung the door open. For just a second he felt an attack of panic coming on, but the darkness in the room bolstered his spirits and he was able to enter with a swagger of confidence.

The long room was lit by one small candle placed on a cutting table in a corner, but even in the faint light he could see the turnout was much better than he'd expected. From the snatches of conversation he caught as he made his way past the rows of filled benches and up to the front of the shop, he could tell Beidler had them very worked up over the robbery. It was the chance of a lifetime, his chance to make it in politics. His arms were tingling and his legs were trembling but thank God there was the blessed darkness.

He began immediately. He felt the same burst of power and glory he always felt just before he commenced a hymn in the church choir, as if his carefully mouthed words could soar right up to the throne of the Almighty. Only he didn't feel like Wilbur anymore. He felt like a budding Abe Lincoln. It seemed to him that his bland face had suddenly become chiseled with character, and his awkward frame and limbs were now lean and agile, and his unmanly voice was coming out grave and sonorous.

"Very disturbing news from the Florence mines, Gentlemen," he said. "Very disturbing news."

He began pacing back and forth. It helped him relieve his excess energy. He looked down at the floor while he filled his lungs with a big gulp of air and then raised his head and turned toward the audience. "A band of more than one hundred Rebels has just destroyed the entire town of Florence, every single business house robbed and looted, every single merchant left absolutely penniless."

A buzz ran through the audience, and then a couple of voices called out questions. It was just the reaction he'd hoped for. But he wanted to stir them up more before he took any questions. He purposely ignored the interruptions and went on with his routine, pacing deliberately and occasionally pausing and gazing down at the floor to keep them on pins and needles. Then he stood still and surveyed the mass of listeners who were almost faceless because of the darkness.

"Gentlemen," he said, "I don't want to alarm you, but you're entitled to know the facts. At this very moment, the band of Rebel outlaws is riding hard for Bannack. These traitors to the Union will be here by Monday morning! Monday morning, Gentlemen, and this is Saturday night!"

He paused to let them chew on the chunk of gristle he'd just tossed out.

Then he said, "Fellow citizens, time is short ..." He lowered his voice so they had to strain to hear him and some of them leaned forward on their benches. He was in complete control, and the sense of power made him feel giddy. He began to pace faster and then halted and quickly whirled around toward them. "We have to act immediately so we can protect our community ... so we can protect our homes, and our businesses, and most of all, protect our families!"

His audience was in a state of serious agitation and he had to be careful or he'd lose the control he'd worked so hard to get. He raised both hands to quiet them. They silenced immediately and he suddenly realized he was able to play with them like a cat does with a mouse, attack and then pause, and then prod and incite again, and then make them wait. He added a fierceness to his voice. He'd always known it was all there inside him wanting to come out.

"These Rebel pirates," he said, "have sworn that on Monday morning their flag will fly over our town! The Rebels are setting up an empire, and they've chosen themselves an Emperor, the Emperor of the West they call him. And, Gentlemen, this tyrant is a traitor living right here among us! Pretending to be a decent man by day, but by night he's ruling his intricately-organized Rebel outlaw gang with an iron hand!"

Several men jumped to their feet and began shouting out questions, and he had to quiet them again.

"No, no, Gentlemen," he said, "sit down. We have to have order. We have to unite to save ourselves and our families! As you probably know, I was a colonel in the Union army, and I've worked out a military defense against this Rebel army that's riding toward us. We'll cut the head off the serpent before it coils and strikes!"

He threw back his shoulders and stretched up to his maximum height and stood in the middle of the room gazing down at them like a general facing his troops. He sensed it was time to take a question.

"What defense?" a voice from the back called out.

It sounded like Chrisman, but Wilbur couldn't be sure.

"Lieutenant Beidler's in charge of carrying out the military plan," he answered. "Naturally the plan's secret. All I can tell you is that the first skirmish will take place tomorrow night. We'll meet here after dark, and the lieutenant will issue weapons."

"Make war on a Sunday?" somebody shouted.

There was a flurry of other questions, but he ignored them and headed for the door. He was waiting for just the right one before he answered. Finally it came.

"Who's the Emperor?" somebody called out. "Who is it?"

He stopped and turned back toward them, and when they saw he was going to speak, they waited with bated breath.

"The Emperor of the West," he said, "is William Henry Plummer."

CHAPTER FIFTEEN

Stinson had promised Sadie he would quit work early so they could be on time for Sunday night service. But he got home late again. He'd been able to beg off patrol duty but before he could get away, Deaf Dick insisted on a haircut. And while he was working on Dick, Cyrus complained that Nellie told him he couldn't come home that night if he didn't get his head sheared down to size.

Stinson barely had time to get into his good clothes. Usually Sadie sat and admired him while he dressed, but tonight she was curled up on the bed with her face turned to the wall.

She was wearing her best dress and he could smell her lavender scent. All he could see was the back of her head but he could tell she'd rolled her long thick brown hair into curls and pinned them up in a topknot. He thought she looked as pretty as any queen, wearing her best dress and sulking on a feather pillow because somebody was keeping her waiting.

He decided to pretend he hadn't noticed she was crabby. "Feelin' bad, Ma?" he asked.

"Yeah," she said, "but I ain't missin' church."

He could tell by the tone of her voice how cross she was. Mama and Papa Toland had already got tired of waiting for him and put out the fire and left for church.

"Ain't no fault o' mine I'm late," he said, "Sheriff didn't ride in till mornin' ... an' that ole consumption it's kickin' up on 'im agin."

Sadie reared up and turned toward Buck. "Sheriff's back?" she asked. "Did he catch them stage robbers?"

"Nope, no luck," Stinson said. He knotted his tie and then wet his long hair and slicked it back. Then he reached down and gave Sadie a love pinch on the arm.

That softened Sadie up a little bit. "I ain't put out, Buck," she said, but her voice still sounded like she was.

He lifted her coat off the peg and blew out the candle. Then he pulled her up and she leaned on his arm as they walked. He noticed she was moving in a sort of waddle, like it hurt her to move her legs, and that worried him. The Tolands had left a candle burning in the front room and there was enough light so he could see Sadie clap one hand to her swollen belly.

"This here ornery little kicker's actin' like it's pop-out time." Her voice was faint and a little breathless.

That alarmed Stinson even more and he stopped in his tracks. His senses were getting sharp, like they always did when he was scared. He could hear Sadie breathing loud in his ears and it sounded like somebody was moving around outside the cabin and her lavender scent was almost overpowering. He knew he had to be careful not to scare her too, but he was thinking they shouldn't try to go to church. On the other hand he hated to disappoint her because she was so fidgety and willful, and if she got upset the baby might come early.

"Reckon I mustn't go after Doc?" he asked. He tried to keep his voice calm but he could hear the edge to it himself.

"I ain't missin' church," she repeated. She was speaking in her normal voice but his ears were making it louder. He knew he had to get a hold on himself if he was going to take charge of the situation and see her through.

She was trying to push on toward the door, but he held onto her arm so she couldn't go any further. He'd always let her be the boss of the family but he was wondering if it wasn't time he stepped in and started taking over.

"Sadie," he said firmly.

They were standing a few feet from the front door and without any sort of warning it suddenly burst in on them and at the same time the candle blew out. In the darkness the sound of wood splintering echoed in his ears and then Sadie screamed and the vibrations rang through his head and nearly split his eardrums. He grabbed her and pulled her close to his chest and hovered over the top of her to shield her.

He could hear people stampeding through the open door and then he felt bodies pressing tight around them and he could smell their ugly old sweat. He didn't know who they were but he could hear them breathing hard and with each snort the air reeked of alcohol. He had a derringer in one boot and a knife in the other but as he tried to go for a weapon, they grabbed his arms and jerked them behind him.

"What y'all want?" he asked. He tried to sound friendly because he didn't want them to hurt Sadie. There was no answer to his question, just the heavy breathing and the intense odors of alcohol and body sweat.

"What y'all want?" he asked again.

"Keep tight hold on 'im now!"

The voice had a nasal twang to it and sounded familiar but it was so loud it addled his brains and he couldn't quite put his finger on who it was and it was too dark to see sizes or shapes.

Sadie screamed again and Stinson broke their hold on him and lunged toward her.

"It's m' wife's time," he said, "please don't y'all hurt 'er none."

Then he felt a blow to one side of his head. The object that hit him was cold and hard and reached from his left temple down to his jaw. He couldn't feel any pain but it was hard to stand up. He kept wanting to fall off to one side. He couldn't think straight either. It was dark and when he closed his eyes it seemed like he could see orange circles chasing each other around inside his head.

They had a new grip on him now and they wrestled his arms behind him and then he felt them binding his wrists together with rope and then they were dragging him toward the gap where the door had been. He didn't resist because he wanted them out of the cabin so Sadie would be safe. Then the smell of lavender flooded over him and at the same time he felt her fling her arms around his neck. She didn't say anything, she just locked her arms there and wouldn't let go. Then she began to cry.

It broke his heart to hear her sob but he couldn't get his hands free to hold her.

"Pry 'er loose," a voice ordered.

It was the same twangy voice as before and it still sounded familiar but Stinson wasn't in any condition to match voices with people. All he could think of was getting away from the house so Sadie wouldn't get hurt ... Sadie and the baby.

But with her hanging on to him this way the three of them were fastened together, Sadie's arms locked around his neck and her cheek pushed up against his cheek and the baby inside her squeezed between the two of them.

Then the odor of alcohol snorted in his face again and the voice shouted out orders and he could feel hands swarming over the three of them and yanking at Sadie's arms, and they were spitting out curse words that echoed through his head.

Finally they broke her grip on him and as they pulled her away, she wailed, "No! No!"

They were rushing Stinson out the door now and he wanted to call something back to her to make her feel better but nothing would work. His tongue seemed puffy, like it filled up all of his mouth so tight it couldn't move, and his jaws wouldn't open. Then he felt something trickling down his face and dripping onto his neck. He knew it must be his own blood.

When they were outside, the cold air cleared his brain a little. The voice was barking out orders again.

"Stay with th' woman! Keep tight hold on 'er!"

The nasal twang again. Beidler of course, Beidler and his Stranglers. He should have known from the first.

They were walking fast, all of them around him and jostling him with every step, but it was a relief to be putting distance between them and the cabin. There was no moon but dim stars lit up the snow on the ground and he could see they were headed in the direction of the creek and the log that crossed over to town.

But when they got to the log bridge, they didn't cross over to the town side. Instead they swung right and kept moving alongside the creek. He was stumbling and they were half dragging him. The men on all sides of him were carrying shotguns and marching like they were an army, and they seemed to be in a square with him in the center. The ones he could see were wearing their overcoats wrong-side-out and had their collars turned up, and their hats were pulled so low their faces were hidden.

Suddenly they swung to the right again and left the creek. Then they stopped. They tightened the square around him till he couldn't move a muscle and somebody behind him twisted one of his arms so hard it felt like they were trying to screw it off. He knew the Stranglers were going to kill him. There was no doubt about that. Sheriff was in bed with consumption, sick like to die, so he couldn't come to save him. Nobody would come to rescue him because nobody else besides Sadie knew what was happening to him. There was no use to pray to God to save him either. Even God couldn't save him from the Stranglers. He was going to die.

Now that it was finally on him, he wasn't as scared as he'd thought he'd be. In fact he felt almost calm. There wasn't anything to worry about anymore. His life was at its end. The sounds around him weren't echoing in his ears and he could think a little bit. It was just leaving Sadie, that and never getting to see the baby, that was what hurt, it was like a knife twisting in his heart. The Stranglers were talking among themselves and the pain in his temple and jaw was coming through now, throbbing like a heart beat. His mind still wasn't working quite right and the regular throbbing made it hard for him to concentrate on their muffled words long enough to make sense of them. The only word he was sure of was "Wait," they kept saying "Wait."

His brain was somewhat scrambled but he was alert enough to know that more than anything he wanted to die game. He wouldn't beg for mercy. Even if they poked out his eyes or cut off his tongue he wouldn't let out a holler. When Sadie found out he was dead, he wanted her to hear that he died game. He wanted her to be able to tell the son he'd never see that his father had died game.

They kept waiting for something. He didn't know what, but he hated them for dragging out his agony. It showed they had no decency. He'd already been waiting too long. Ever since that morning when he slipped the noose over the boy's head he'd known something was coming and now he just wanted it to finally be over with. Hanging the boy wasn't right and now it was bringing them all down, just like he'd known it would.

He tilted his face up toward the sky. The stars were getting fainter but he could still make them out and they gave him a feeling of peace. He had faith God would give him the strength to die game and he also had faith that when he was gone, God and Mama and Papa Toland would take care of Sadie and the baby. But as he gazed at the heavens, dark clouds began drifting over the stars. It was so dark now he couldn't even see the men pressing in on him. He could only feel them and smell them and hear them breathing.

Then in the distance, a flame burst into the darkness. Further down the creek somebody had lit a torch and was holding it up in the air. A spark of hope lit in Stinson's soul. He was thinking maybe Sadie had broken away and run to the hotel and rousted Sheriff out of his sick bed. Maybe Sheriff and Ray were searching for him ... coming to save him. Now the torch was moving, leaving the creek and heading in the direction of the Bluebird.

Then as he anxiously watched, the torch suddenly went out.

CHAPTER SIXTEEN

It was cold outside and Deputy Ray was worn out and wanted to go home and get in bed, but he was the only one left to patrol main street. Plummer was laid up with a severe case of consumption, and the Reb had to take his wife to church. Night patrol was supposed to be Stinson's job, but everybody knew Sadie led him around like he was a bull with a metal ring hooked through his nose. When Sadie said, "Jump, Buck!" he didn't even ask how high. He just hopped two feet off the ground and when he lit, he promised, "I'll do better next time, Ma." And when Sadie said, "I wanna go t' church, Buck," he bustled around to get his suit and tie on and slick down his hair as fast as he could.

But Stinson and his wife were crazy about each other so what difference did it make. Ray knew what it felt like to be crazy about a woman. When Libby was alive, there wasn't anything in the world he wouldn't do just to make her smile.

He took a candle-lantern to light his way and locked up the sheriff's office. Then he tromped through the snow in the back alley and crossed over to the stable and started his rounds there. The miners had already left for their claims and the town was nearly empty. He didn't like seeing Bannack so deserted, it gave him a lonely feeling.

Snow had drifted several inches deep on the boardwalk and as he walked past the assay office, his feet were beginning to feel the cold and that made him think about what had happened to Rawley. It was something he didn't like to think about because the little carpenter wasn't taking his accident well. Vera Grizzert had told Stinson she thought Rawley was trying to starve himself to death. And evidently he held it against Ray and Plummer for riding out to find him.

As Ray approached the carpenter shop, he could see it was dark at the front but there was a light burning toward the back. He stopped and leaned up to the window to see if everything was all right inside and spotted Vera Grizzert standing at the table and pressing a pair of trousers with the flat iron. The family was probably getting ready to go to church. It was about that time of night.

As he passed by the Elkhorn, he could see it was almost empty. Then he turned his head toward the barber chair and noticed Stinson clipping away at Deaf Dick's hair. At first he felt like going in and telling the little weasel to get out here in the cold and do his own work, but he decided not to get himself upset. There was no use to start a ruckus with the Reb just because he begged off patrol one night a week.

It wasn't really the Reb he was thinking about anyhow. For some reason, Libby was strong on his mind tonight. Of course it wasn't unusual for him to think about his dead wife because he was still in love with her. There wasn't a day or night went by when he didn't remember her and miss her. When the two of them had been together, life had been good, and it had been simple.

But that was in the days before he met Caroline and she got her eagle hooks fixed in him. Lately she'd been making his life miserable instead of happy, like it'd been when he first moved into her cabin. Ever since that day he'd made the mistake of calling her his wife in front of old Edgerton and saying how he intended to take her back to New York state, she'd been after him in one way or another.

She never came right out and asked him about it again, like she had that time on the bed when he saw her cry for the first time. She just kept hammering at him with what her simple mind probably thought were subtle little hints. "I expect it gets right cold in New York, don't it, Edward Ray?" she'd ask. And she was always bringing up something like, "The gold's goin' t' run out in Bannack one o' these days. We gotta be thinkin' o' somewheres else t' live." While she was harping on the topic, she always used her syrupy-sweet voice.

And it wasn't just the things she said. It was what she did too. Lately she'd been hounding him to try to remember how his mother made bread pudding so she could bake him up a batch. When they first met, he'd mentioned the pudding to her only she hadn't shown any interest then, and now all of a sudden she was anxious to make him his favorite home-baked dessert. Besides that, she was sewing him "a frontier suit," as she called it. "If you're goin' t' live on th' frontier, Edward Ray," she said, "you oughta dress in a frontier suit."

That was the same argument she'd used when she was trying to persuade him to wear his hair long, and now she was trotting it out again to try to force him to wear buckskin. By the way she was trying to take over his life, Ray could see he was in a precarious position. He'd pretty well decided to leave for New York in the spring all right, ... but alone. He hadn't broken the news to Caroline yet. He felt awfully bad for her because he knew how much she'd miss him. She'd be very lonely there in the cabin all by herself.

He did have one thing to be grateful for though. At least Cyrus hadn't heard about Caroline wanting to go to New York, or about the bread pudding or the buckskin suit either. Otherwise, Cyrus would be rubbing Ray's nose in it every time he walked through the doors of the Elkhorn to play a game of cards. Cyrus was almost as bad as Caroline when it came to bringing up things other people wanted to forget.

But no matter how much Caroline hinted about moving to New York, Ray was determined to act like he missed the point. Not that it solved the problem. Later, she'd just bring the subject up again. He longed for the good old days before old Edgerton came pounding on the cabin door and ruined their peace and happiness.

Nearly every business on main street was closed up tight, and his rounds were going fast. After he passed the Goodrich Hotel, he turned and looked back at the second story. Plummer's room was still lit, so he figured the Sheriff must be too sick to get any sleep. When he'd gone up to the room to visit him earlier, he noticed that Plummer's face was very pale, and it seemed like he could hardly get his breath. In fact Ray had been struck with the impression that Plummer didn't have long to live.

The hurdy-gurdy house was dark and so were the restaurant and the butcher shop. The new butcher, Conrad Kohrs, wasn't much of a gambler or drinker, and he usually went to bed with the chickens. When Ray crossed to the opposite side of the street, he noticed Peabody's saloon didn't have any more customers than the Elkhorn. He tapped on the glass and saluted the bartender and kept moving. His boots were wet and his feet were beginning to ache from the cold, and he walked faster so he could get done.

The last building on that side of the street was the big log cabin where Edgerton and his family lived. There were candles burning inside and as he looked across the creek, he also saw lights in most of the houses on Yankee Flat. The big hogan where the religious folk held church was already lit up. The preacher always went over an hour early and built a fire so the building would be warm during service.

Ray didn't like looking at the hogan ... not after the comment Caroline had made that very morning. "That big old church tepee would shore be a romantic spot t' hold a weddin'," she said, "don't you think, Edward Ray?"

That was what confused him so much about her. She swore up and down she didn't ever want to get married. "Ain't no man ever goin' t' tie me down," she liked to say. That was why he'd felt comfortable with her at first, but he was beginning to have a suspicion she just said that to throw him off guard. It was part of her ploy. Simple as her mind was, she was the shrewdest businesswoman he'd ever met and probably she viewed him as just another business venture. When he thought of it that way, he supposed that actually he was a pretty good catch.

Ray turned around and headed back toward the cabin. Even though Caroline had him worried, their little cabin still felt like home. He wasn't sure why. When he opened the door he saw live coals on the hearth, and there was the sweet scent of fresh-baked food in the air. Even when Caroline wasn't there, her presence still filled up the place.

As he put the candle-lantern on the table, he saw she'd left his place set. There was a little cut-glass dish filled with bread pudding and a silver spoon and a long-stemmed crystal glass filled with white wine.

He pulled off the damp boots and wiggled some circulation back into his toes. Then he took off his overcoat and suit coat and hung them on the row of pegs next to the door. That was one thing he and Caroline agreed on, keeping the place neat and orderly.

He was so hungry he didn't bother to loosen his tie or find a pair of moccasins to warm his feet. He just sat down at the table and ate every single bite of the pudding. It didn't taste anything like his mother's but it was good.

After he poured himself another glass of white wine, he moved over to the bear rug in front of the fireplace and tossed a handful of twigs on the embers. When little flames came curling up, he added some small sticks and sat there sipping the wine.

He felt very content. But that only made him feel guilty ... because of Libby. He gazed into the fire and watched flames dancing out of the sticks and thought how very much he loved Libby. And she'd loved him just as much. Then he had a rather disturbing thought. If Libby still loved him, wherever she was, then she'd want him to be content ... that's exactly what she'd want. He wondered why he'd never thought of it that way before. It took quite a burden off his shoulders.

When he finished the wine, he put a small log on the fire so it would still be warm when Caroline got home and then took the candle-lantern and headed for the bedroom. As he was turning back the satin sheet, he saw the frontier suit. It was laid out on top of the quilt spread. She'd finished it and of course she'd left it there because she wanted him to try it on. "How'd th' frontier suit fit?" That'd be the first thing that came out of her mouth when they woke up in the morning.

Ray set down the light and undid his tie and then took off his shirt and trousers and carefully hung each one on the correct peg. When he picked up the buckskin clothes to examine them, he was surprised that the material felt rather smooth and soft, not rough and stiff like he'd expected. And she'd gone to the trouble of foxing the shirt front and sleeves with long buckskin fringe.

After he wiggled into the new clothes, he stood in front of her mirror and admired himself. He had to admit that with the frontier outfit and the long hair, he looked like a regular Westerner. For some reason it excited him and he wanted to go somewhere and show himself off. Caroline was always trying to get him to stop by the Bluebird but he hated the place and would never go there unless it was on law business. Of course he could make up some excuse for being there, say he'd heard there were some drunken rowdies who'd stayed in town so he needed to stop by as part of his rounds.

She saw him as soon as he stepped through the door. She was standing at a gambling table and dealing faro and she was wearing his favorite dress, the pale blue one, and in the candlelight the gold jewelry on her fingers and wrists and ears was flashing. She kept on dealing but she gave him her big easy smile and then took a second look and saw he was wearing the buckskin outfit. At first her face lit up, and then it got a little grave, like she might be going to cry.

He grinned at her and sat down at an empty table in the corner, and the bartender hurried over with a drink on the house. The violinist was lounging at the bar, but he looked over at Ray's new garb and grabbed up his violin and began fiddling "Oh, Susanna."

Caroline must have been doing lots of bragging about the frontier suit she'd sewn for him because nearly every eye in the house was on Ray and he was beginning to feel a little embarrassed. All of the girls were waving their fingers at him, and the stout white-haired little prosecutor raised his whiskey glass like he was making a silent toast. Ray decided to play along. He lifted his drink in Billy's direction and they both drained their glasses dry.

The bartender must have been watching because he bustled over with another drink on the house.

Ray couldn't keep his eyes off Caroline. He'd never seen her look so bright and sparkly, and he'd never noticed before how much natural poise she had. He watched how sure her hands were as she flipped the cards and then swept in the coins. It occurred to him she could probably get any man she went after, but she wanted him. He'd intended to just show her how well the suit fit and then get out as quick as he could, but now he was toying with the idea of staying and waiting for her.

It was hard for him to picture the woman running the faro game with so much finesse and authority as the same person who waited on him hand and foot at home. But the more he thought about it, the clearer it all became. The way she'd been acting lately wasn't a mystery to him anymore. All she was doing was offering him love. The pudding and the buckskin suit, they were both offers of love, and he was thinking that maybe he shouldn't be so afraid of taking them. Maybe he should just reach out and grab love with both hands.

While he was considering the idea, the front door swung open and three men bundled in overcoats and scarves stepped into the building. For a few seconds they stood there ogling the girls in their low-cut dresses and then they began slowly making their way over to Ray's table. He didn't recognize any of them at first sight, but it was hard to say if he knew them or not because they had their collars turned up and the brims of their hats were pulled down so their faces were shadowed.

They didn't take a chair. They just stood beside the table and looked down at him. They seemed to be carefully examining his fringed shirt, just like everybody else in the place had. Then one man leaned over and said in his ear, "Say, Deputy, you're needed at the Elkhorn. Two drunks quarrelin' and Stinson's already gone home."

Ray had no choice. He was the only lawman on duty, so he stood up and followed the men to the door. The three of them went out ahead of him and as he passed the bartender, he paused and said, "Tell Caroline I'll be right back."

As he was walking down the front steps and being careful not to slip on the packed snow, he stopped and looked around for the three men but they seemed to have disappeared. He cautiously put one foot on the last stair and was just lowering the other foot when dark figures sprang out from both sides of the building and surrounded him. In the faint light coming from the Bluebird's front windows he saw the glint of shotgun barrels. He had his revolver tucked under the buckskin shirt but they got to it before he did and then pinned his arms behind him and tied his hands together.

At first he was filled with disbelief. He couldn't believe he'd let himself be taken so easily. The three men hadn't been admiring his fringed shirt, they were looking for a bulge made by a revolver. Sheer terror began to set in and it was a new feeling for him. They were forming a square around him, trapping him inside, and then they started marching rapidly in the direction of the creek, not staying on the trail but breaking fresh snow as they tramped. It was so dark nothing around them was visible. They were moving forward from darkness and entering into darkness, and bodies were leaning in on him and jabbing him with shotgun barrels. He could feel his heart pounding against his chest. Nobody spoke a word.

Finally they halted. There were still no words spoken, but their group seemed to be joining with another bunch and then somebody gave him a hard shove and he collided with a body that reached only to his shoulder.

"Yank?" a voice whispered. "That y'all?"

The words were muffled, like they were being forced out between clenched teeth but he knew it was the Reb, and he knew the two of them were in the hands of the Stranglers. He was shocked at how many volunteers Beidler had been able to round up ... in shock, and trembling with fear of what he still couldn't believe was ahead.

There was only one glimmer of hope. When he didn't get back, Caroline might come looking for her Edward Ray. Maybe she'd go to the hotel and rouse Plummer out of his bed. That was his only chance, but if she didn't start out soon enough, when she finally found him he'd be swinging from the beef scaffold beside the butcher shop.

They were forming a new square around the two of them now, and then the merged group stood waiting in the dark and the cold. He could feel the Reb's stocky little body squeezed against his own and it made him think how this was the first time they'd ever known any fellowship. They couldn't stand to work together, but now they were going to die together. He wondered which one would go first and which one would have to stand and watch the other one twist at the end of a rope.

The waiting went on. He was grateful for it though because the delay should make Caroline start worrying about him. He started counting the seconds so he'd know if Caroline had enough time to get alarmed.

The seconds began adding up to minutes and still they stood in the snow and the dark and the cold without moving a muscle. He went on counting. It kept his hope alive, but it also occurred to him he might be doing nothing more than ticking off the final seconds of his life.

Suddenly a torch lit the sky somewhere further up the Grasshopper. He knew it was a signal but he didn't know what it meant. The high torch began moving away from the creek, heading in the direction of the houses on Yankee Flat, and then suddenly it blacked out.

CHAPTER SEVENTEEN

Plummer lay on the cot in his hotel room and watched the shadows cast by the candlelight playing across the log rafters of the ceiling. He was in too much pain to sleep. Over the years he'd gotten used to the consumption attacks, the dry cough that seemed to tear at his lungs and then the taste of blood coming into his mouth. But this attack was worse than usual. He was fighting hard for every breath, and he was also fighting to keep the thought he was dying out of his head.

It wasn't really a thought. He was too feverish to think clearly, but a series of images were passing through his mind, as though he were watching a pageant. The scenes were hazy and would linger for a few minutes and then slowly dissolve. He saw himself laid out on a table. He was dressed in his best suit, and dim candles were flickering at his head and feet, but there was no one there to mourn him. The picture was rather cloudy, but his face appeared to be ghostly pale and his eyes were closed.

That image gradually faded away and was replaced by Electa. Her face was hazy too ... hazy but bathed in a soft golden light. Her hair was down and it flowed on both sides of her face and gave off glints of golden-red, like it was reflecting firelight. As he watched, the golden hair gradually dissolved into yellow leaves shimmering on the rippled surface of the Sun River. Then Electa's slender hands dipped into the river and split the yellow cottonwood leaves apart to let in a long slash of pale blue sky and soft cottony clouds.

For just a moment the reflection of her face appeared in the patch of blue sky and white clouds, and then her long thick hair fell around her face and drooped into the water. At the same instant, a flash of pain racked his body, and he sat up in bed and clutched at his chest till the sharp ache gradually subsided.

His face was beaded with perspiration and he wiped it dry with his handkerchief and then lay down again. Now it seemed that he was able to think clearly again, and he felt quite sure he was going to die. There was only one thing left that he desperately wanted, and that was to be with Electa when his life ended.

He got out of bed and steadied himself against the wall while he dressed. He put on the same shirt and suit he'd left draped over the chair by his cot and grabbed his overcoat and put it on too. Then he blew out the candle and felt his way out of the room.

There was no light burning on the second floor of the hotel, but a bright fire on the large hearth below lit up the stairway. As he hurried through the lobby, Bill Goodrich reached out and handed him a candle-lantern.

"Here, Sheriff," he said, "you'll for sure need this. Pitch-black out there."

The boardwalk was drifted in snow but the flakes had stopped falling and the wind had calmed. The cold air he was drawing in felt like needles pricking his lungs, but he kept walking fast, hurrying toward the cabin. Most of the business section was dark but light glowed from the small windows of a few homes on Yankee Flat, and also from the log hogan where they were holding church service. He could faintly hear them singing "Bringing in the Sheaves."

Carefully he stepped along the log slung across the creek and reached the other side without once slipping into the water. As he walked the lane to the cabin, he thought he could feel her presence beside him, and that was what he'd come for.

Then he was inside. It was the first time he'd gone to the cabin since she left and he held the light high and looked about him, examining the gray calico curtains and everything else her hands had touched. The fast walk had tired him and he was breathing hard and coughing and hurting badly. He set the light on the table by the divan and snuffed it out and the thought came to him that he was only thirty-two years old and his life was being snuffed out. He lay down on the divan and pulled the blanket over him.

He was shaking with a chill, but then the fever flaired up again and he had to throw off the blanket and then take off his overcoat too.

Though he was so sick, it felt good to be home. If he were going to die, he wanted it to be here. Lying there in the darkness, he sensed her presence again. He closed his eyes and she seemed to be leaning over him and letting her hair fall onto his chest and hands, and then he was able to get his breath again and he felt himself drifting into sleep.

He was wakened by a pounding on the door and someone calling, "Sheriff, Sheriff!" The voice had an urgent tone, and he stumbled to his feet and groped his way to the door. He couldn't see who it was but while the door was still swinging open, a shadowy figure began speaking.

"Sheriff," the voice said, "them damn Stranglers, they're gettin' ready t' do some stringin' up. Claim they caught the stage robbers."

Plummer stepped outside and closed the door behind him. The cold air entered his nostrils and then stung as it penetrated his lungs but he was determined not to appear sick.

"Where are they?" he asked.

"Down creek a piece. Come on, I'll show ya."

Plummer followed the man. The moon was hidden by clouds but dim starlight reflected off the creek beside them and barely lit the snow-packed path. Suddenly the two of them were surrounded on all sides. The men were wearing their coat collars turned up and had pulled their slouch hats low over their faces. All around him, he caught the glint of shotgun barrels.

They didn't approach any further, but instead held back as though they were afraid to come close to him, and that calmed him. It was hard for him to get enough breath so he could speak forcefully, but he knew he had to say something to save the suspects they were holding down creek.

"Gentlemen," he said, "these men may be guilty of robbery, but we'll be guilty of murder if we put them to death without a trial."

There was a long silence, and then he could see the men

around him lowering their guns and resting them at their sides.

For good measure he added, "You know I'll see that justice is done."

The group around him shuffled about in the snow for what seemed like endless minutes. Overhead, the haziness began to break up and drift, and the increased light coming from the newly exposed stars brightened the snow. Then a pale moon barely showed its face through a rift in a mass of dark clouds. He could now see there were more than twenty men around him and he was trying not to give the appearance of being sick, but he had to take quick shallow breaths to keep the cold air from going deep into his lungs.

He waited. He didn't want to say anything more unless it was necessary ... and they were also waiting ... waiting as though they were very carefully considering his words.

Then the group slowly began to disperse. Several men headed in the direction of main street, and for a second Plummer thought he recognized one of them as Chrisman. He decided he must be wrong; he couldn't believe a man as decent as Chrisman could ever be talked into joining the Stranglers.

The sudden military order that came from behind them was so sharp it sounded almost like a dog barking.

"Forward march!"

The order came from the direction of the Wilbur Sanders cabin, and Plummer turned back to look. Standing in the shadows against the side wall was a lanky figure wearing an overcoat and hat and leveling a rifle directly at him.

The men who had been leaving now quickly turned back. Then they also leveled their guns on him.

"Do your duty, men!"

Again the order was crisp and sharp, and the Stranglers began hurriedly surrounding him. They did not press in on him, but instead held off at a respectful distance. Then the entire body began to march. They had formed a square with him in the center.

They were walking rapidly down creek, and then they were joined by a horde of excited men armed with shotguns. Recklessly the new group shoved themselves a passageway and marched two prisoners in beside him. Even before he saw their faces, he knew they were his two deputies.

"Forward march!" Sanders barked out again.

Row by row, the small army of men began splashing through the creek. They were heading in the direction of main street. He could hear his own labored breathing and the pain in his chest was burning like fire. He splashed through the creek too and kept up with their pace while they crossed main street. Then he looked up the narrow lane rising to the hills ahead of them and caught a glimpse of the delicate pine gallows glowing like silver in the pale moonlight.

CHAPTER EIGHTEEN

Electa woke in the night with the feeling she was suffocating. A heavy weight seemed to be pressing down on her breast and forcing the breath out of her. She sat up in bed and pulled the quilts around her and shivered as she sucked in deep gulps of air.

She was sleeping in the bedroom she'd known as a child but the shadowy pieces of furniture in the cold room no longer seemed familiar to her. Through the tall window beside the bed she could see a pale moon high in the sky. It was sternly watching her like a giant white eye.

She knew she'd committed a grave sin, and now she was suddenly gripped by a strong fear that something terrible was going to happen because of it. She bowed her head and closed her eyes and folded her arms across her breast and began to pray out loud. She begged for forgiveness and asked for His protection and help, but when she finished she didn't feel any better.

The Bible told her that the sheep can hear the Shepherd's voice, and all her life she'd listened for His voice and gradually learned to recognize it. And now the voice inside her head was saying, "Sinners bring tragedies upon themselves, tragedies that even God cannot prevent."

She thought of the great distance separating her from Will and felt sick with fright. From the minute she'd begun packing her steamer chest, she knew it would be wrong to leave him. In fact she'd never wanted to leave him, and she'd never expected that Will would let her go. That was why she'd asked him first. Then when he gave his permission, she was sure that at the last minute he'd come with her.

And he had—just like she'd expected. She didn't like remembering what had happened at Salt Lake. When he turned around and headed back for Bannack, she couldn't believe it.

The new stage pushed further and further east, but she kept thinking he'd catch up to them. At every station she stood outside gazing back toward the western horizon in hopes she'd see the silhouette of a rider on a long-legged horse. But Will hadn't come. He'd chosen Bannack instead of her.

It hurt very deeply to accept the fact that he could live without her. He'd always told her he couldn't. But now she knew different. She'd never said it to him, but she'd always known she couldn't live without him, and nothing could ever change that.

There was a hope left, the hope she was carrying his child inside her. Because when she wrote and told him about it, he'd be sure to give up Bannack and come to Ohio and then everything would be like it was at the mission on Sun River. They'd go on long strolls under the big trees beside the river, and as they walked, they'd watch for wildflowers and birds, just like at the mission. And they'd gaze up at the sky like they always did and say that cloud over there looked just like a hound with its tongue hanging out and its long ears drooping down, and the one beside it looked more like a horse galloping, with its tail raised and flying to the winds. Then before their very eyes, the hound and horse would start shifting into new shapes.

Then they'd stop and stand quietly beside the river and look down at the reflection of themselves and the trees and the sky and the clouds. She'd hold onto his arm like she always did and he'd put his face down to brush against her hair.

And the best part of all would be that his only concern in life would be for her ... her and the child they were going to have, and nobody else.

She fastened her eyes on the moon and it didn't look so stern anymore. In fact it looked rather kind ... kind and forgiving. She thought how in far-off Bannack, that beautiful glowing circle that God had created and set in the heavens so there would be light at night was looking down on Will too. It was watching over both of them and they were both looking up at it.

From the very first, she'd known their marriage was ordained in heaven. During the wedding ceremony, God had even taken care to spread sunshine over them just at the very moment the priest united them as one person. It suddenly occurred to her that they were still one person, and now God was using the moonlight to make them whole again. Even though they were so very far away from each other, the moon could see them both and it was shedding light on both of them. And God could see them too, and in the palm of His hand, He was still holding the two of them together as one.

She fluffed up the high feather pillows and lay back on them and then tucked the quilts tight around her neck and shoulders. But the shivers running through her body kept on coming. She glanced up at the moon again, and it seemed to her it had suddenly turned ghostly pale, shifted into something else altogether just like the clouds at Sun River always did.

Then as she watched, a film of feathery clouds began slowly drifting over the silvery disk. The clouds kept on getting thicker, and then finally she couldn't see the moon at all.

CHAPTER NINETEEN

They were marching fast through unbroken snow. The frothy plumes coming from the nostrils and mouths of the marchers hovered above them in the icy air. Plummer was fighting for every breath. The pain in his chest had spread through his entire body, and his legs were wavering but he was determined to appear game. No matter how weak he was he would never forget he was a Plummer. Every difficult step he forced his legs to take brought them nearer to the slender pine gallows shining silver against the black hills.

Memories of the morning they had hanged young Peter Herron filled his mind. He saw the frail body in the oversized clothes jolt at the end of the rope and when the thin arms and legs began to flail, he'd had to turn his eyes away.

Beside him he could feel the bodies of Stinson and Ray, moving in step with him, rubbing their arms and shoulders against him. By the stiff way they were holding their shoulders, he knew their hands were tied behind them. But his hands were free, and that was a good sign. The Stranglers had not dared to touch him.

He heard Stinson give a low moan. He knew it was his duty to save his deputies. He'd helped persuade them to work for the miners. Whatever it took, he was obligated to save them.

As soon as they stopped so he could catch his breath, he would speak. He would speak calmly and with authority and the Stranglers would listen. They had listened to him on Yankee Flat. And the lynch mob in the streets of Lewiston had listened. And the mob in California had also listened. They had listened, and then they had dispersed.

His lungs felt ready to burst but still they marched on. They were almost to the gallows now. They were so close he couldn't see the uprights anymore, only the crossbar rising above the army of Stranglers ahead of him. His arms were free but they were tingling all the way to his fingertips. He was determined not to let his hands shake. He recalled the California mob, how the man beside him had nudged him and said, "Skeered, aintcha?" and he had held out his hands and answered, "Are they shaking?" He'd be sure they didn't shake this time either.

The forward troops came to an abrupt halt and he nearly bumped into the marchers in front of him. He held himself back so he wouldn't touch them. It was important not to touch them so they would keep on being afraid to touch him.

He drew a deep breath and noticed the pain in his body was gone. In fact he could no longer feel his body. He seemed to be only a mind, and pictures of his mother and father and Becky were passing through it. But when he thought about how much he loved them, his chest began to ache again.

A tall lanky man pushed past him and then elbowed his way forward. Apparently Wilbur thought the wrong-side-out overcoat and the slouch hat hid his identity, but Plummer recognized him immediately. Beidler was close at Wilbur's heels. He was also easy to identify because he was the shortest man there, and his black overcoat hung nearly to the ground.

Wilbur bent down to Beidler and they began exchanging comments. Plummer couldn't hear what they were saying but both men seemed very nervous and agitated. He was struck by the absurdity of the pair in their costumes, and felt a surge of confidence. Then both of them began working their way toward him. It was nearly impossible for him to believe Wilbur had joined the criminals, but there was no doubt he was the one who barked out the order at Yankee Flat and now he was giving more orders.

It was Wilbur he'd have to deal with. Whatever chance for life his deputies had depended on the decency he could arouse inside an ambitious greenhorn who was willing to act as his uncle's fool and lackey.

When the two of them reached him, Wilbur held back and stepped behind another tall man. He seemed to think Plummer still hadn't recognized him. But Beidler planted himself directly in front of Plummer.

"Last words?" he asked. The scent of alcohol was strong.

Plummer took another deep breath. "Yes," he said. "We'd like a fair trial."

He wasn't looking at Beidler. Instead he looked over him and fixed his eyes on Wilbur. He saw the soldiers around him lift their heads and guessed they were doing the same thing, watching Wilbur and waiting for his answer. There was a long silence. It was so silent it seemed to him that all the men gathered around him were holding their breath the same as he was.

Wilbur made the noise of clearing his throat, but then he apparently decided not to speak. Beidler shot Wilbur a ferocious look and began hopping around on his toes in the clear space between Plummer and the soldiers. It was hard to tell if he was in a fit of rage because of Wilbur's bungling or if he was gleeful.

Beidler tipped his head back and shouted, "Up there!" Then he flung one short arm toward the gallows crossbar. "Up there! Yer damn trial'll be up there!"

It appeared Beidler was trying to take the command away from Wilbur, and their recruits seemed to be getting uneasy. They were watching both men closely. Plummer was sure Beidler had no conscience to touch and felt a moment of panic. Then he tried to clear his head. His success depended on staying calm. It always had.

Beidler pushed his way back to the gallows. "Bring up th' first!" he shouted. He was in a flurry of excitement, gesturing with his arms and giving random orders to everybody around him.

But there was no response. The soldiers were confused about who was in charge.

Then a second order rang out.

"Do your duty, men!"

Sanders had come to life again but he didn't approach the gallows. Instead he stayed behind the only man in the crowd who was as tall as he was. But his voice had the same military bark to it that had stirred the men on Yankee Flat.

Ray was standing closest to the gallows and a squad of four

men rammed their shotguns into his back and began shoving him toward the gallows. When he was directly beneath the bar they halted him.

Plummer knew it was his last chance to say something that would move Sanders, and he turned toward him.

Just then Beidler hollered out, "Where th' hell's th' damn rope?"

Wilbur cleared his throat again but he didn't speak, and Beidler scurried over to him.

"Where th' hell is it?" he shouted.

"The rope's at my Uncle's cabin." Wilbur spread his hands in a gesture of apology. "I just forgot and ... well anyway, Lieutenant, just send somebody to get it."

"Oh Gawd!" Beidler said, "Oh m' Gawd!" Then he collared a teenage boy standing near him and sent him running toward main street.

It was a reprieve and Plummer was weak with gratefulness. It gave him precious minutes to think. He began formulating the words he should say to Wilbur, the words that would save them from a disgraceful death.

He was starting to feel the pain in his chest again and it was hard to stay on his feet. His mind seemed to be clouding up and when he tried to concentrate on the words he should choose, all he could think of was Electa.

CHAPTER TWENTY

While they waited for the rope, the vigilante soldiers kept Ray under the crossbar. He wasn't counting the seconds and minutes anymore. He knew he was going to die and he felt proud he hadn't shown his fear. He was going to die the same way he'd killed Peter Herron. Then it occurred to him that he wasn't. His neck wouldn't snap because the Stranglers wouldn't use a drop. They'd noose him and then slowly hoist him in the air and his legs and body would flail while he fought for air. He wasn't sure if the terror was gone or if he was just getting so used to it he couldn't recognize it anymore.

A short distance away he could see Stinson standing with his head bowed, as though he were praying. Plummer was slowly pacing in the clearing the Stranglers had left for him out of respect, or maybe out of fear.

Plummer stopped walking and turned toward Wilbur. "If you don't give this man a trial, Sanders," he said, "you'll be guilty of murder. It doesn't matter what political office you rise to, eventually your name will go down in history as a murderer."

While he listened to Plummer speaking, Ray kept his eyes on the lane, watching for the boy to return from Edgerton's home with the rope. The old man had been right after all when he made the threat that morning at the cabin. Ray did have regrets. He regretted giving up his life as a civil engineer, and most of all he regretted consenting to be a lawman for the miners.

He saw the mob of men pulling apart. They were opening a lane and then he could make out the teenage boy. He was carrying three separate lengths of rope wrapped around one arm. For just a moment Ray thought he was going to fall, but he spread his legs to keep his balance and was able to stay on his feet. He bowed his head and closed his eyes but he wasn't able to pray.

The carpet of snow silenced the sounds of the men moving about him. Then he felt the coarse fibers of the rope sting his neck. He opened his eyes and saw Beidler next to him, standing on his tiptoes and stretching up to help someone else tighten the noose, only he couldn't reach that high. Then the taller man yanked the rope collar so tight it was already beginning to choke him.

Ray heard a whack as the other end of the rope was tossed over the gallows crossbar. He was thinking that dull whack of rope on wood would be the last sound his ears would ever hear on this earth, and then her cry shattered the stillness.

"Where's my Edward Ray? ... Where's my Edward Ray?"

He tried to turn his head to look at her for one last time but they were already beginning to hoist him. His feet were being lifted off the ground. The blood was gathering in his head, it was trapped there and he could feel it boiling to get free.

He heard Caroline wail. He wanted to see her. He wanted to look at her and tell her with his eyes that he was her Edward Ray. She wailed again and he flung his legs toward the upright and wrapped them around it so he was holding himself up instead of dangling. Then he turned his head and looked over his shoulder and saw her fighting her way toward him.

Below him, Beidler was reaching up to break the grip his legs had on the pole, and as Beidler jerked, he felt his legs beginning to slip and then he looked back for Caroline again. At first he couldn't see her and then just as he spotted her within only a few yards of him, one of the Stranglers slung the butt of his shotgun against the side of her face. She screamed as she fell to the ground.

Ray felt his legs being yanked from the pole and then he fell too.

* * *

Rawley sat up in his bunk. He was certain he'd heard a woman scream and he was afraid it might be Vera. It was about time for the Grizzerts to be on their way home from church. He didn't take time to light a candle. Instead he fumbled under his bunk until he found the pegs French had built for him. Hurriedly he strapped them on and stood up and began awkwardly shuffling toward the dim light coming through the windows at the front of the shop. He felt like he was walking on stilts. It was hard to keep his balance and the pegs and straps hurt his tender stumps.

As he opened the front doors and peered out, he saw Cyrus dash from the saloon and run in the opposite direction. He pushed himself on, hobbling along in the tracks Cyrus left on the boardwalk and using his left hand to steady himself against each building he passed. Behind him he could hear somebody running and he paused and hung onto one of the square pillars in front of the Goodrich Hotel so he wouldn't be knocked down.

He saw that the hefty form rushing toward him and then passing him by was H. P. A. Smith. As Rawley began to inch forward again, Smith turned left and ran up the lane that led to the gallows. Rawley followed after him as fast as he could shuffle.

It was slower going in the lane because there was nothing to hold onto and his stumps were hurting so badly he felt sure they were bleeding. About halfway up the gulch he slipped and fell, but he pushed himself up and hobbled on. He discovered it was safer to slide the pegs on the packed snow rather than trying to lift them. Ahead of him he could see a crowd gathered around the gallows and then a small group broke away from the solid mass and headed in his direction.

As they approached him, he could see two men gripping a woman by the arms and pulling her along. He was relieved to see the woman was too large to be Vera. When they brushed by him, one of the men knocked him down and he sat in the snow and watched the strange group pass by. The men had their coat collars turned up and their hats were pulled so low he couldn't see their faces. But he could tell who the woman was. It was Caroline Hall. She was crying and holding one hand to the side of her face. He couldn't be sure but he thought he saw blood running from her nose. There was no way to know whether the men were helping her or whether they were the ones who had hurt her in the first place.

While he was wondering what he should do, he heard Smith's voice ring out and then echo up the gulch.

"Stop! In the name of God stop!"

Rawley struggled to rise and then balanced himself on the pegs and shuffled on. Guards bristling with shotguns and facing out from the mob were blocking him, and he swung wide around them and made his way toward Smith. As he turned his head toward the gallows, he saw two forms dangling from the crossbar. Judging by their sizes, he was deathly afraid they were the two deputies.

Beside him Smith was still shouting, and then there was a louder shout with a strong nasal twang.

"Bring up Plummer."

Rawley realized for the first time that somehow the mob had been able to capture the Sheriff. The shock made him so dizzy he had to reach out and grab onto Smith to keep from falling down. He turned his head to see who had given the order. Evidently the words had come from a small man bustling around under the crossbars. He was holding some coiled rope in his hands and giving orders to everybody around him. There was no doubt it was Beidler.

"Bring up Plummer!" Beidler shouted again.

The entire crowd fell silent and held their same positions, and Beidler also became very still. He was waiting like everybody else.

"They won't touch Plummer," Rawley said. He kept his eyes pinned on Beidler standing there under the crossbars and holding the rope and waiting. Not a man in the mob moved to obey the order.

"They won't touch Plummer," Rawley repeated. "They wouldn't dare touch him."

It seemed to Rawley the long moment of waiting was frozen in time, that it was too horrible and momentous to ever come to an end.

Nobody stirred. Then finally Beidler pulled out his Bowie knife and sliced a short piece off the rope he was holding. He handed the large coil to the man beside him and kept the short piece and began shoving his way toward the center of the mob. Through the path he cleared, Rawley could see Plummer standing alone and then Beidler reached him. Beidler didn't touch the Sheriff. Instead he turned toward a tall man standing a few feet from Plummer.

"Ichabod Crane," Rawley said.

Wilbur's shoulders heaved with a sigh and then he straightened up and barked out, "Men, do your duty!"

Beidler began sidling behind Plummer. Rawley couldn't see Beidler any longer but he knew he must be binding Plummer's hands with the short piece of rope. Plummer did not protest or resist in any way. Rawley was weak with horror and clutched onto Smith with both hands to keep from collapsing.

Then four armed men began escorting Plummer toward the gallows. Beidler darted out from behind them and danced ahead so he could get to the crossbar first. He grabbed the coil of rope out of the other Strangler's hands and stood there holding it and waiting.

As the procession of five passed, the other Stranglers backed off and Plummer was now in plain view. Rawley was overwhelmed by the dignity of the man. He stared at Plummer's bound arms and suddenly remembered the ride back from Badger Pass. While he was half-conscious, those same arms had held him on the horse for hours.

Rawley sank into the same feeling as before, the moment being frozen in time, Plummer walking calmly to his death ... never getting there. Then Plummer was under the bar and Beidler was standing on his tiptoes, but he had to give up and pass the noose to a taller man. Rawley felt sick to his stomach and quickly turned away from Smith and wretched up the whiskey he'd drunk from the jug that evening.

While he was facing away from the gallows, it was easier for him to think and he decided what he had to do. He had to work up the courage to stop the lynching, even if it meant the Stranglers killed him. After all he was to blame for not stopping it before. He turned back and took a firm hold on Smith.

"Murderers!" he shrieked. "Don't murder the best man in

the Territory ..."

He didn't see which direction the blow came from but he felt himself tumbling and then he skidded on his face through the snow. He felt Smith kneeling beside him but then Smith was grabbed and dragged away. Rawley heard a collective gasp from the crowd and knew it was too late to try to stop it now, it was all over. It seemed to Rawley that everything was all over for him too.

* * *

He didn't know how long he'd been lying in the snow unconscious, but suddenly Rawley recognized Cyrus's face hovering above him. Cyrus scooped him up in his arms and began walking rapidly away from the gallows. On all sides of them armed men were flocking by.

"Shush up now," Cyrus whispered to him. "You shush up. They're in control now."

Rawley could hear Cyrus's words but he couldn't understand them. All he was aware of were the arms holding him and the pain caused by the constant movement. Then it wasn't dark anymore. There was a glare of brilliant light that hurt his eyes even while they were closed and he decided he must be on the horse coming back from Badger Pass. His feet were completely numb, but he could feel the warmth of Plummer's body and arms. Then as they rode down Cemetery Hill, he heard the low gentle voice say, "We're home."

CHAPTER TWENTY-ONE

Vera Grizzert was upset at her husband for purposely keeping her away from the baby's grave. She felt like crying about it but she couldn't. That was because she'd cried herself dry when she lost the baby girl so she didn't have any more tears left inside her. She liked to visit the cemetery every day, but for the past week he hadn't let her step foot out of the carpenter shop. He said it wasn't safe.

He wouldn't tell her what had happened last Sunday night. He said it was too awful for a Christian woman to hear. All he'd say was they didn't have Sheriff Plummer to protect them anymore, and they were going to leave Bannack just as soon as it got warm enough to travel. Her husband had been acting strange ever since he found out about the trouble. He was worried all the time, and he seemed like he was scared half out of his wits. At any sound he jumped and looked all around him. No matter how much she tried, she couldn't get him to talk about what was bothering him.

In fact he didn't want to talk at all and that was very unusual for him. Usually he'd tell his life story at the drop of a hat, and to anybody who'd listen. She couldn't begin to count the hours she'd had to sit and listen to him drone on and on about every single thing that ever happened to him since the day he first poked his head out of his mother's womb. By now she knew it all by heart and was sick and tired of hearing it. She was also getting tired of having him behave like a yellow-bellied turntail.

She wanted to tell him she thought he was about as brave as a stray cur with its tail between its legs but she didn't dare. He had a temper and she was especially afraid to cross him when he was this upset. But sooner or later she was going to have to tell him she had no intentions of going off and leaving the baby alone up on the hill, not the way the wolf packs came down at night and howled around the graveyard.

No matter how bad things got in Bannack, she'd have to spend the rest of her life right here with the baby girl. Even if all the gold ran out and Sheriff and everybody else in the whole town left, and even her husband too, she'd stay with the baby.

She supposed the trouble that had her husband so crazy was just another stage robbery. That made sense because it also explained why Sheriff wasn't in town to protect them. He was off chasing the robbers just like he had the time before.

Everybody knew he was the best lawman ever so she felt sure he'd eventually catch the road agents. And then her husband wouldn't have to be scared anymore. And even if Sheriff couldn't find them, the robbers wouldn't be likely to stop by the shop and bother her family anyway. Everybody in town probably knew the Grizzerts were poorer than church mice.

By the time Sheriff got back she should have his stockings finished. She'd been working on them every time she got a free moment. It was the least she could do for him. He was the only friend she'd made in Bannack. All the ladies at church were too standoffish. But she knew Sheriff liked her because he was always giving the family gifts to keep them going. Last time it was a venison roast fresh from the butcher shop. He had Deputy Stinson carry it over to her on a sharp stick because the butcher didn't have any paper to wrap it in.

Sheriff hadn't caught her off guard though. She had the neck scarf she'd knitted for him all folded and ready. She took the roast and put it in the cupboard and then handed the folded scarf over to Deputy Stinson and asked him to please deliver it to Sheriff, and the Deputy promised he would. Even though she didn't get a chance to see Sheriff anymore since they were living at the carpenter shop, she could still think about how right this very minute he'd be wearing the scarf around his neck while he was out hunting for the robbers.

It did keep her busy though just trying to think up things she could make for him and send back every time he sent a gift.

Of course she couldn't work on his stockings today. She never knitted on the Sabbath. Besides, she'd had to waste a good part of the day persuading her husband they should go to church like usual.

"Ain't gonna be no church this Sunday," he kept saying, but she was sure he was lying. It was evening by the time he finally gave in and said they could go and then she had to rush around to get their Sunday clothes ready.

She ironed a shirt for the boy and a dress for herself so the only chore left was pressing her husband's trousers. While she was working on them she got to thinking maybe she should invite Mr. Rawley to go along with them to service. It might perk him up a little. He was even worse than her husband. He'd gone out last Sunday night and tried walking on his pegs and got so sick he passed out and Cyrus Skinner had to carry him home and put him in bed.

Since then he hadn't stirred off his bunk except to use the chamber pot. The man acted like he was completely out of his mind. From behind the curtain that partitioned off his room she could hear him muttering to himself, and his voice sounded downright mean and crazy. All week he'd hardly touched his food and sometimes at night she thought she heard him crying. She'd never seen a grown man carry on so in her entire life.

She finished pressing the trousers and folded them over a chair and then set the flat iron back on the stove. She thought it was really her husband's duty to offer the invitation but he was reading a Bible passage to the boy and she didn't want to interrupt him. It took her a while to work up the nerve to speak to Mr. Rawley. He'd been cranky since the day they moved to the shop but she hadn't minded that. She was just grateful to him for taking them in so they were out of the snow and had a roof over their heads. And of course till the day she died she'd never forget how he'd carved the beautiful lamb on the baby's coffin.

But since he'd taken this turn for the worse last Sunday, she hated to even talk to him. She could hear him mumbling behind the curtain and decided she'd better speak up before he mumbled himself to sleep.

"Say, Mr. Rawley," she said. She tried to make her voice sound kind but she could hear it didn't. Since the baby died she'd let herself fall into the habit of being sour and nasty all the time, almost as bad as Mr. Rawley. She was resentful at her husband for leaving Missouri and bringing them to this Godforsaken wilderness and she was resentful at the doctor for not coming quicker and saving the baby and she was resentful at the boy for being alive when his little sister was dead and she was also resentful because she never had a chance to see her only friend at the mines anymore.

She stepped closer to the curtain and raised her voice to be sure he could hear. "Mr. Rawley, hand me them trousers out so I can press 'em. Then you come along to service with us."

The muttering behind the curtain stopped and she stuck her hand inside and waited for quite a while. He slept in his clothes now so it would take him a while to pull the trousers off. She kept waiting but he didn't plop them in her hand so finally she just went away. She couldn't stand around all night waiting for him to make up his mind. She had to wash the boy and put his fresh shirt on him and then she had to get herself ready.

All the while they were putting on their Sunday clothes, her husband kept trying to talk her out of going. "Ain't safe out," he said. But anyhow he put on the pressed trousers and washed his face and hands and raked a comb through his wiry beard and hair.

Then he went on with the grumbling but she didn't pay him any mind. She just grabbed the comb out of his hand and began working the tangles out of the boy's hair.

"Ain't safe out," he said again.

She could scarcely hold her tongue. All week it'd been hard for her to keep from saying what she thought. She didn't think she could ever forgive him for keeping her away from the grave, and she decided it was just about getting time to speak up to him. Let his temper go ahead and fly. She didn't care anymore. All he ever did anyway was shake her a little bit.

"Ain't no stage robber gonna stop me from keepin' the Sabbath holy," she told him. She stood up to him and looked him right in the eye and he didn't say a word. He just grabbed his coat and put it on.

As they walked on the snowy path toward Yankee Flat, she could see the big log hogan was still dark and that worried her because it wasn't like the preacher to be late. He wasn't much of a speaker and his sermons were pretty odd but at least he always tried to be prompt. Every Sunday evening he came early and built a fire so the congregation could sit still and listen to him without having their fingers and toes freeze.

"Ain't gonna be no church," her husband said.

She wanted to tell him she was sick of hearing him say that but she was afraid to push him any further so she kept her mouth shut and just thought to herself that she'd never forgive him for trying to stop her from keeping the Sabbath holy.

Her husband tried to open the door to the hogan but it was locked.

"Preacher'll be here purty soon," she said. She tried to sound like she wasn't worried.

An icy wind was blowing and they stood in the untrampled snow at the front door of the hogan and shivered. After a while the boy began to whine because he was cold and her husband had to pick him up to get him out of the snow.

Then her husband started walking back toward main street, holding the boy in his arms.

"Go on back if you want," she said. "I'm stayin' here. I ain't afraid."

Her husband whipped around and grabbed her by the arm and shook her, not hard, but just the way he usually did.

"Looky here!" he said. "Ya ain't mindin' me and I won't have that." Then he began walking again and kept hold of her arm and tugged her along after him. She felt ashamed to be dragged so she shook loose and came on her own.

"Let's walk by the preacher's cabin," she pleaded, "maybe he's holdin' service there."

Her husband considered for a minute and then he turned back to Yankee Flat and headed for the tiny little cabin down by the creek where the preacher lived. The snow was unbroken all the way so they knew he hadn't been out, and when they got to where they could see his window, it was dark.

"Just like I told ya ... nary a light," her husband said. He had that bossy tone to his voice that she hated so much. "Satisfied now?" he asked. Then he began hurrying for home and she came behind, stepping in his tracks.

When they got to the carpenter shop they found the front doors standing open. Her husband gasped and then handed her the boy and went inside by himself. He'd been warning her all week that the town wasn't safe anymore and now she finally believed him. She held her breath until she saw the candle-lantern flare up and then stood watching through the window glass as the light moved slowly through every nook and cranny of the shop. She didn't know what he might find in there, maybe a robber with a Bowie knife hiding someplace.

The boy began to whine again and she pressed him close to her and rocked him. Then she saw the light moving toward the door and he was beckoning for them to come in.

"It's all right," he said. "Ain't nothin' gone."

She wanted to see for herself so she put the boy down and took the light and started her own inspection. "Flat iron's gone!" she said. "I left it on the stove. Somebody stole the flat iron!"

Her husband didn't seem particularly anxious. "Mr. Rawley maybe used it," he said. "It's his anyways."

"Where is he?" she asked.

"He ain't here. He's gone." Then he began pulling off his clothes to go to bed.

They slept three to the bed, with the boy in the middle so he wouldn't fall out or take a chill and come down with the pneumonia. Vera lay beside her boy in the dark and tried to piece it all together. Something very bad must have happened in Bannack. Her husband was afraid. Sheriff was gone. There was no church service. Somebody had stolen the flat iron. And now Mr. Rawley was gone. That meant he was out again trying to hobble around on those pegs in the snow and on top of that with the wind blowing. She knew she'd never be able to sleep till he made it home.

She was so tired she was afraid she might drift off to sleep anyhow but she didn't. For hours she lay awake, but Mr. Rawley didn't come home. She lay there waiting for him to come back and listening to her boy breathing peacefully and her husband snoring. She couldn't turn over or move any because the boy might wake up and that'd make her husband cross. She was lying there trying to hold still and wanting in the worst way to move when the horrible thought popped into her head. Her husband must be keeping her away from the cemetery because the wolves had dug up the baby girl's grave.

Once she thought of it she couldn't stay in bed any longer. She had to know.

She edged out of bed as soft as she could so the boy wouldn't wake up and dressed in the dark. Then she bundled up in her coat and wrapped her head in a wool scarf. She had to fumble around in the dark till she felt the candle-lantern. Then she tiptoed into the big room to light it. She went out the back door and didn't go over to main street. Instead she took the alley, behind the row of businesses and straight over to the gulch. The wind cut right through her coat and the snow had drifted and she couldn't hold her skirt up high enough to keep it from getting wet and her shoes were soaked. But she could hardly feel any of it. She had to know.

Then the wind died down to a complete standstill and she didn't feel so cold. She was just opposite the gallows and was starting to climb up cemetery hill when she noticed three fresh mounds dug just off the path. Before she could get close enough to look at them, something caught her attention off to her left. She swung the light in that direction and saw a man standing only a few feet from her. He wasn't moving, just standing perfectly still under the gallows with his back turned to her. He wasn't wearing a coat and she could see that a piece of fabric in the shape of a flat iron was missing from the back of his white shirt. She stuck out her arm and moved the light closer and could make out his burned flesh showing through the iron-shaped gap in the shirt. The man had his head tipped off to one side like he was gazing up at the sky. Suddenly the breeze picked up and he began to gently sway with it. She raised the light a little higher and then saw the rope around his neck. He was dangling from the crossbar.

Her first thought was he might still be alive. She needed to get him down. Her legs were trembling so much she could hardly stay on her feet but she set the candle-lantern on top of the snow and reached up to the body. As soon as her fingers touched it she knew it was too late. The body was already frozen stiff.

Her knees buckled under her and she felt herself sinking into the snow. Her eyes were at the level of the dead man's trousers now and the candle-lantern resting on the snow was lighting the cuffs up and she could see there weren't any feet sticking out of them. Then a powerful gust of wind swept up the gulch and the body above her twisted. In the wavering candlelight she could see a bone sticking out of each trouser leg.

At the same time she saw the stumps and knew they belonged to Mr. Rawley, a lone wolf howled on the hill just beyond the gallows. She sprang to her feet and grabbed the light and began running down the lane. She'd thought she couldn't cry anymore but she could feel tears streaming down her cheeks. Her first thought was to run and find Sheriff but then she remembered he wasn't here. By now she was panting for breath.

Her eyes were stuck on the snowy path the candle-lantern was lighting for her, but inside her head she could see the footless bones sticking out of the trouser legs. And then the picture of the flat iron gap scorched through his white shirt and the patch of burned flesh under it would flash right over the top of the picture of the bones in his trouser legs.

She had to spend the rest of her life here in Bannack and she knew she'd never be able to get the pictures out of her mind. Those two pictures of Mr. Rawley's stumps and his burned back were frozen in her mind for all time.

THE END

HISTORICAL NOTE

By F. E. Boswell

The Vigilantes of Montana carried out their lynchings for several years. Sidney Edgerton, who supported the vigilance activities, was appointed the first governor of Montana Territory, and his nephew Wilbur Sanders became the state's first senator. The plaque on X. Beidler's gravestone contains the Vigilantes' secret symbol 3-7-77 and reads, "PUBLIC BENEFACTOR, BRAVE PIONEER, TO TRUE OCCASION TRUE."

As for Henry Plummer, Montana histories describe him as a miners' sheriff by day, but by night, the leader of a huge outlaw band that terrorized the gold camps. According to these histories, the so-called "Plummer Gang" robbed, murdered, and then mutilated more than one hundred victims, though a list enumerating the victims who were supposedly murdered was never issued.

Together, author R. E. Mather and I have researched and written four Western history books which have been published by university or other scholarly presses: *Hanging the Sheriff: A Biography of Henry Plummer, John David Borthwick: Artist of the Gold Rush, Gold Camp Desperadoes,* and *Vigilante Victims: Montana's 1864 Hanging Spree.* These books appear in some of the most prestigious university libraries in the United States, such as Yale, Berkeley, and Stanford.

Yet during the decades we spent researching the Gold Rush

era, we were never able to uncover one shred of evidence that an outlaw gang actually existed at the Montana mines. Instead, evidence indicates that crimes—such as the two relatively unprofitable stage robberies that occurred between Bannack and Virginia City, and a few claimed, but undocumented, robberies of individual travelers, sometimes amounting to no more than two to ten dollars each—were committed by small groups of rather inefficient individuals working alone.

Nevertheless, during the winter of 1864, Vigilantes lynched twenty-two untried men for allegedly belonging to a huge outlaw band that supposedly had plans of taking over the mines. "These road agents," the Vigilantes claimed, "had said the pirates' flag would wave over the town before Spring."

Deputies Buck Stinson and Edward Ray, as well as saloonkeeper Cyrus Skinner, were among the twenty-two untried victims lynched during the extended spree. Vigilantes also threatened to hang attorney H. P. A. Smith, and he had to flee the territory. Later, R. C. Rawley was lynched for publicly expressing "sympathy ... with the men who had been hanged, stating that they were good men."

Vigilantes did not deny that Sheriff William Henry Plummer was one of the most promising young men to come West during the Gold Rush era. But they claimed Plummer was an efficient law officer only by day, and that by night, he directed the largest, most intricately organized, and most murderous outlaw band in the West. Without holding an investigation of what was no more than a rumor—or even so much as questioning or charging the suspect—a group of approximately seventy-five heavily armed Vigilantes captured the ailing Sheriff by using the pretense they needed his help in dispersing a lynch mob. Plummer got out of his sickbed and left his cabin unarmed in order to prevent a lynching. But Vigilantes escorted the miners' sheriff up Hangman's Gulch, where they strangled him—and his two deputies—on the gallows that had been constructed to legally execute convicted murderer Peter Herron.

But a problem remains. If crime at the Montana mines was not organized, as our research indicates, then *William Henry Plummer could not have been a gang leader. There was no outlaw gang for him to direct. And if that is the case, then on that cold, dark night in the winter of 1864, the Vigilantes strangled an innocent man on the Bannack gallows.*